Secrets
of a
Wallflower

Lords & Ladies of Mayfair

Laura Beers

Chapter One

England, 1813

The sun was low in the sky as Miss Simone Delacourt stood in the gardens. She brought her wrist back, and with expert precision, aiming for a mark at least twenty yards away, released the dagger towards the target. It embedded in the center, just as she had intended.

Simone had been gifted her first dagger by her mother when she was eight years old. They had spent countless hours together as she perfected her aim and it was a time that she cherished, especially since her mother died nearly two years ago.

Throwing daggers was an odd skill for a genteel lady to be proficient in, but her mother had been anything but conventional. She loved learning new skills, just for the sake of learning. And that had been something Simone had admired about her mother. It was something she wished to emulate.

The sound of approaching footsteps drew her attention and Simone watched the butler come to a stop a short distance away. "Your father wishes to see you, Miss," Clarke informed her.

Simone hesitated. Her father had hardly uttered a word to her in weeks, and when he had, it had been in passing. It had been this way since her mother had drowned. She felt as if she had lost both parents that fateful day. Her father seemed lost in his grief, unable to move on.

"Are you sure?" Simone asked.

Clarke's face softened, and she knew that he understood why she had asked such a thing. "I am," he replied. "And it is best if you don't keep him waiting." His words were spoken with kindness that was all too familiar.

Simone smiled at the white-haired butler. He had been working for their family since before she was born. As of late, he felt like more of a father figure than her own. "Let me collect my dagger," she said before she approached the target.

After she retrieved the dagger, she slipped it into an opening in her gown that her lady's maid had created for her.

They started walking back towards the townhouse and Simone found herself curious as to why her father had summoned her. An uneasy feeling came to her stomach, and she had learned long ago not to discount her emotions so easily.

Once they arrived at the study, Clarke stopped at the open door and offered her an encouraging look. "You will be just fine."

Simone was grateful for the butler's comforting presence. She was not one to get nervous, but standing outside of her father's study, a wave of nervousness washed over her.

"Thank you," Simone responded before she stepped into the study.

Her father was sitting at his desk, his head hunched over his ledgers. She took a moment to study him. He was tall, dark-haired, but the wrinkles on his face were starting to deepen, marking his advancing age. He had a commanding presence about him, one that had terrified her when she had been a child. But she was not so young anymore and he had never treated her harshly. He just treated her with indifference now.

Simone thought it was best to make her presence known and not keep him waiting. "Father, you wished to see me," she said, walking further into the room.

Her father rose from his seat and gestured towards a chair that faced the desk. "Yes, please sit down."

Her father sounded cordial enough, she thought, as she lowered herself down onto the proffered chair.

Returning to his seat, he dispensed with pleasantries. "You are on your third Season, and it is time that you wed."

Simone felt her back grow rigid. His declaration surprised her, at least the timing of it, but she thought it was best if she was honest with her father. "I do not wish to marry."

"You wish to be a spinster then, an utter drain on my finances?" her father asked. There was a harshness to his voice that she couldn't help but notice.

"I did not mean to imply such," Simone responded. "I have an inheritance from my grandmother that I can live on."

"That much is true, but not in the style you have been accustomed to living."

"I can live on much less," Simone insisted.

Her father leaned back in his seat. "I don't doubt that but I can't keep providing Seasons for you, only to be disappointed, time and time again," he said.

"It has only been three Seasons, Father," she argued.

"Three is far too many for someone of your beauty and connections," he stated. "Your mother was married during her first Season."

"True, but I have not found a suitor that has piqued my interest yet," Simone said. Which was the truth. But, then again, she hadn't truly been looking for a suitor.

Her father let out a frustrated sigh. "I have been watching

you, Simone," he remarked. "You sit with the other wallflowers, along the back wall, and you don't make yourself available to dance with the unattached gentlemen."

"No one has given me any heed," Simone attempted.

"That is because you show no interest," her father said. "It is time for you to come out of your shell and find a suitor."

Simone shifted uncomfortably in her seat. "But I do not wish to marry, Father."

"Why?" her father asked. "Your dowry is more than sufficient to attract a worthy suitor, and that is in addition to the inheritance your grandmother allotted for you."

"Yes, but once I marry, it all belongs to my husband."

Her father gave her a blank stare. "Is that an issue?" he asked. "He is, after all, tasked to take care of you."

"I don't want someone to 'take care of me.' I want more out of a marriage," she said. "If I ever did marry, it would be for love."

Simone didn't dare tell her father that if she wed, then she would have to stop working as a spy. And she didn't want to give that up. It provided her with a sense of accomplishment every time she completed an assignment. It may be dangerous, but it gave her the adventure that she so desperately craved in her life.

"You reach too high, just as you always do," her father stated. "Marriage is more mutual toleration than love."

"Didn't you love Mother?" she asked.

His jaw tightened and she wondered if she had gone too far in her line of questioning. "I did love your mother," he replied after a long moment. "But it didn't start that way. We had to work for what we had, and it wasn't always easy."

"I didn't mean to imply such."

"I am not without compassion," he said. "You have until the end of the Season to select a suitor or I would be happy to arrange one for you."

Simone reared back. "Surely you cannot be serious?"

"It is far preferable to being on your own," her father said. "It is lonely not having a spouse to lean upon."

Simone could hear the pain in his words and she knew he was speaking from his own experience. But that didn't soften her resolve. She would rather remain unwed than marry a stranger. It was almost unfathomable to think of.

"Are you so quick to get rid of me?" Simone asked. In truth, she needed to keep having Seasons to keep her cover intact. She may play the part of a wallflower, but she used that time to observe the members of high Society.

Her father frowned. "I am hoping this motivates you to make the changes necessary in your life to be happy."

"I am happy."

"Are you?" her father asked. "Mrs. Fernsby has informed me that you hardly leave the townhouse, and you spend your days in your bedchamber."

Simone quirked her lips, knowing her father truly had no idea how she spent her time. Her companion was hardly a match for her, but she needed to at least pretend she had an objection to Mrs. Fernsby. "I do not need a companion to watch over me."

"You do." He abruptly rose from his seat. "This conversation is over. I have much more pressing issues at hand."

"More pressing than me?" Simone asked as she attempted to keep the hurt out of her voice.

A look of annoyance flashed in her father's eyes. "You would be wise to remember your place, Simone. I am needed at the House of Lords and I don't have time to lollygag around the townhouse."

Simone's gaze grew downcast as she knew fighting with her father would accomplish nothing. He was stubborn, almost to a fault, and would talk down to her. How she hated being treated in such a fashion, but she had little choice in the matter.

"Now run along," her father ordered.

Knowing what was expected of her, Simone rose and dropped into a curtsy before departing from the study.

Her father didn't know what she was capable of. He only saw her as a weak young woman that relied solely on him. Which was far from the truth. She was strong and determined, but she couldn't risk revealing her true self. Quite frankly, she doubted her father would ever accept her if he learned of the truth.

Simone hurried up to her bedchamber on the second level. Once she stepped inside, she saw her lady's maid, Felicity, waiting for her on the settee.

Felicity jumped up when she saw her, an eager look on her face. "What did your father want?"

Tossing her hands in the air, Simone replied, "He wants me to get married."

"Married?" Felicity repeated. "Why now?"

"Apparently, he is tired of paying for my Seasons and three has been enough," Simone replied.

Felicity harrumphed. "I am surprised he has even noticed you are in your third Season."

Simone nodded in agreement. Felicity had been her lady's maid since they had left their finishing school and they bore a striking resemblance to one another. It had come in handy a time or two since she had become a spy.

"What am I to do?" Simone asked. "I won't marry for the sake of it, and I have far more important matters to deal with. I have yet to track down those two French spies."

Felicity grew serious. "Have you spoken to Mr. Bolingbroke about this?"

"I have not," Simone replied. "I can handle it on my own."

"I thought you were assigned to work together?" Felicity asked.

Simone dropped down onto the bed. "I can't work with

Mr. Bolingbroke. He vexes me. I just wish Kendrick had assigned someone else, frankly, anyone else, to work with me."

"If you can't stand him, why did you break cover and save his life?" Felicity asked knowingly.

She playfully narrowed her eyes. "Whose side are you on?"

Felicity laughed. "There are no sides. I am merely curious."

"I need to leave soon and speak to my informants," Simone said. "I hope they have discovered something of use."

"What about Mrs. Fernsby?"

As if on cue, the door opened and her white-haired companion stepped into the room. She adjusted the thick, rounded spectacles on the top of her nose. "There you are, Child," she admonished as she looked at Felicity. "I have been waiting for you in the drawing room."

Felicity opened her mouth to no doubt correct her, but Simone spoke first. "She will be right down," she said.

"What?" Mrs. Fernsby asked as she brought a hand to her right ear. "You must speak up."

"Miss Simone will be down in a moment," she said, raising her voice. "She just needs a moment to change."

Mrs. Fernsby perused the length of Felicity, who wore a simple brown service gown. "Simone looks fine to me. Come along."

Felicity lifted her brow and Simone clasped her hands together, silently pleading her to play along. After a moment, Felicity conceded, "Perhaps we can work on our needlework in the library."

"Library, yes," Mrs. Fernsby agreed. "The lighting is much better in there. I might just close my eyes for a minute while you work on your embroidery."

Simone stood back as they departed from her bedchamber, pleased that she had time now to meet with her informants. But she did have to hurry. Mrs. Fernsby usually was fooled for only so long, but her father wouldn't notice. He never did. She could be invisible for all he cared.

She changed into a simple cotton gown and headed towards the main level.

Clarke met her in the entry hall. "I see that you tricked Mrs. Fernsby again by switching places with Felicity," he tsked. "I wouldn't feel as bad if she wasn't such a crotchety old woman."

Simone giggled. "You shouldn't say such awful things," she said lightly. But the truth was that she appreciated his honesty.

The humor left Clarke's face. "Dare I ask where you are going now?"

"It is best that you didn't know," Simone replied. "Is the coach out front?"

"It is."

Simone tipped her head. "Thank you, Clarke," she said. "I shall be back shortly."

"I won't lie for you," Clarke stated.

"Nor would I ask you to, but we both know that my father won't ask about me," Simone said dejectedly. "He hasn't cared about me since my mother died, and don't you try to deny it."

Clarke's eyes held compassion. "Your father cares for you," he attempted.

"I do believe his actions speak louder than his words," Simone said before she departed from the townhouse.

She knew Clarke meant well, but her father cared more about his reputation than his own daughter. Perhaps one day she would make him proud and he would finally see her for who she truly was. Until then, she was going to find these two French spies and finish the assignment.

Mr. Caleb Bolingbroke was tired of this blasted assignment. He had been scouring London for any sighting of the French spies, but he kept coming up empty-handed. It was as if they had vanished. But that was impossible. Someone must know where they had gone, or what their purpose was for being in England.

He would find them; it was only a matter of time. But what kind of havoc would they have released before he did so?

Caleb stood just beyond the entrance to The Dark Raven Tavern, observing the patrons as they came and went from the disreputable establishment. He was to meet his informant soon, yet he hesitated to step into the dim, musty confines of the tavern. Not that it was much better on the narrow, uneven pavement in the rookeries.

The air reeked of desperation, and as people with hollowed-out faces brushed past him, Caleb couldn't escape the palpable sense of misery that clung to the surroundings. The buildings, blackened and collapsing in on themselves, housed entire families in uninhabitable rooms. It was a place of torment. There was no hope in a place like this. Despite Society's inclination to turn a blind eye to such realities, the misery persisted, regretfully undeniable.

Caleb saw his informant approaching. Matthews was rather short and had a patch over his right eye. It was a sailing accident, or at least that is what Matthews had told him. But Caleb had his suspicions, considering his informant's line of work.

Matthews came to a stop in front of him. "Shall we go inside for a pint of ale?"

Caleb had no desire for the watered-down ale that was served in this establishment but it was best if they got off the street. No good came from loitering there. He was dressed in tattered clothes with disheveled hair and dirt strategically smeared on his clothing. Despite being the son of a viscount, he convincingly portrayed the role of someone down on his luck.

Opening the door wide, Caleb said, "After you."

Caleb followed his informant into the loud, rowdy tavern and they found a table in the back. Once they were situated, Matthews leaned in and revealed, "You are not the only one asking about information on the two French spies in London."

"Who else is asking?" Caleb inquired.

Matthews rubbed his chin. "I don't recall, but a guinea would refresh my memory."

Caleb retrieved a coin and slid it across the table. "How is your memory now?"

"It is much better," Matthews replied, depositing the coin into his worn jacket pocket. "A beautiful young woman named Hope has been asking questions. I do fear that she is in over her head but she pays well for information."

Who the blazes was Hope, he wondered, and why was she asking questions about the French spies? "What have you told her?" Caleb asked.

"The same as I will tell you," Matthews replied. "I don't have any information on the whereabouts of the French spies. No one matching their descriptions has drawn attention."

"They must be somewhere," Caleb said.

Matthews shrugged. "Sure, but they are most likely hiding out somewhere, waiting to make their move."

Caleb frowned. "That is what I am afraid of."

As the tavern door swung open, a hush fell over the room. Miss Delacourt entered with poise, her head held high, displaying no sign of hesitation. Her blue gown was simple enough, doing little to flatter her figure, and her dark hair was neatly gathered in a tight chignon at the nape of her neck. She was tall, with a thin frame, but she had the most striking green eyes. They seemed to assess everything, making him wonder what she truly saw.

Miss Delacourt's eyes roamed over the room until they landed on him. Annoyance flashed in her eyes, and she did not appear eager to see him. Not that he blamed her. The feeling was mutual. They were supposed to be working this case together, but Simone had made herself completely unavailable to do so. Which was fine. He would rather work this case alone than work with someone that clearly disliked him.

Matthews spoke up. "That is her. Hope," he said, gesturing towards Miss Delacourt.

"I should have known," Caleb muttered.

"You know her?"

Caleb kept his gaze on Miss Delacourt as he replied, "Unfortunately."

Miss Delacourt ignored the jeering of the patrons as she approached his table. "I need to speak to you," she said firmly.

Caleb took his foot and pushed out a chair. "Have a seat, then."

With a glance at Matthews, Miss Delacourt said, "Alone, if you don't mind."

Matthews shoved back his chair and rose. "That is my cue to leave. Good day."

Miss Delacourt watched Matthews' retreating figure for a moment before turning her gaze back towards Caleb. "I need your help."

His brow lifted. That was the last thing he expected to hear from Miss Delacourt. "What is it that you need my help on?"

"I understand that you have intercepted a French code, and I am in need of it."

With a nod, he asked, "What you have heard is true, but why do you need it?"

"Is the reason important?"

"It is to me," Caleb replied.

Miss Delacourt let out a frustrated sigh as she reached into the folds of her gown, retrieving a piece of paper. "I think I have discovered how someone is communicating with the French spies."

Now Miss Delacourt had his attention. "How?"

Miss Delacourt lowered herself down onto the chair and extended him the piece of paper. "Someone is placing ads in the newssheets and they don't make any sense. They are just a bunch of random words and letters."

"Why do you assume this is related to the French spies?"

"Because the first ad was placed the day after Lord Drycott was declared dead by the newssheets," Miss Delacourt explained.

Caleb looked at the ad and saw that it was a muddled mess. But that didn't prove it was related to the French spies.

"Furthermore," Miss Delacourt continued, "the person always pays for the ad in person and is very specific about what is to be written."

"How do you know that?"

Miss Delacourt pressed her lips together. "Surely you didn't think I wouldn't do due diligence when it came to discovering who posted the ad."

"Did you get a name?"

"The person was not forthcoming about that particular information so I had to get creative."

Caleb gave her a knowing look. "You mean break into their offices and look at their files?"

"Perhaps, but how I discovered the information is not as important as the fact that I *did* discover the information."

"What is the man's name?"

"Hugh Crowe," Miss Delacourt replied. "Does that name mean anything to you?"

Caleb shook his head. "It does not," he replied. "That still doesn't prove that these ads are coded messages to the French spies."

"That is why I need the code so I can decipher it," Miss Delacourt said.

"Unfortunately, I gave the code to Kendrick and he turned it over to the agents that handle linguistics," Caleb remarked.

Annoyance once again etched itself onto Miss Delacourt's features. "Why didn't you just tell me that to begin with? It would have saved us a considerable amount of time."

"It would have, but I would have missed a chance to converse with a beautiful young woman," Caleb said, a smirk playing on his lips.

"You are useless to me, then."

Caleb placed a hand over his heart. "You wound me, Miss Delacourt," he mocked. "How can I earn your approval?"

Miss Delacourt reached down and snatched the paper out of his hand. "I don't know why Kendrick ever thought we could work together. You are impossible."

"I have never had a complaint before, especially from a young woman," Caleb joked as he leaned back in his seat.

"Perhaps they were just being polite," Miss Delacourt retorted.

A burly man approached their table and his bloodshot eyes were fixated on Miss Delacourt. "Is this man bothering you?" he asked, his words slurring.

"Yes," Miss Delacourt promptly responded, "but it is nothing that I can't handle."

"We don't take kindly to men mistreating womenfolk here," the burly man said, waggling his finger at Caleb.

Miss Delacourt flashed her protector a smile. "You are kind, sir, but you do not need to worry about me. I am fine."

The man eyed her for a long moment before bobbing his head. "All right. You've convinced me, but we will be watching him."

As the man returned to his own table, Miss Delacourt gave Caleb a knowing look. "You think you would be nicer to me, considering I saved your life once already."

"I believe I have already thanked you for that," Caleb said.

"Yes, but you could stand to thank me more," Miss Delacourt responded.

Caleb glanced at the broken, grimy window along the side

wall. "Kendrick wants us to work together. Should we not at least make an attempt to do so?"

"I don't need a partner."

"Neither do I, but here we are," Caleb said, putting his hands up. "We both haven't made much progress on the assignment working alone. What would happen if we combined forces?"

Miss Delacourt held up the paper. "I did find this clue."

"Until we get the French code to decipher it, you have nothing, and you know it."

Emotions flickered on her expression as she seemed to assess him. "Fine. You may call upon me tomorrow to discuss the case," Miss Delacourt said.

"I may call upon you?" Caleb tipped his head. "Thank you for the invitation. I feel honored that you would bestow such an honor upon me."

Miss Delacourt crossed her arms over her chest. "It isn't as if I could call upon you," she said.

"I would rather go someplace that doesn't have prying ears," Caleb remarked. "What if we met in Hyde Park on the bench near the south entrance?"

"I am amenable to that."

"Good, let's say we meet at noon," Caleb said.

Miss Delacourt abruptly rose. "I will see you tomorrow."

Rising, Caleb asked, "Would you like me to see you home?"

"No," came her curt reply.

Caleb gave her a pointed look. "I am not your enemy, Miss Delacourt," he said.

"I know."

"Do you?" Caleb asked. "Because you keep me at arm's length, and you clearly do not trust me."

"Trust is to be earned," Miss Delacourt asserted. "Regardless, I doubt that you trust me either."

Caleb knew that Miss Delacourt had a point. He didn't

trust her, because, quite frankly, he didn't know anything about her. She was an anomaly to him. She may be beautiful, but she was also dangerous.

"You are right," Caleb sighed. "But this is not a good start to our partnership. Perhaps if we got to know each other better."

"I know everything that I need to know about you," Miss Delacourt said. "You are a somewhat competent agent, except when you are careless and let Lord Drycott discover your true identity."

"That was unfortunate, but I assure you that I am a proficient agent."

"Are you?" Miss Delacourt asked.

Caleb was not about to engage in a debate with Miss Delacourt. He assumed she was the type of woman who would rather fall on her sword than lose an argument.

"Until tomorrow, and don't try to follow me," Miss Delacourt said before she walked off, drawing the unwanted attention of every man in the hall.

"Botheration," Caleb muttered. Why had Kendrick assigned him to work with the most obstinate young woman in all of London?

Caleb waited a moment before he headed out of the tavern. He had meant what he had said before about how working together might yield more results. He no more wanted to work with Miss Delacourt than chew glass. But he was first and foremost a spy. And a spy always finds a way to complete the assignment. Even if that means he was to engage in a battle of wits with Miss Delacourt.

Chapter Two

With the morning sun streaming in through the windows, Simone sat in the library of her townhouse as she read the newssheets. She had to do so in private because her father would never condone her actions.

Her father was no different than most of the gentlemen of the *ton*. They didn't want a woman to hold an opinion on serious topics, such as politics or religion. But she could have as many opinions as she wanted on ribbons or other frivolous subjects.

She had long suspected that her father was disappointed that she had been born a girl. He didn't have his heir and his title would be passed to a distant cousin. But Simone didn't mind being born a girl. It enabled her to hide in plain sight as a spy. No one would dare suspect that a lady would be an agent for the Crown.

For the most part, Simone enjoyed being a spy. She was able to wear a mask of her own making and kept a part of herself hidden from the world. It was a way to protect herself from the harsh realities that she had to face. Alone.

A knock came at the door before a young maid stepped

into the room and announced, "Miss Emilia Sutherland has come to call."

Simone folded the newssheets and placed them onto a table. "I will be down shortly," she replied.

The maid departed from the room, just as quickly as she arrived, to do her bidding.

Rising, Simone couldn't help but wonder why Miss Sutherland had come to call. The last she had seen of her was after she had helped save her from death at the hands of her half-siblings. But that had been nearly a week ago. Now Miss Sutherland was happily engaged to Lord Chatsworth and the banns had been posted.

Simone arrived at the drawing room on the main level and saw Miss Sutherland was holding a large, overflowing basket of goods in her hands.

Miss Sutherland's eyes lit up when she saw her. "Miss Delacourt," she greeted. "Thank you for agreeing to see me."

"You are always welcome in my home," Simone said.

Miss Sutherland extended her the basket. "I brought you something. I wanted to do something nice, considering you saved my life."

Simone accepted the basket and glanced inside to see a random assortment of items. "Thank you."

"I wasn't sure what to get you so I compiled items that I particularly enjoy," Miss Sutherland explained. "There are biscuits, ribbons for your hair, dry sweetmeats, some delicate fabric for needlework, and a book that was written by A Lady. I don't want to give anything away but it was a splendid book."

"You are kind, but this was unnecessary. I am just glad that I was there to help."

Miss Sutherland smiled. "When you first arrived on the path that night, I thought you were just in the wrong place at the wrong time. I had no idea you were so proficient at throwing daggers."

"It is a talent that I have perfected over the years," Simone admitted.

"Do you think I should carry a weapon?" Miss Sutherland asked. "I only ask because Lady Roswell carries a pistol in her reticule and you carry daggers on your person. Are the streets of London so terribly unsafe?"

"They are unsafe," Simone replied. "But can you shoot a pistol or know how to properly handle a dagger?"

Miss Sutherland shook her head. "No, but I can learn."

"I can teach you how to throw a dagger, assuming Lord Chatsworth approves. I do not wish to make an enemy of him," Simone responded.

"He will approve," Miss Sutherland said matter-of-factly.

"Then we shall start right away," Simone stated. "Throwing a dagger isn't overly complicated, but it will take a lot of practice to become somewhat proficient."

Miss Sutherland stepped closer and lowered her voice. "What is it like being a spy?"

Simone blinked, taken aback by the unexpected question. "Why would you think I am a spy?" she inquired.

With a knowing look, Miss Sutherland replied, "It wasn't hard to deduce since you are acquainted with Fredrick and Lord Roswell." She hesitated. "Was I wrong to assume so?"

Simone had a choice. She could lie, just as she was accustomed to, or she could confirm what Miss Sutherland had so easily deduced. Very few people knew of her secret, but she knew enough about Miss Sutherland to know that she was trustworthy.

"No, you weren't wrong," Simone replied, keeping her voice low, "but no one knows about me here."

Miss Sutherland nodded her understanding. "Say no more."

Simone gestured towards the settees. "Would you care to have a seat?" she asked. "I can request a tea service to be brought up."

Miss Sutherland made a face. "No tea, please," she said. "All I seem to do is work on my needlework and drink tea."

"What about spending time with Lord Chatsworth?" Simone asked.

A very telling blush came to Miss Sutherland's cheeks. "I do enjoy spending time with him when he comes to call."

Simone sat down on a settee and placed the basket onto the table in front of her. "I am glad since you two are engaged."

"I don't think I will ever tire of being in Fredrick's presence," Miss Sutherland shared as she sat across from her. "He completes me in a way I didn't even realize I needed."

"I am truly happy for you," Simone said.

Miss Sutherland clasped her hands in front of her. "I must admit that I had an ulterior motive in coming today."

"You did?"

With a bob of her head, Miss Sutherland continued. "I was hoping we could become more acquainted with one another, and perhaps, if you are willing, become friends. I could use some more friends. I have three now."

"Three?"

Miss Sutherland held up three fingers. "Lady Roswell, Lady Lizette and Lily, my lady's maid. I know some might not count a lady's maid as a friend—"

"I would, wholeheartedly," Simone said, cutting her off. "My lady's maid is one of my dearest friends, as well."

"Lily and I became friends when we both started working at the same boarding school," Miss Sutherland revealed. "I convinced her to come work for me as a lady's maid and now she works as a teacher at the boarding school I just opened."

"Yes, I heard about the boarding school. I think it is a remarkable feat on your part. You should be proud."

Miss Sutherland dismissed her praise with a wave of her hand. "It is rather easy to do good things when one has the funds available to do so."

"Unfortunately, not everyone feels the same as you," Simone said.

"Regardless, I only finished what my father envisioned."

Simone leaned against the back of the settee. "How are you adjusting to life in high Society?"

Miss Sutherland shrugged. "People have been much more accepting of me now that I am engaged to Lord Chatsworth."

"Marrying a lord will do that, especially one that declared he wasn't going to fall prey to the parson's mousetrap," Simone joked. "People are curious as to how you ensnared him."

"I did not ensnare him," Miss Sutherland declared.

Simone laughed. "I know. You two are so clearly in love. Which no doubt irks the *ton* even more," she said.

"I love Fredrick with my whole heart."

"Then I am glad that it worked out for you two," Simone responded. "Not everyone gets a happily-ever-after."

Miss Sutherland eyed her curiously. "Are you one of those people?"

"I do not intend to ever marry."

"Fredrick said that same thing," Miss Sutherland teased.

"In my case, I am in earnest," Simone asserted. "I do not want to give up the freedoms that have been afforded to me."

"I understand," Miss Sutherland said. "By marrying Fredrick, I am no longer in possession of my fortune. It belongs to him."

"Does that worry you?"

With a shake of her head, Miss Sutherland replied, "Not at all. I trust Fredrick, wholeheartedly."

"That is a rarity amongst the *ton*. You must know that," Simone said. "There is always a certain level of mistrust, even among spouses."

"Did your parents have mistrust?"

Simone grew silent. "My mother was rather opinionated,

and sometimes I believe that my father barely tolerated her. He claims that he loved my mother, but I have my doubts."

"Why is that?"

"After my mother died, my father was insistent that we weren't to mourn her," Simone revealed. "She was here one day and gone the next. I didn't even get a chance to say goodbye."

Miss Sutherland's eyes held compassion. "That must have been hard."

"It is all I know," Simone admitted softly.

"My mother lingered at the end and I wanted her to be at peace," Miss Sutherland shared. "It made her passing much easier knowing she was no longer in pain anymore. Not that it was easy to say goodbye."

Simone felt the tears prick the backs of her eyes and she blinked them back. It would do her no good to cry and show emotion. Her mother was dead and nothing could be done about that. She could only fix what she was able to.

Miss Sutherland offered her a weak smile. "Perhaps we should move on to another topic," she suggested. "The weather?" A glint of humor came into her eyes, informing Simone that she was just teasing.

"I abhor talking about the weather."

"As do I." Miss Sutherland paused before saying, "I asked around about you. I was taken aback by how many people knew of you, but how few people actually knew you."

"That is not surprising since I tend to keep to myself," Simone admitted.

"Why is that?" Miss Sutherland questioned. "You shouldn't be standing back with the wallflowers when you are so evidently meant to stand out."

"You are kind."

Miss Sutherland arched an eyebrow. "You aren't going to answer my question, are you?"

Simone glanced at the open doorway before saying, "I

don't want people to take notice of me. It allows me to slip in and out of halls and ballrooms without garnering any attention. To the *ton*, I am a nobody. I am merely someone who just takes up space in the corner of the ballroom."

"But we both know that isn't true," Miss Sutherland contended.

The long clock in the corner chimed, alerting Simone to the time. She was to meet Mr. Bolingbroke in Hyde Park soon and she didn't dare be late.

Simone rose from her seat. "I apologize but I'm afraid I must depart soon for a meeting in Hyde Park."

Rising, Miss Sutherland asked in a hushed voice, "Is this spy related?"

"Yes, but I cannot say anything more than that."

"Then you must go and save England," Miss Sutherland said with such a dramatic flair that it made Simone giggle.

"I shall try," Simone promised.

Miss Sutherland dropped into a curtsy. "I shall see my way out, Miss Delacourt."

Simone found that she rather liked conversing with Miss Sutherland and was looking forward to getting to know her better. "If we want this friendship to work, you must stop with the formalities and call me Simone."

"I will, but only if you call me Emilia."

"Thank you for coming to call, Emilia," Simone said. "You are truly a delight, and I see why Lord Chatsworth is so enamored with you."

Emilia smiled so broadly that it spilled into her eyes. "It has been my pleasure, and I am pleased that I now have four friends."

Simone watched as her newfound friend departed from the drawing room, and she knew she was going to enjoy getting to know Emilia.

Sitting on a bench in Hyde Park, Caleb could sense the perspiration trickling down his spine. There was a faint breeze, but it did little to ease his discomfort.

He adjusted the top hat on his head as he waited for Miss Delacourt to arrive. He had come early to their meeting so she wouldn't chide him for being late. She seemed to always find fault with him, no matter what he did. Which was odd. He had never had to work so hard to win a young woman's favor before.

He was his father's heir and would one day inherit a large, thriving estate. Young women would always bat their eyelashes at him and cast him coy smiles. But not Miss Delacourt. She seemed to find his mere presence to be insulting.

Caleb watched as Miss Delacourt approached the bench, a maid trailing behind her. When their eyes met, her eyes seemed to flash with the usual annoyance. At least she was consistent. If she suddenly was nice to him, then it might worry him.

Miss Delacourt positioned herself on the opposite end of the bench, her gaze fixed straight ahead as she addressed Caleb. "I am here, per your request."

He glanced at her and noticed her face obscured by a large straw hat. "Did you have to wear that hat?"

Miss Delacourt gave him an innocent look. "Do you not like it, sir?" she asked.

Caleb had a suspicion that she had deliberately chosen the hat to annoy him, a tactic that had indeed succeeded. How were they supposed to have a meaningful conversation if he couldn't see her face?

"I would have preferred to see your face," he admitted.

"And I would prefer if I didn't see yours," Miss Delacourt responded. "I guess we both don't get what we want."

Caleb looked heavenward. Why did he even try with Miss Delacourt? She was maddening. But he did have one thing that she wanted. Perhaps he might even bring a smile to her lips.

Reaching into his jacket pocket, he pulled out a piece of paper. "I have something for you," he said.

"Which is?" she asked, feigning little interest.

"It is the French code that you requested," Caleb replied.

Now he had her attention. She turned towards him and reached for the paper, but he moved it out of her reach. "I will give it to you on two conditions."

She let out a frustrated sigh. "Of course you have conditions," she muttered.

"The first condition is that you will inform me if the code works," Caleb said.

"I can agree to that." She paused. "And the second?"

Caleb smiled, hoping to disarm her. "You will allow me to take you on a carriage ride through Hyde Park."

"No," came her quick reply.

"Whyever not?" Caleb asked. "Surely there is no harm in taking a carriage ride with me."

Miss Delacourt shifted back on the bench so her face was concealed. "Just being here with you, right now, could cause people to talk."

Caleb's eyes roamed over Hyde Park. "No one appears to be giving us much heed. Are you afraid that being seen with me could damage your reputation?"

"No, but I do not want people to gossip about me," Miss Delacourt explained. "If the *ton* starts to take notice of me, I'm afraid of what they will see. My cover depends on anonymity."

"You are much too beautiful to be a wallflower," he praised. Perhaps if he charmed her, she would be more cooperative.

But it didn't seem to work.

Miss Delacourt visibly stiffened. "I would prefer if you didn't use flattery to achieve your purposes."

"It was merely the truth," Caleb defended.

"Well, do try to keep your opinions to yourself," Miss Delacourt said. "My appearance does not affect my ability to be an agent."

"I never said that it did."

Miss Delacourt gave him a pointed look. "Did you ever tell Lord Roswell that he was beautiful when you worked with him?"

"I see your point," Caleb admitted. "But we digress. If you are opposed to a carriage ride, may I at least call upon you?"

"For what purpose?" Miss Delacourt asked.

Caleb resisted the urge to groan. "I am trying here," he replied. "Please at least try to meet me halfway."

Miss Delacourt pursed her lips, appearing as though she might reject his plea. However, her expression softened, if only slightly, but it was enough. "Very well," she conceded. "I suppose you may visit me, assuming you do not overstay your welcome."

"Thank you," he acknowledged.

She tipped her head. "Now may I have the code?" she asked.

He extended it towards her. "You will tell me what you discover, won't you?" he asked.

"I said that I would, didn't I?" she responded as she accepted the paper.

Caleb watched as she studied the paper in her hand and couldn't help but admire her lovely face. For it was indeed lovely. Not that he should be noticing such a thing.

Miss Delacourt abruptly rose. "Thank you for this, but I should be going," she said.

Rising, he asked, "May I see you home?"

"That is not necessary," she replied. "I am more than capable of seeing my way home."

"I know you are capable, but it would be my privilege."

Indecision flashed on Miss Delacourt's features before she said, "I will allow you to walk me to my coach."

It might not be much, but he would take it as a small victory. "I would like that very much," he said as he held out his arm.

Miss Delacourt glanced down at his arm before she reluctantly placed her hand on his sleeve. "Did you often escort Lord Roswell around Town?"

"No, but he wasn't as beautiful as you," Caleb replied as he started leading her down the dirt path.

"Mr. Bolingbroke, you go too far..." she started.

Caleb put his other hand up. "I know. You seem to have an aversion to compliments."

"Not an aversion, but I would prefer it if we maintained some boundaries between us," Miss Delacourt said. "We are not friends, but merely agents that are assigned to the same case."

Caleb chuckled. "You mean we are partners."

"Yes, but it is under protest."

His curiosity was piqued. "Why are you so opposed to having a partner?"

"I do not like answering to anyone," Miss Delacourt replied. "It is the only thing in my life that I have control over."

"Are you terribly stifled at home?"

Miss Delacourt glanced away as she admitted, "My father hardly pays any attention to me now that my mother is gone."

"That must be hard."

"It is all I know," she said.

Caleb could hear the sadness in her voice, and he assumed that admission cost her a great deal. "That doesn't make it any easier."

"My father is a very busy man, and it has allowed me to

come and go as I please," Miss Delacourt said. "If anything, I should be grateful for his aloofness."

"My parents are very attentive, almost too attentive," Caleb admitted. "My mother is adamant that I find a wife, and quickly."

"Are you opposed to marriage?"

Caleb nodded. "My life is not conducive to having a wife. I do not wish to cause that complication in my life."

"I agree," Miss Delacourt replied. "Although, my father wishes for me to marry this Season. He has even offered to arrange a marriage for me."

"That is most gracious of him," Caleb teased.

Miss Delacourt grinned, just as he had intended. "I would rather be a spinster than have to answer to a husband. Furthermore, I would have to give up working as a spy and that is not something I wish to do."

"Oh what a tangled web we weave," Caleb said, referencing Sir Walter Scott's poem, *Marmion*. "We both would rather work for the Crown than pursue our own happiness."

"I am happy," Miss Delacourt asserted.

"I did not mean to assume otherwise," Caleb said.

With a curious glance, she inquired, "Are you not happy?"

Caleb brought a smile to his lips. "I am." It was the same lie that he had been telling himself for months now. He wasn't happy, but he didn't quite know why that was. He had everything that he wanted, but he seemed to long for more. But what he longed for, he couldn't say.

As he led her out of Hyde Park, he was grateful for the lull in their conversation. He didn't want to reveal too much of himself to Miss Delacourt. As she so graciously pointed out earlier, they were not friends.

Miss Delacourt pointed towards a black coach that was waiting down the street. "That is my coach," she said.

"Out of curiosity, how is it that you elude your companion so easily?" Caleb asked.

"Mrs. Fernsby is mostly blind and deaf in one ear," Miss Delacourt explained. "She is my father's second cousin and came to live with us after my mother died. I hardly knew her then, and it hasn't gotten much better. We are such different people."

"Does anyone in your family know that you are a spy?"

With a glance over her shoulder at the maid, Miss Delacourt replied, "Felicity does, and I am confident that she will never betray my trust." She cocked her head. "What of your family?"

"My sister knows the truth, but that is only because she was abducted and was told of my unusual profession."

Miss Delacourt reached up and adjusted her straw hat. "Kendrick told me that Lady Roswell's actions were nothing less than heroic when she shot Mr. Barnard."

"Yes, and she is constantly reminding me of such," he said lightly.

They arrived at the coach and Miss Delacourt removed her arm from his sleeve. "Thank you for escorting me to my coach, sir."

"You are welcome," he said. "Until tomorrow."

"Tomorrow?" she asked.

Caleb lifted his brow. "I was going to call upon you so we could become better acquainted with one another."

Miss Delacourt worked hard to keep the displeasure off her face, but she was unsuccessful. "Wonderful," she muttered.

Leaning in, he whispered, "Careful, Miss Delacourt. It almost seems as if you don't enjoy my company."

A laugh escaped her lips, and she delicately covered her mouth with a gloved hand. "You aren't as terrible as I once thought."

"And with that, I shall walk away before you change your mind."

A footman stepped off his perch to open the door for Miss

Delacourt. As she held Caleb's gaze, she said, "Thank you." There was a quiet sincerity in her voice.

"Whatever for?" he inquired.

Though subtle, her gaze softened just enough to captivate him. "For making me laugh," she responded.

He bowed, replying, "It was my pleasure."

As Miss Delacourt settled into the coach, Caleb started walking down the pavement, feeling a sense of accomplishment. He had made some progress with Miss Delacourt, albeit small. He was determined to break through the walls she had built around herself until she could trust him.

That is what any good partner would do, he thought.

Chapter Three

Beneath the midday sun, Simone stood alongside Emilia as she hurled a dagger at the target and watched as it bounced off.

Emilia's shoulders slumped as she turned to face Simone. "What am I doing wrong?" she asked. "That is the fifth time that the dagger bounced off the target."

As Simone went to retrieve the dagger, she said, "As you release the dagger, you must flick your wrist forward. This motion should be smooth and controlled."

"Am I not doing that?" Emilia inquired.

Simone smiled. "You are doing just fine," she encouraged. "Throwing daggers is a skill that develops over time. You must practice and then practice some more."

"I can do that."

"I know you can," Simone said as she extended the dagger to Emilia. "Now allow your arm to follow through after releasing the dagger. Be sure to keep your eyes on the target."

Emilia faced the target and brought her left foot slightly forward. She took a deep breath before she released the dagger. It embedded in the target, slightly off center.

"I did it!" Emilia cheered.

"That you did," Simone said. "And you hit the target."

Emilia wore a bright smile. "I did, and now I am one step closer to being proficient at throwing daggers."

Simone walked up to the target and removed the dagger. "How are your shooting lessons going with Lady Roswell?"

"I am spectacularly bad at shooting a pistol," Emilia admitted. "I will not be a spy any time soon."

"Do you want to be a spy?"

Emilia shook her head. "No, I think I will leave that to you and Fredrick. I am much more content with cheering you on from the safety of my townhouse."

Simone laughed. "I greatly enjoy being a spy," she admitted. "I am able to pretend that I am someone else, even just for a moment. I have been a serving wench, a factory worker, and a beggar. Sometimes I even dress like a man."

"I could never be that brazen," Emilia said as she ran a hand down her pale blue gown. "Besides, I just got a whole new wardrobe. I wouldn't want to waste those."

"Don't get me wrong, I do enjoy wearing gowns as well, but there is something liberating about wearing trousers."

Emilia glanced at the townhouse. "Are you not worried about what your servants think?"

"They are used to my odd behavior by now," Simone replied. "I come and go so often that I am sure they have just given up trying to figure me out."

"What of your father?" Emilia asked. "Does he not worry about you?"

Simone pursed her lips together as she worked to keep the displeasure out of her voice. "My father is a very busy man and doesn't pay me much heed," she replied. "Besides, the servants are loyal to me and won't betray my confidences."

Emilia offered her a weak smile. "I'm sorry."

"For what?"

"Your father being a jackanapes."

Simone blinked. "Why do you think my father is a jackanapes?"

"Anyone who would ignore a daughter that is as incredible as you deserves to be called a jackanapes," Emilia replied. "Am I wrong to say so?"

"No, you aren't wrong."

Emilia placed a hand on Simone's sleeve. "You are in good company," she said. "I only knew of my father after he was dead and left me his fortune. I wish he had made himself known to me while he was still alive."

"My father has never been an overly affectionate man, but he grew distant after my mother died," Simone shared.

"Grief affects everyone differently," Emilia attempted.

"I know, but he rarely speaks of my mother," Simone said. "He even had her portrait removed from the main level and placed in the attic."

Emilia lowered her hand to her side. "Perhaps it was too hard to look at her every single day."

"But what of me?" Simone asked. "Shouldn't he take my feelings into account when making decisions that affect both of us?"

"The easy answer is yes, but grief grays that line. Some people can't see past themselves when mourning a loved one," Emilia counseled.

Simone knew that Emilia was trying to help, but she found herself growing angry all over again. How could her father tuck her mother's portrait away as if she meant nothing to him? Her mother deserved better.

Emilia briefly glanced up at the sky. "I should be going," she said. "Fredrick is taking me on a carriage ride today during the fashionable hour."

"That sounds rather terrible," she teased.

"You are welcome to join us," Emilia offered.

Simone grinned. "That is kind of you, but I think my time will be better spent on saving England from outside threats."

"That is smart," Emilia responded.

As they started to head back to the townhouse, Simone remarked, "I heard that Calvin and Clarissa have been transported."

Emilia released a despondent sigh. "I wish things had been different between us, but Calvin and Clarissa never wanted a relationship with me. I was naive to think otherwise."

"There is nothing wrong with hoping for things."

"There is when my half-siblings try to kill me to gain my fortune," Emilia said. "I am just glad that they won't ever have the opportunity to hurt me again."

Simone's lips quirked. "I have had many people try to kill me, but none of them have been family. That must have been hard."

A footman opened the door for them and they stepped into a corridor. They continued on to the entry hall where they were greeted by the butler.

Clarke tipped his head as he announced, "Mr. Caleb Bolingbroke is waiting for you in the drawing room, Miss. He didn't want me to interrupt your time with Miss Sutherland."

Emilia turned to face her, curiosity evident in her gaze. "Do you have an understanding with Mr. Bolingbroke?"

"No, he is just an acquaintance," Simone replied.

It seemed Emilia was on the verge of further inquiry, but thankfully, she held back. Instead, she remarked, "I will leave you to it then."

Once Emilia had taken her leave, Simone entered the drawing room to find Mr. Bolingbroke standing pensively by the window. She paused to study him. His dark hair framed a face distinguished by a square jaw, and his tall stature commanded attention. He was undeniably handsome, but that was not something she should notice about her partner. He was just a man who vexed her.

"Mr. Bolingbroke," she greeted.

He turned to face her. "Caleb."

She arched an eyebrow. "I do not wish to be so familiar with you."

"We are partners, are we not?"

With a glance over her shoulder at the open door, she lowered her voice. "Do you intend to let my whole household staff know that I work as a spy?"

Caleb took a step closer to her. "You are making a big ado out of nothing," he replied. "I watched you as you taught Miss Sutherland how to throw a dagger."

"That must have been rather boring for you," Simone muttered.

"It was interesting, especially when you would hit the target from nearly twenty yards away," he said. "It was impressive."

Simone brushed off his praise with a slight shrug of her shoulder. "I have had a lot of practice."

"Throwing daggers is not a common practice for ladies."

"No, but my mother was Scottish," Simone explained. "They had a tradition in their family that everyone, male and female, would receive a dagger on their eighth birthday. I have since started using daggers that are designed for throwing."

Caleb held his hand out. "May I see your dagger?"

Simone reached into the folds of her gown and removed the dagger from the scabbard. As she extended it to Caleb, she advised, "Be careful with it."

With an amused look, he said, "I know how to handle a dagger."

"I wasn't sure since your weapon of choice is a pistol."

Caleb admired the dagger before saying, "The hilt has a rather ornate design. Where did you get such a fine dagger?"

"I had it commissioned after my mother died," Simone shared. "The design is of my mother's favorite flower. Every time I hold the dagger, it reminds me of her."

He extended the dagger to her. "Do you think your mother would approve of you being a spy?"

Simone accepted the dagger and slipped it back into the scabbard. "I don't rightly know," she replied. "She caught me once sneaking out to attend a lecture at university and I was wearing men's clothing. But to my surprise, she didn't stop me from going."

"That is a surprise."

"My mother was rather progressive in her views, and she saw nothing wrong with a woman trying to better herself," Simone said. "I think a small part of her wanted to go as well."

Caleb wore a pensive expression. "Anette may wear trousers to ride horses but I don't think she would ever be brazen enough to go to university."

"That is how Kendrick found me," Simone shared. "He followed me out of the hall and asked if I wanted to do more with my life than sit in drawing rooms. I don't know how but he saw through my disguise."

"Kendrick is a spymaster, after all."

"It hardly took me a moment before I agreed to work for him," Simone said. "He started me off small by eavesdropping on conversations. Soon I started going out on my own and completing tougher assignments."

Caleb nodded. "Kendrick found me at university as well. He recruited me and Roswell at the same time. We have been working together ever since."

"Except on this assignment," Simone pointed out. "Why do you suppose that is?"

"Frankly, I am not sure."

Simone extended a gesture towards the settees. "Would you care to have a seat and maybe a cup of tea?"

"Does this mean you aren't trying to get rid of me?" Caleb inquired, a hint of mirth lacing his voice.

"I haven't decided yet," Simone quipped.

An older maid stepped into the room, taking a position in the corner.

Simone went to sit down and was pleased when Caleb sat on the opposite settee. Surprisingly, the conversation was proving less burdensome than she anticipated and she even found herself enjoying it.

"Would you care for some tea?" Simone asked as she reached for the teapot on the tray.

Caleb bobbed his head. "I would, thank you."

Simone poured two cups of tea and offered him a cup and saucer. Their fingers brushed against one another, and she felt something. Something that she couldn't quite explain. It almost felt like a spark, which lingered like a sweet bruise. Which was impossible. That would imply that she felt something for Caleb. And she most assuredly did not. She could barely tolerate the man.

Caleb leaned back in his seat, appearing completely unaffected by their touch. What a relief. At least he had the good sense to feel nothing.

Caleb was working hard to keep the emotions off his face, but something had happened when they had touched. It was most extraordinary, and not at all welcome. He felt something, but he would never act upon those feelings.

Simone was complicated, and messy. Both things he did not need in his life. He would just pretend that nothing had happened and move on. It wasn't as if he couldn't find a young woman to court if he wanted to. But he did not want to court anyone. He preferred being on his own, much to his mother's chagrin.

He took a sip of his tea as he observed Simone. He still couldn't fathom how the *ton* had completely overlooked her. Her beauty alone should have made her the envy of the other young women, but she didn't flaunt it. Perhaps she didn't realize how truly captivating she was.

But he wasn't visiting Simone for a social call. He wanted to get to know her and see if she had deciphered the code.

Caleb knew he had to be discreet since they weren't alone. A maid was working on her needlework in the corner, but he had little doubt that she was listening to their conversation.

Leaning forward, he placed the teacup onto the table and asked, "Did you have a chance to read the newssheets?"

Understanding dawned on Simone's features. "I did," she replied. "I was up most of the night reading the newssheets, and the only thing that sparked my attention was the words- Noble Snapping Turtle." She paused. "Do those words mean anything to you?"

Caleb nodded. "There is a pub known as The Noble Snapping Turtle and it is where French sympathizers spend their time," he informed her. "Was anything else of impor- tance in the newssheets?"

Simone shook her head. "Nothing. At first, I thought the paper you gave me was of little use, but eventually I started seeing a pattern in the words," she said. "Shall we start at the pub?"

With a glance at the maid, Caleb replied, "Perhaps I should go alone."

"Why would you do such a thing?" she asked, her words curt.

Not wishing to stoke Simone's anger, Caleb gently explained, "The pub is in Shadwell and is no place for a lady. Your appearance might cause a disruption amongst the patrons."

"You underestimate me," Simone asserted. "I am more than capable of blending in, if the situation warrants it."

Caleb knew there was no point in arguing with Simone. He could see the determination in her eyes, and he knew she wasn't about to give up this fight. There was no denying that

Simone was a formidable young woman, but even she had limitations. Did she even realize what they were?

"Very well," he replied. "When would you care to travel to the pub?"

Rising, Simone replied, "Now."

"Now?" he asked, awkwardly rising.

"Yes," she said. "Did you bring your carriage with you?"

With a frown, he replied, "I did, but—"

She spoke over him. "Perfect. We can go on a carriage ride," she said. "I will just bring my lady's maid with me."

Turning towards the maid in the corner, Simone ordered, "Will you inform Felicity I am in need of her?"

The maid tipped her head. "Yes, Miss."

As the maid departed from the drawing room to do her bidding, Simone gave him a smug look. "Everything is working out perfectly."

"Do you always get your way?"

Her lips twitched. "Most of the time," she admitted.

Caleb perused the length of her. "Do you intend to change first?" he asked. "I only ask because your gown is rather fine for a pub."

"Good, I want to attract attention," Simone said.

"Dare I ask why?"

Simone held her skirt out. "By doing so, it doesn't make me look like a threat. It will just appear that I am a naive young woman who is bored and is courting trouble."

Caleb crossed his arms over his chest, a playful smile on his lips. "That is a shame. I would have liked to see you as a serving wench again."

"When I am a serving wench, I am practically invisible to the patrons of the pub," Simone said. "They have no qualms about speaking freely in front of a serving wench."

"How are you able to even work as a serving wench?"

Simone grinned. "I ask nicely, and I pay a pretty penny for the honor," she admitted. "It is not a cheap endeavor."

"I guess I hadn't considered that before," Caleb remarked.

An older woman stepped into the room, wearing thick, rounded spectacles. Her eyes squinted as they settled on Simone. "I heard you are going on a carriage ride," she said, her voice unusually loud for the refined atmosphere of the drawing room.

"I am," Simone confirmed.

The woman walked closer to Simone. "I will go with you."

"That won't be necessary," Simone said. "Felicity will accompany me."

"Who?" the woman asked, tilting her left ear towards Simone.

Simone raised her voice as she replied, "Felicity. My lady's maid."

Caleb had to assume that this was the companion that Simone had told him about. The companion turned her attention towards him. "You will behave, sir," she ordered in a firm tone.

"That is my intention, Ma'am," Caleb replied.

"Good, because I know for a fact that Miss Delacourt carries a dagger on her person and she is not afraid to use it," the woman said.

Caleb offered a smile, attempting to disarm the aged companion. "I am well aware of Miss Delacourt's dagger abilities."

The companion scrutinized him in silence, causing his smile to dim. He shifted uncomfortably in his stance, unsure of what she was looking for. After a prolonged moment, her gaze shifted to Miss Delacourt. "I will expect you home shortly, and no lollygagging."

"I understand," Simone said. While her words were straightforward, her eyes betrayed a mischievous gleam.

"Very well," the companion urged.

Simone's lady's maid stepped into the drawing room and she was holding a blue bonnet in her hands. She extended it towards Simone. "I thought you would like to wear this on your carriage ride, Miss."

"Thank you," Simone acknowledged as she accepted the bonnet.

Once Simone tied the strings under her chin, Caleb offered his arm towards her. "Allow me to escort you to my carriage."

Simone placed her hand on his sleeve and he led her out of the townhouse. Once she was situated inside of the open carriage, Caleb sat across from her.

The carriage moved into traffic and Caleb inquired, "So that was your companion?"

"Yes, Mrs. Fernsby," Simone replied. "She is blind as a bat, and possibly sleeps as much as they do."

Caleb chuckled. "She is very good at intimidation. I think the agency could use her."

"She probably was staring at you to see if you were a real gentleman," Simone joked. "It has been a long time since a gentleman has called upon me."

"Why is that?" he asked. "You are a beautiful young woman."

With a huff, Simone responded, "What did I say about flattery?"

"I am merely trying to understand," Caleb replied.

Simone's eyes grew guarded. "Finding a suitor is like a game. You take the hand that you have been dealt and use it to your advantage. But I am not interested in playing the game. I sit on the sides and watch the young women fall over themselves to secure a husband. A part of me feels sorry for them that they so desperately want a husband to control them."

"Not every husband is controlling of his wife," Caleb pointed out.

"That may be true, but it is not a gamble I wish to make," Simone said. "I am doing just fine on my own."

Caleb heard Simone's words, unsure if she genuinely believed them. A hint of sadness lingered in her voice, prompting him to wonder if she was even aware of it.

"Please stop looking at me like that," Simone said.

Realizing that he had been caught staring, he asked, "Like what?"

"You are analyzing me, searching for something that is not there," Simone replied.

Caleb lifted his brow, challenging her. "Is there something that you think I might find?"

Simone rolled her eyes. "You are an infuriating man."

"Thank you," Caleb said.

"That was not a compliment."

Caleb shrugged one shoulder. "I took it as one."

Simone turned her attention towards the shops as Caleb decided to ask the one question that had plagued him. "What is it about me that you don't like?"

"I beg your pardon?"

"It is a simple enough question," Caleb said. "Did I do something to offend you?"

Simone stared at him for a moment before admitting, "I don't entirely *dislike* you." Her words were hardly convincing.

"What does that mean?" he asked, hoping for more clarification.

She let out a sigh. "You seem like a decent enough person, but I don't need a nursemaid on this assignment."

"Is that what you think I am doing?"

"It is what every man does," Simone replied with a wave of her hand. "They can't seem to help themselves because they think they know best. And what are women but just weak and simpering, not worthy of their time or notice."

"I have never thought of you as weak or simpering. In fact, I believe you to be a proficient agent," Caleb admitted.

"But?"

Caleb leaned forward in his seat. "There is no 'but.' I'm beginning to see you for who you truly are."

Simone eyed him warily. "And who is that?"

"You are hiding behind a mask of your own making," Caleb replied. "You want to project to the world an image of yourself, but it is yourself who you are lying to."

She grew rigid in her seat. "I am doing no such thing."

"You want me to see you as a woman with no weaknesses, but sometimes it is those so-called 'weaknesses' that make us strong." Caleb gave her a knowing look. "I believe that people are the strongest when they come face to face with their greatest weaknesses."

"You presume too much," Simone said, her eyes wary.

Caleb straightened in his seat and continued. "I want you to be honest around me, Simone. Trust that I won't let you down."

"That is a big ask."

"I know, but when the time comes, I know you will keep me safe," Caleb said. "It is who you are."

Simone grew silent as she shifted her gaze away from him. Perhaps he had gone too far in his bold speech, but he didn't care. He needed Simone to know that he trusted her. She had saved his life before, and she would do it again. He was sure of that.

Chapter Four

Simone felt a sense of relief as they finally reached The Noble Snapping Turtle. She appreciated what Caleb was attempting to do, but she didn't want to let him in. She couldn't. It was much safer to keep him at arm's length.

Caleb spoke of weaknesses as if they could be strengths but she disagreed. She couldn't afford mistakes; any error might lead others to doubt her ability to handle the challenges of being a spy. She had to surpass her male counterparts, working harder and being better- an unfair reality she had come to accept.

"We are here," Caleb announced as the carriage halted in front of a two-level, red-brick building nestled between two larger structures. A modest sign displayed the establishment's name.

A footman opened the door, assisting Simone onto the dirt-encrusted pavement. Caleb joined her there and asked, "What is our plan?"

She looked at him in surprise. "You are asking me?"

"Who else would I ask?"

"I just assumed you would tell me what our next move was," Simone replied.

Caleb looked displeased by her remark. "I would be more than happy to take the lead, but something tells me that you have already come up with a plan in your head."

That much was true. Perhaps Caleb knew her better than she thought. "My plan was rather simple. We will go in and listen to what is being said around us. With any luck, someone will say something that will help aid in our investigation."

"All right," came Caleb's quick reply.

"You are in agreement, then?"

Caleb shrugged. "I think we will need to modify your plan once we get inside, but for now, it is good enough."

Felicity approached her and asked, "Would you like me to accompany you inside the pub?"

"That won't be necessary," Simone replied. "Remain with the carriage and the footmen. They will keep you safe."

"Yes, Miss," Felicity replied before she took a step back.

Simone adjusted the bonnet on her head before turning her attention towards Caleb. "Shall we?"

Caleb offered his arm. "Did you notice the boarding house that was just up the street?" he asked. "If the French spies spend their time here, one might assume that they are residing at the boarding house."

"That would be a good assumption, but we tend to work in facts."

"We do, but in good time," Caleb said as he stepped over to open the wooden door that was decorated with brass handles.

They entered a cozy hall with low ceilings adorned by wooden beams. The back wall was dominated by a sizable hearth, and round tables occupied the space. The atmosphere was lively as the patrons engaged in conversation, while a few men focused on card games.

Caleb guided her towards an unoccupied table, helping her into her chair before taking his own. "This place is almost pleasant."

"It is," Simone said as her eyes strayed towards a door that was along the side wall. "Where do you suppose that door leads to?"

"I don't know, but I am assuming you want to find out."

Simone grinned. "You know me well."

"I'm starting to," Caleb said, returning her smile.

A barmaid approached the table, wearing a simple brown gown with an apron tied around her neck. "What can I get you?" she asked.

"I would like an ale," Caleb replied.

The barmaid turned her attention towards Simone. "And for the lady?"

"Nothing for me, but I was hoping for some information," Simone said as she retrieved a gold coin from her reticule. "Where does that side door lead to?"

The barmaid perused the length of her. "Nowhere that will interest you."

"Humor me, please," Simone said.

With a glance over her shoulder, the barmaid lowered her voice. "It leads to a private room but it is not for the casual observer. The conversation that dominates the room is of a serious nature."

"What kind of serious nature?" Simone asked.

The barmaid took a step back. "I have said too much. Excuse me," she said before she walked away.

Caleb lifted his brow. "I think you scared her off."

"I did, but she is not the only one we can get information from," Simone said. "You can go ask the barkeep."

"I was thinking as much," Caleb replied as he shoved back his chair. "Will you be all right while I am gone?"

Simone shot him an irritated glance. "I will be fine."

Caleb tipped his head in acknowledgement before he headed towards the bar area.

Her eyes swept over the room, and she noticed a few of the patrons casting curious glances in her direction. Ladies seldom frequented pubs so their reactions weren't completely unexpected.

Simone turned her head, observing Caleb engaged in conversation with the barkeep. He laughed at something the man said and she begrudgingly admitted it wasn't an unpleasant sound—it held a certain charm. There was something about his laugh that brought a smile to her face. How could he laugh so freely, especially considering the weight of their chosen profession? It was odd, really.

Leaning casually against the polished bar, Caleb looked at ease in this place. He accepted a tankard from the barkeep and took a sip.

A commotion in the corner caught her attention. A group of patrons at a table engaged in an increasingly heated conversation about politics, expressing their discontent with England's treatment of the poor. It was a familiar discourse, one she had heard many times before, and she doubted it would be the last. The war had taken a severe toll on the less fortunate, with the exorbitant cost of food being just one of their many challenges.

From behind her, a woman's voice inquired, "Dare I ask why you are here?" The words carried a hint of a French accent.

Simone turned in her seat to face a dark-haired woman of slender build. She was older than her, but she hadn't reached an age where wrinkles had marked her features. Her hair was neatly pulled back into a low chignon, and she wore a simple cotton gown. Suspicion lingered in her eyes, a subtle detail Simone couldn't ignore.

"I have come to participate in a lively debate," Simone replied.

"Women do not debate politics," the woman remarked.

Simone nodded. "True, but I heard that this place was different," she responded. "I was under the impression that a woman had a voice here."

"Does a woman have a voice anywhere?" the woman questioned.

"I hope so," Simone said. "There is nothing more damning than a Society that turns a blind eye to the suffering of women."

The woman seemed to study her before gesturing towards a chair. "May I?"

"Please," Simone replied.

As she moved around to sit, the woman said, "My name is Juliette, and I find you to be rather intriguing. Women of your class do not usually frequent pubs. Nor are they escorted by such a handsome gentleman."

"He is just my friend," Simone replied.

With a glance at Caleb at the bar, Juliette said, "This is a dangerous place for you two. I would recommend you leave and never come back."

"I thank you for your concern, but we are more than capable of taking care of ourselves," Simone responded.

Juliette tsked. "You could just as easily be robbed in here than served the watered-down ale."

"I don't drink the ale," Simone said. "Why, pray tell, are you here if it is so dangerous?"

She put her hands up. "These are my people. They wouldn't harm me."

"Your people?" Simone inquired. "But you are French, are you not?"

"I am, but we are like-minded individuals, making them 'my people,'" Juliette explained. "Go home to your fancy townhouse and be tended to by your servants. Leave the serious business to the people who can handle it."

"Like you?"

Juliette nodded affirmatively. "I am one of those people."

"What if I told you that I was one of those people, as well?" Simone asked.

Leaning her head back, Juliette released a laugh. "Thank

you. I needed a good laugh today." She rose from her chair. "Go home, my lady."

"I am not a lady," Simone said.

"You look like one and act like one," Juliette observed.

Simone maintained her gaze. "Looks can be deceiving, but I would prefer if you called me Simone."

A smile came to Juliette's lips. "I can't help but wonder if you are delusional, but I'm intrigued," she said. "What is it that you want?"

Glancing at the closed door, Simone replied, "I wish to go into the back room."

"Why?" Juliette asked. "There is nothing for you there."

Simone had an idea of what was being discussed in the back room. No doubt it was treasonous in nature. "I want to do more than sit in a drawing room and practice my needle-work. I can do more to help the people that are suffering," she asserted.

"What are you willing to do?" Juliette asked.

In a firm voice, Simone replied, "Whatever it takes."

"And your friend? Does he feel the same way as you?"

"He does."

Juliette returned to her seat and leaned closer. "I need to know whose side you are on. Are you loyal to Britain or France?"

Simone raised an eyebrow and asked a question of her own. "Why do you think I came all this way to be with French sympathizers if I didn't believe in their cause?"

"Interesting," Juliette muttered, as if seeing her for the first time. "I do believe you might be of use to me, but I do not wish to explain it here. I want you to meet me at the boarding house up the street tomorrow morning."

Rising, Juliette continued. "And bring your handsome friend. I do not think I could get tired of looking at him."

"He isn't that handsome," Simone remarked.

Juliette grinned. "I disagree, my lady."

Simone opened her mouth, but Juliette spoke first. "I know. You aren't a lady, but I think I shall call you that. It fits."

After Juliette walked off, exiting the pub, Caleb approached the table and sat down. "What was that about?"

"I don't know, but I think I might have found one of our French spies," Simone said. "She wants us to meet at the boarding house up the street tomorrow morning. I think she has a job for us."

Caleb placed his tankard down on the table. "If the barkeep is to be believed, he said that woman comes and goes from this place but spends most of her time in the back room with the more ardent French sympathizers." He paused. "And she doesn't always come alone. Her brother is often seen with her."

"If they are the French spies that we have been looking for, we need to proceed with caution until we find out their purpose for being here," Simone said.

"I agree." Caleb pushed his tankard away from him. "I think it is time we depart before I even think of drinking more of this ale."

"Is it terribly watered-down?"

"I think that water is the main ingredient," Caleb joked.

Simone pushed back her seat and rose. "Let's depart before my companion comes searching for me."

Caleb chuckled. "We do not wish for that."

"No, we most assuredly don't," Simone said.

As they exited the pub, Simone was pleased that everything was falling into place. But an uneasy feeling came to her stomach. It all seemed too easy- almost unnervingly so. If Juliette was, in fact, a French spy, why had she sought her out?

One thing was certain, they had to be cautious.

Keeping his gaze straight ahead, Caleb said in a hushed voice, "We are being followed. How do you want to play this?"

"I think it would be best if we gave them a tour of Town until we can lose them," Simone responded.

"Then a tour of Town it shall be," Caleb declared. "It shouldn't be too difficult to lose them in the crowded streets."

———

The carriage came to a stop in front of Simone's townhouse and Caleb promptly stepped down onto the pavement. Extending his hand, he assisted Simone out of the carriage.

Simone withdrew her hand once she stood beside him. "Thank you for the carriage ride."

"Allow me to escort you inside," Caleb said.

"That isn't necessary—" Simone began.

Caleb interrupted, "Let me be a gentleman, please."

Simone pressed her lips together before she reluctantly conceded. "Very well," she muttered.

As he led her inside, Caleb said, "I shall return tomorrow morning for our carriage ride." He kept his words intentionally vague since there were prying ears around.

"I shall look forward to it."

Once they were in the entry hall, Simone removed her hand off his sleeve and gave him an expectant look. "Is there anything else, sir?"

"No," he replied, seeing no reason to tarry. It was evident that Simone didn't want him there. He bowed. "Good day, Miss Delacourt."

Simone dropped into a curtsy. "Good day, Mr. Bolingbroke."

Caleb exited the townhouse and entered the carriage. It was a short drive back to his townhouse and he knew he had a lot of work ahead of him. Not just as an agent, but as his father's heir. He was to review the accounts and meet with their man of business. He didn't mind working on the accounts since one day it would all belong to him. But he hoped that day didn't come for many years. He loved his father and didn't want to imagine life without him.

Once he stepped into the entry hall, he was met by his mother and his sister. Both wore solemn expressions, and he grew concerned. "What has happened?"

"Something terrible has happened, Brother," Anette replied.

He rushed closer to them. "What?" he asked, his voice rushed. "Is it Father? Did something happen to him?"

"No, it has nothing to do with Father, but everything to do with being deceived by you," Anette replied.

Caleb furrowed his brow. "Pardon?"

Anette gave him a pointed look, her gaze unyielding. "I was driving by Miss Delacourt's townhouse this morning and I saw you escorting her into the carriage," she said. "In my opinion, it was the ultimate betrayal."

"I hadn't realized you took issue with Miss Delacourt," Caleb said.

"You misunderstand me. I have no issue with Miss Delacourt, but I do take issue with you not telling us that you are courting her," Anette clarified.

Caleb frowned, the realization dawning on him. So that is what this was about, he thought. "I am not courting Miss Delacourt," he asserted, his voice carrying a hint of frustration.

"It certainly appeared that way," Anette responded. "You two appeared to be a rather lovely couple."

"Looks can be deceiving," Caleb said.

His mother spoke up. "Why have you been keeping this a secret?" she asked. "I was acquainted with Lady Hungerton, and I could not be more delighted you are pursuing her daughter."

Caleb put his hands up in front of him. "I am not pursuing anyone, much less Miss Delacourt. We just embarked on a pleasant carriage ride this morning."

"What is wrong with Miss Delacourt?" his mother asked.

"Nothing is wrong with her, but I am not interested in getting married at this time," Caleb replied.

His mother tossed her hands in the air. "You are impossible, Son. You need to marry, and I need grandchildren."

"Anette will give you a bushel of grandchildren," Caleb attempted. "Just pretend that I am not here."

"You know I can't do that. It is my job... no, my duty, to ensure you are properly wed and are blissfully happy," his mother said.

Anette interjected, "You must know that the gossips will catch wind of this and Miss Delacourt's name will be tied to yours."

"I am hoping that won't happen," Caleb said.

"If I saw you two together, other people did as well," Anette expressed. "I must admit that Miss Delacourt is an interesting choice. I am not acquainted with her."

Caleb didn't want to have this conversation. Not with his sister or his mother. He didn't dare break Miss Delacourt's confidence by sharing that she was a spy. So, for now, he would have to skirt the truth.

"It was one carriage ride. Can we leave it at that?" Caleb asked, attempting to quell further discussion.

His mother, undeterred by his objections, persisted. "I do find it odd that Miss Delacourt is a wallflower, considering her mother was anything but when she was in high Society. Lady Hungerton was opinionated, stubborn and an utter delight to be around."

Caleb bit his tongue, knowing that Simone sounded precisely like her mother. How she convinced the *ton* otherwise was beyond him.

His mother continued. "Fortunately for you, I have taken

it upon myself to invite Miss Delacourt and her father for dinner this evening."

"*You did what?!*" Caleb exclaimed.

"There is no reason to raise your voice," his mother said. "I am hoping to become more acquainted with Miss Delacourt."

Caleb stared at his mother. "You have no right to interfere with my life."

"I have every right; I am your mother," she asserted. "Besides, it is just one dinner. I am not quite sure why you are getting so worked up by this."

"You have gone too far with this one, Mother," Caleb fumed.

His father's voice came from the corridor. "What is all the shouting about?" he asked.

With a look that exuded innocence, his mother replied, "Caleb is upset that I invited Lord Hungerton and his lovely daughter, Miss Delacourt, to dinner."

"Are you intending to play matchmaker, my dear?" his father asked, knowingly.

"Perhaps, but Caleb doesn't need a gentle push anymore to find a wife. He needs to be shoved," his mother defended.

Caleb turned his attention towards Anette. "You went along with this, willingly?" he asked.

Anette had the decency to look ashamed. "I didn't realize Mother was going to invite them to dinner, but it isn't such an awful idea."

"No, it is a pretty awful idea," Caleb responded. "Mark my words. I do not intend on courting Miss Delacourt."

"You seem rather adamant about that," his mother said.

Caleb let out a frustrated sigh. "I am done with this conversation," he stated. "I need to go work on the accounts before our dinner guests arrive." He didn't even bother to keep the annoyance out of his voice as he headed towards the study.

How dare his mother and sister interfere in his life? He had no desire to marry, but they didn't believe him. They thought they knew what was best for him, but they were wrong to do so. Why couldn't they have left well enough alone?

He entered the study and walked over to the desk, dropping down into the chair. How was he to work when he was so upset?

His father stepped into the room and said, "You must know that they mean well."

"They are meddling in my life," Caleb grumbled.

"Your mother is just worried about you."

Caleb leaned back in the chair. "There is no reason to be worried about me," he argued. "I am doing just fine on my own."

"Are you?" his father asked. "I don't know what you are involved in, but I know it is dangerous. I have seen it firsthand."

"I can't discuss that—"

His father spoke over him. "I know, and I am not asking you to," he stated. "I haven't told your mother any of this because I do not want her to worry about you."

"Thank you," Caleb said.

Walking closer to the desk, his father shared, "I have spent more time on our accounts than on politics, per your recommendation."

"It wasn't my recommendation," Caleb remarked. "But I am glad that you heeded my words. By doing so, certain people were willing to overlook what you had to do to keep our family safe."

His father sat on a chair that faced the desk. "Dare I ask who those people are?"

"It is best that you don't know."

"Very well," his father said. "But your mother is right. You need an heir."

Caleb groaned. "Not et tu?"

"If you do not have an heir, then my title will be passed to your cousin, David," his father said. "He is an imbecile."

"David is not an imbecile," Caleb attempted.

His father lifted his brow. "Surely you can't say that with a straight face," he remarked. "I blame it on when he fell off his horse and hit his head."

"That was when David was ten, and it was just a bump on the back of the head," Caleb said.

"Which no doubt caused his simple-mindedness," his father pressed. "Do you truly want David to be responsible for our thriving estate?"

"This is assuming David is still alive when I die," Caleb pointed out.

Putting his hands up, his father said, "You are right. The title might pass to the imbecile's son."

Caleb grudgingly acknowledged that his father did have a point. David might not be the most astute individual, often ignorant, but he wasn't inherently a bad person. The question lingered- was mere ignorance reason enough for marriage?

His father stood up. "Just think on what I said," he urged. "There are hundreds of people that are dependent on us for their livelihoods. We have a duty to not let them down."

After his father departed from the room, Caleb reached for a ledger and started to review it. However, his focus wavered, repeatedly revisiting the same line.

Frustrated, he slammed the ledger shut. Blast it all. He understood duty, more so than anyone else. His duty was to his King and Country. He wouldn't enter into marriage solely for the sake of producing an heir. They all deserved better; he deserved better.

And now he was forced to endure a dinner with Simone and her father. He had little doubt that Simone was equally annoyed by his mother's matchmaking attempt. She had made her thoughts on matrimony rather clear to him.

Anette stepped into the room and asked, "Are you still upset with me?"

"Yes," Caleb replied.

"You have only yourself to blame," Anette said. "You have never shown favor to a young woman before."

"It was just a carriage ride."

"So you keep saying, but I think it is something much more," Anette said, approaching the desk. "You were smiling when I saw you with Miss Delacourt."

Caleb shot his sister an exasperated glance. "Should I have been scowling instead?" he asked in a frustrated tone.

"No, you wouldn't want to scare the poor girl," Anette said.

Her innocent remark caused him to let out a dry chuckle. "I doubt that would scare Miss Delacourt."

Anette, lowering her voice, leaned in. "Is she a spy, too?"

Caleb maintained a composed expression, carefully choosing his words. "Why do you ask?"

"If you aren't courting her, then that is the only explanation that I can come up with," Anette responded, her tone carrying a hint of curiosity. "I thought the agency didn't employ ladies."

"Does this conversation have a point?" Caleb asked, his eyebrows raised.

Anette narrowed her eyes, the curiosity intensifying. "You aren't going to answer my questions, are you?" she asked.

"No, I am not."

"By not answering them, you are answering them," Anette stated.

Caleb looked heavenward. "I do not have time for your misguided logic, Sister," he said. "I need to get ready for a dinner party this evening."

Anette took a step back but held his gaze. "Fine. Do not tell me, but I will root out the truth. I always do."

Rising, Caleb replied, "Not this time."

"All right. You win, for now," Anette said. "If you will excuse me, I need to return home and prepare for this evening."

Caleb watched his sister's retreating figure and he knew tonight was going to be an utter disaster.

Chapter Five

Simone sat at her dressing table in her bedchamber as Felicity styled her hair. She was not looking forward to this evening. Not one bit. She wondered why Caleb had invited her to dine with him this evening. She had no desire to spend additional time with him. They were partners, not friends. Although, she had to admit that line was starting to blur.

Felicity took a step back and asked, "Are you pleased with your hair?"

Simone turned her head to the side to look at her reflection in the mirror. "I am," she replied. "But I do not know why you were insistent that you put pearls in my hair."

"You are going to dine with Mr. Bolingbroke and his family. I daresay that you need to look your best, if not for your sake, then for your father's."

Simone shifted in her seat to face her lady's maid. "I can't believe my father agreed to go this evening. It is just so unlike him."

"It surprised me as well."

"What if he thinks Mr. Bolingbroke intends to court me?"

Felicity shrugged. "What if he wants to?"

Simone shook her head. "No, Mr. Bolingbroke and I can

hardly stand one another. He has no intention of courting me. Which makes this invitation to dine with his family that much more perplexing."

"You two did not look at odds with one another in the carriage," Felicity pointed out.

"I will admit that Mr. Bolingbroke does have a pleasant demeanor about him, but we are just partners on this one assignment."

Felicity eyed her curiously. "If you are sure…" Her words trailed off.

"I am."

Her lady's maid didn't look convinced. "I shall drop it, for now."

"Thank you," Simone said, rising. "I should be going. I wouldn't want to make my father wait for me."

"I wish you luck."

"I don't need luck, do I?"

Felicity smiled. "A little luck never hurt anyone."

Simone acknowledged her words with the tip of her head before she departed from her bedchamber. Once she arrived in the entry hall, she saw her father was waiting for her with his usual solemn expression.

"Good, there you are," her father grumbled. "Let us get this over with."

Simone shared her father's sentiments, but she just bit her tongue. It would be nice to spend some time with her father, even if it meant that she had to dine with Caleb and his family.

Her father led her towards the coach, and they stepped inside. The journey to Lord Oxley's townhouse was brief. Upon arrival, they exited the coach and made their way to the main door, which was promptly opened by the butler.

"Do come in," the butler said as he stood to the side.

As they came to a stop in the entry hall, the butler continued. "Allow me to show you to the drawing room."

They both followed the butler into the elegantly furnished drawing room and saw that they were the first ones there.

"The family will be down shortly," the butler informed them before he departed from the room.

Her father's eyes roamed over the drawing room with its blue-papered walls. "This place has not changed much since the last time I was here."

"When was that?"

"We attended a soiree here once before your mother died," her father replied, his eyes growing reflective. "I did have a whole other life before that fateful day."

Not sure what she could say, she just murmured, "I'm sorry."

"There is no reason to be sorry," he replied. "It was a different time, and I am a much different man now because of it."

Simone could hear the pain in his words but she knew that no truer words had ever been spoken. The day her mother died, her father had changed. And not for the better.

A silence hung heavily in the air but Simone wasn't sure what she could say to help her father. He was hurting, but so was she. Losing her mother in such a dramatic fashion had taken a toll on her. She hadn't even had a chance to say goodbye to her.

Lady Oxley entered the room with a bright smile on her face. "Lord Hungerton, it is so good to see you again," she said in a pleasant voice.

Her father bowed. "Lady Oxley," he greeted.

"It has been ages since we have last seen one another." Lady Oxley turned her attention towards Simone, her eyes exuding warmth. "And this must be Miss Delacourt. You are most welcome here."

Knowing what was expected of her, Simone dropped into a curtsy. "My lady," she greeted.

Lady Oxley perused the length of her. "You look so much like your mother," she said. "It is almost uncanny."

"It is a blessing and a curse," her father remarked, his voice curt.

"I can only imagine," Lady Oxley remarked.

Her father glanced at the doorway. "Will Lord Oxley not be joining us this evening?"

"He will be here shortly," Lady Oxley replied. "He is just finishing up his meeting with his man of business. It used to be that I couldn't keep him away from the House of Lords, but now he devotes all his time and energy to our country estate."

Caleb stepped into the room and his eyes landed on Simone. In his gaze, she saw something. An apology, perhaps?

He bowed. "Miss Delacourt, you are looking enchanting this evening."

Simone dropped into a curtsy. "You are too kind, Mr. Bolingbroke."

Caleb turned his attention towards her father. "Lord Hungerton," he said. "Thank you for coming this evening."

"It was our pleasure," her father responded. His words were cordial enough but they seemed to lack sincerity.

Lady Oxley gestured towards the mantel and addressed her father. "Did you see the vase that we just acquired from China? I recall how you love antiquities."

As Lady Oxley and her father conversed about the vase, Caleb approached Simone and said in a hushed voice, "I'm sorry about this."

Matching his low tone, Simone asked, "Why did you invite us to dine with you?"

"I didn't invite you. My mother did. She is under the impression that I am attempting to court you."

"Why would she assume such a thing?"

"Because my sister saw us on our carriage ride," Caleb explained. "My mother is relentless about me finding a wife."

With a glance at her father, Simone asked, "What are we to do about this, then?"

"I will deal with it," Caleb replied. "Just try to be nice to me this evening."

"That will be rather difficult," Simone said, softening her words with a smile. "I would have you know that I can be rather pleasant."

Caleb grinned. "I have yet to see that side of you."

"That is because you only say things that vex me, constantly," Simone joked.

"I do believe everything out of my mouth vexes you," Caleb said.

Her smile grew. "You wouldn't be wrong."

Caleb perused the length of her, and in his eyes, she saw approval. "I was in earnest earlier. You are looking especially lovely this evening."

"Flattery, Mr. Bolingbroke?" she asked.

"It is merely the truth."

Simone was secretly pleased by his compliment, but she would never admit that. She didn't want him to think she cared about what he thought.

Caleb's grin transformed into a smirk. "Did I do the impossible and make you speechless?"

"You did no such thing," she asserted. "I was just thinking about all the ways I could insult you, but I do not wish to do so in front of your mother."

"Should you practice complimenting me?" Caleb asked.

Simone arched an eyebrow. "What would I even compliment?"

Caleb waggled his brow as he tugged at the end of his waistcoat. "You could tell me how devilishly handsome I look this evening."

"I thought you wanted truth between us," Simone quipped.

"Humor me," he said with amusement in his eyes. "Just offer me one genuine compliment."

Simone pursed her lips together, feeling rather foolish. "This is absurd," she muttered.

"Can you not do it?"

With a glance at her father, who was admiring the vase in his hand, Simone attempted to think of something that would appease Caleb. There were many things she admired about him, but she didn't dare admit that. Not to him. He would become even more unbearable than he already was.

Simone turned her attention back to Caleb and studied him from head to foot. After a long moment, she said, "I like the way you brushed your hair this evening."

He chuckled. "Are you truly complimenting me on how I brushed my hair?"

"Yes, it is more brushed forward than normal, is it not?"

"I don't rightly know," he replied. "I do not keep track of such things."

"Pity," she said.

Caleb leaned closer to her. "There are surely other things that you have noticed about me," he remarked. "My smile or perhaps my chiseled jawline."

"I haven't noticed those things but clearly *you* have," Simone said, secretly enjoying his nearness. He smelled of orange and musk. It was the most intriguing combination of scents, and it was as unique as he was.

"You disappoint me," Caleb said, his words light.

"And you, sir, are supposed to be charming," Simone retorted.

A subtle smile played at the edges of his lips as he remarked, "I like how you styled your hair this evening, as well. The pearls are a nice touch."

"Thank you. I shall pass along your compliments to my lady's maid," Simone said.

Caleb's eyes darted towards the open door and informed

her, "Wonderful. My sister and her husband just arrived." He winced slightly. "I'm sorry. I am not quite sure what my sister will say or do on any given occasion."

Simone watched as Lord and Lady Roswell approached them with smiles on their faces.

Lady Roswell came to a stop in front of her. "Hello, Miss Delacourt," she said.

As Simone gracefully descended into a curtsy, she greeted, "Lady Roswell. It is a pleasure to meet you. I have heard much about you, all good things, I assure you."

Lady Roswell gestured towards her husband. "Are you acquainted with my husband?"

"I am," Simone replied, exchanging a look with Lord Roswell. "We were introduced at Miss Sutherland's ball."

Lord Roswell tipped his head towards her. "Miss Delacourt," he said.

Lady Roswell's lips twitched, as if she were privy to a secret. "Miss Sutherland is a dear friend. I believe her to be a delight."

"I agree, wholeheartedly," Simone responded.

"I am teaching Miss Sutherland how to shoot a pistol," Lady Roswell shared.

Clasping her hands together, Simone said, "She informed me of this when she came to call. I have had the privilege of teaching her how to throw daggers."

"Daggers?" Lady Roswell repeated.

"Yes, I am rather proficient in throwing daggers," Simone replied.

Lady Roswell shifted her attention to her husband and inquired, "Do you think I should learn how to throw daggers?"

"No, I think that is a terrible idea," Lord Roswell replied, his words softened by a smile directed at his wife.

"I would be happy to teach you, but I should warn you

that it takes a lot of practice before one becomes proficient," Simone said.

Lady Roswell's face brightened. "I shall take you up on that. I have never had a desire to toss daggers until now, but it sounds exciting."

The butler stepped into the room and announced supper was ready.

Caleb stepped closer to Simone and offered his arm. "May I escort you to the dining room?" he asked.

"Thank you," Simone replied, placing her hand on his sleeve.

While Caleb led her towards the dining room, Simone snuck a glance at him. He truly was an intriguing man. She enjoyed his playful side, and how he bantered back and forth with her. But it would do her no good to develop feelings for him. They were partners and both were smart enough not to complicate their relationship with something as trivial as emotions.

Caleb ate his soup as he listened to the conversation that was going on around the dinner table. He felt no need to speak up and interject his thoughts, considering everyone was speaking on polite conversational topics.

He glanced at Simone and noticed that her demeanor had changed. She seemed much more timid and her eyes remained downcast. It appeared that her ruse of being a wallflower was one that extended outside of the ballroom.

Simone turned her head and caught him staring. Instead of looking away, or feeling embarrassed, he asked, "Are you not enjoying your soup?"

"It is delicious, but I have had enough," she replied.

"But you hardly ate any of it."

Her lips quirked. "Do you monitor all of your guests' intake of soup?"

"Only yours," he teased.

As the footmen collected the bowls, his father stepped into the dining room and said, "I do apologize for being late, but my meeting with my man of business went longer than expected."

"It always does," his mother remarked lightly.

His father sat down at the head of the table as he acknowledged his guests. "Miss Delacourt. Lord Hungerton," he greeted. "Welcome to our humble home."

Lord Hungerton tipped his head. "We appreciate the invite to dine with your family this evening."

"You are always welcome," his father said. "You and your lovely daughter."

In a soft voice, Simone spoke up. "Thank you, my lord."

His father smiled kindly at her. "I'm afraid it has been some time since we saw you last. You were just a child then."

"Simone is not so young anymore and is in her third Season," Lord Hungerton said, his voice gruff.

"Time certainly does go by quickly, especially when it is not one's own child," his father remarked.

Anette interjected from the other side of the table as she addressed Simone. "What occupies your time?"

With a brief glance at her father, Simone replied, "I enjoy working on my needlework, practicing the pianoforte, and reading books."

"Are you reading anything of importance?" Anette asked.

Reaching for her glass, Simone replied, "I am reading a book of poetry right now."

"Poetry?" Anette made a face. "How boring."

Roswell chuckled. "Not everyone has an aversion to poetry as you do, my dear," he said. "Some people actually enjoy bettering themselves."

With a loving glance at her husband, Anette continued

questioning Simone. "Have you read the book that was written by A Lady?"

Before Simone could reply, Lord Hungerton answered for her, "My daughter would not read such dribble. Can you imagine the ramblings of a madwoman?"

Anette's displeasure was etched on her features. "Why do you suppose she is mad?"

"What kind of woman would have a desire to write a book?" Lord Hungerton asked. "I daresay that no sane woman would."

Caleb opened his mouth to argue with Lord Hungerton, but Roswell spoke first. "I hope more women write books. They have stories that need to be told, and I for one, want to hear them."

Anette looked at her husband with approval. "Thank you, Roswell."

Lord Hungerton put his hand up. "I do apologize. I did not mean to start a debate," he said. "We clearly do not see eye to eye on this issue, and that is all right. But as for me and my house, we do not read books written by women."

Caleb knew Anette objected to Lord Hungerton's words most profusely and he held his breath to see if she was going to continue arguing. However, she turned her attention back to Simone and asked, "Besides throwing daggers, do you have any other interesting hobbies that I should be made aware of?"

"I'm afraid not," Simone replied. "I am not that interesting."

Anette didn't look convinced. "I am not quite sure that is true."

"Simone speaks true," Lord Hungerton said. "She has aligned herself with the wallflowers, much to my chagrin, and the *ton* hardly notices her."

The footmen started placing plates in front of them and Caleb reached for his fork and knife. It was fascinating to him that Simone had managed to fool her father into believing that she was something that she wasn't. How was it possible that he lived with her and didn't see what was right under his nose?

His father's eyes held compassion. "Everyone blossoms at their own pace. It is not Miss Delacourt's time to shine yet, but I have no doubt that she will."

"Thank you," Simone acknowledged.

A silence descended over the table as they started eating their food. After a long moment, Lord Hungerton shifted in his seat to face his father. "Did you have a chance to review the bill that was being proposed by Lord Chatsworth?"

With a glance at Caleb, his father replied, "I have not, but I have heard that it is garnering more attention."

"That it has," Lord Hungerton agreed. "If Lord Chatsworth can push this bill through, it could make a real difference for the poor."

"I doubt it will pass," Anette remarked.

Lord Hungerton lifted his brow. "Are you familiar with the bill?"

"I am, and the House of Lords will never agree to lowering the taxes, especially during a time of war. If anything, the Tories will push to raise the taxes," Anette replied.

"With all due respect, young lady, you know nothing about politics," Lord Hungerton stated. "Lord Chatsworth believes he has the support of the Tories and Whigs."

"He would be wrong," Anette said.

Lord Hungerton wiped the sides of his mouth with his napkin before responding, "I am not quite sure where you get your information, but I suspect it isn't coming from the Social pages of the newssheets."

"I tire of reading the Social pages," Anette expressed. "Why should I care about what color ribbon someone wore when our poor are suffering?"

"This is why women cannot be in politics," Lord Hungerton said. "You deal in emotions, whereas men deal in facts."

His father pushed back his chair and rose. "I believe we should continue this conversation over a glass of port in my study."

With a glance at his plate, his mother asked, "Are you not hungry?"

"I am not." His father patted his stomach. "And I think it would be a good thing if I skip dessert this evening."

Lord Hungerton rose. "I think a glass of port is a fine idea," he said. "Mr. Bolingbroke? Lord Roswell? Will you be joining us?"

Caleb nodded as he placed his cloth napkin onto the table. "I think I shall."

Roswell remained seated and said, "I would prefer to stay and finish dinner with my wife."

"Very good," his father responded. "Gentlemen?"

As his father and Lord Hungerton departed from the room, Caleb leaned closer to Simone and asked, "Will you be all right without me?"

She tilted her chin, a smile playing on her lips. "I have managed to do so my entire life. Why do you think tonight would be any different?"

Caleb chuckled. "I will miss you, too."

The smile disappeared. "I never said that," Simone said, most ardently.

"No, but I can tell you are thinking it."

"You would be wrong."

Caleb playfully raised his eyebrows. "I will return later to beat you at a game of whist. I am quite good at that particular card game."

"As am I, and I do not intend to go easy on you," Simone said.

"Nor would I expect you to, which will make beating you that much more satisfying," Caleb remarked, rising.

Simone held his gaze, a mischievous glint to her eyes. "I will be looking forward to taking you down a peg or two."

Caleb placed a hand over his heart. "You wound me," he joked.

"I doubt that. I have never met a more cocky man than you," she retorted.

"I would prefer the term 'confident.'"

Simone rolled her eyes. "You have found yet another way to vex me."

"Then my work here is done," Caleb said as he performed an exaggerated bow.

After he exited the dining room, he walked towards the study that was in the rear of the townhouse. He stepped into the room and saw his father and Lord Hungerton already had a glass of port in their hands.

"It is about time you showed up," his father teased as he went to sit on the settee that faced the hearth.

Lord Hungerton looked at Caleb with a solemn expression. "What exactly are your intentions towards my daughter, Mr. Bolingbroke?"

Caleb knew this question was coming, but he was no more prepared for it. He needed to proceed cautiously or else he would risk stoking the baron's anger.

"I have immense respect for your daughter, but I am not interested in getting married at this time," he replied.

Displeasure marred Lord Hungerton's expression as his brow furrowed. "Is my daughter not good enough for you?"

With a shake of his head, Caleb replied, "That is not what I meant."

"But that is what you said."

"No, I merely said I was not ready to marry," Caleb argued.

Lord Hungerton tossed back his glass of port before he

grumbled, "Her dowry is fifteen thousand pounds and I still can't marry her off."

His father held up his drink. "She is only in her third Season. Give her time, and she might surprise you."

Lord Hungerton huffed. "I doubt it. She is rather dull."

Caleb looked at him in disbelief. "You believe your daughter to be dull?" he asked.

"Is that why you aren't interested in her?" Lord Hungerton asked. "All she does is sit around our townhouse and practice her needlework with her companion. I try to encourage her to go call upon people and I am met with resistance."

Lord Hungerton dropped down on the settee and continued. "I blame her mother," he said. "Rebecca filled her head with nonsensical nonsense when Simone was younger and now she isn't here to guide her."

"It is hardly Lady Hungerton's fault that she died," his father remarked.

"I should have taken more interest in Simone's upbringing," Lord Hungerton said. "Perhaps if I had, she would already have taken a suitor."

Caleb worked hard to keep the annoyance off his features. It did not sit well with him that Lord Hungerton was criticizing his daughter, especially since he was wrong to do so. Simone was nothing like how he described.

"I might just have to pay someone to take her off my hands," Lord Hungerton declared.

Caleb walked over to the drink cart and picked up the decanter. As he poured himself a drink, he asked, "Do you truly think Miss Delacourt would go along with an arranged marriage?"

"Not at first, but she will do as I tell her," Lord Hungerton replied. "Although, she has this absurd notion that she can live on her own."

"Why is it madness?" Caleb asked.

Lord Hungerton looked at him as if he were a simpleton. "Simone hardly leaves the townhouse. How could she possibly care for herself? She is just a weak, defenseless woman and someone would take advantage of that."

Caleb gripped the glass tightly in his hand. He wanted to correct Lord Hungerton's perception of Simone, but he knew it was not his place to do so. He just did not like the way the baron was disrespecting his daughter.

His father leaned forward and placed his glass onto the table. "I used to worry about Anette, but she found a fine match in Roswell. Sometimes we must give our children the space they need to find themselves."

"Your daughter does have some unique views," Lord Hungerton commented.

His father's voice filled with pride as he stated, "I raised her to have a voice, and I am pleased that Roswell is encouraging her to use it."

"My wife was similar, and I do miss having riveting conversations with her," Lord Hungerton shared. "Heaven knows I can't have those same conversations with Simone."

Caleb went to sit down on an upholstered armchair. "I do think Miss Delacourt would surprise you, given the chance."

Lord Hungerton's eyes held annoyance. "I know you mean well, but I am more familiar with my daughter than you are."

Putting his hand up, Caleb said, "I did not mean to imply otherwise."

While Lord Hungerton and his father engaged in conversation, Caleb resisted the urge to excuse himself and seek out Simone's company. She was far more entertaining than her father. And he knew the truth about her. Simone was obstinate, headstrong, and utterly delightful. She was someone that he could fall for, but he was not foolish enough to do so.

Chapter Six

With a cup of tea in her hand, Simone sat in the drawing room with the ladies as they waited for the gentlemen to return from having a glass of port. The conversation was pleasant enough, but Simone did not see a need to interject her thoughts. She was, after all, playing the ruse of being a wallflower.

Lady Roswell shifted her gaze towards Simone. "What are your thoughts on our Prime Minister, Lord Liverpool?"

"I have none," Simone lied. She had many, but she didn't dare express her opinion. Not here. Not now.

With a lifted brow, Lady Roswell responded, "You have none? Not even one?"

Simone leaned forward and placed her teacup onto the table. "A lady does not express her opinions on politics."

Lady Oxley spoke up. "Well said, Miss Delacourt," she praised. "Anette would be wise to remember that."

"I am married now, and my husband encourages me to speak up," Lady Roswell remarked. "I do not believe that Miss Delacourt is truly this boring."

"Anette! That was uncalled for. Apologize to Miss Delacourt," Lady Oxley chided.

Lady Roswell put her hand up. "My apologies, Miss Dela-court, but I think you do have an opinion on a myriad of things. Quite frankly, I would like to hear them, all of them."

Simone found Lady Roswell's directness to be refreshing, but she didn't dare reveal too much about herself. But she could, at the very least, share one or two opinions about which she felt passionately. "Very well. I do believe Lord Liverpool is doing a decent enough job, but his attentions are more focused abroad rather than the suffering of his own people."

"I agree," Lady Roswell said with approval in her eyes. "The taxes that are being inflicted on the poor are unjust and something should be done to alleviate their suffering."

Lady Oxley frowned. "I do not think this is an appropriate conversation to be having in the drawing room."

"When is it appropriate, Mother?" Lady Roswell asked.

"Miss Delacourt is a guest in our home, and I do not want to make her feel uncomfortable for any reason," Lady Oxley replied.

Lady Roswell shifted in her seat to face Simone. "I daresay it takes much more to make Miss Delacourt uncomfortable. Am I wrong to assume so?"

"No, you are not," Simone admitted.

With a curious gaze, Lady Roswell asked, "What are you truly reading? And please do not say a book on poetry. No one reads poetry for their own enjoyment."

A laugh escaped Simone's lips and she brought her gloved hand up to cover her mouth. "You wouldn't be wrong. Poetry is dreadfully boring." She glanced at the empty doorway. "I am, in fact, reading the book that was written by A Lady."

"I knew it!" Lady Roswell exclaimed. "It is all the rage right now."

"Miss Sutherland gifted me the book, and I found it to be captivating," Simone shared. "I started devouring it the moment I received it."

Lady Roswell took a sip of her tea before asking, "Why are you hiding it from your father?"

Simone hesitated before revealing, "My father is not progressive at all. He is set in his ways and I am forced to tiptoe around him."

"I am most fortunate that my parents supported me," Lady Roswell remarked.

Lady Oxley bobbed her head. "Yes, most fortunate, and you would be wise to remember that," she said with a smile.

"My mother was much more progressive," Simone revealed. "She encouraged me to read whatever books I could get my hands on, and to have a voice. But my father is different. He expects me to fall into line and keep my opinions to myself."

"That must be awful for you," Lady Roswell said.

Simone gave her a weak smile. "It is all I know now," she expressed. "I do what is expected of me, and my father doesn't pay me much heed."

Lady Roswell's eyes held pity. "My parents were too attentive of me," she said lightly.

"That is far better than being overlooked," Simone responded.

A silence fell over them and Simone retreated to her own thoughts. How she missed her mother. She had always felt loved, and more importantly, understood. But now she was a mere afterthought for her father. She didn't feel loved, or valued. She almost felt like a burden at times.

Lady Roswell's voice pierced through her thoughts. "I'm sorry," she said. "I should never have pressed you."

"You did nothing wrong. I just miss my mother," Simone admitted.

"Of course you do, Child," Lady Oxley asserted. "She was a good woman, and an even better mother. On the few occasions I visited with her, her eyes would always light up when she spoke of you. It was evident that she was very proud of the woman you were becoming."

Simone felt the sting of tears at the backs of her eyes. "I just wish I had the opportunity to say goodbye. Her death was so sudden, so unexpected."

Lady Oxley leaned forward, extending a comforting hand towards Simone. "Your mother was much too young to have been taken from us."

"She said that she would never leave me," Simone said, her voice hitching on her words. "She promised."

"It wasn't her choice. You must know that," Lady Oxley stated.

Simone blinked back the tears, feeling a twinge of embarrassment at her display of emotions. "Forgive me, I don't usually cry when I speak of my mother."

Lady Roswell offered her a warm smile. "Mothers hold a special place in our hearts."

"That they do," Simone agreed.

As she released Simone's hand, Lady Oxley said, "But enough of this conversation. It has grown far too serious for my liking."

Lady Roswell reached for a plate on the tray and extended it towards Simone. "Biscuit?" she asked. "I have learned that biscuits make every situation better."

Simone expressed her gratitude with a thankful smile, then reached for a biscuit. She took a bite as she tried hard to quell her emotions. She wasn't one to be so emotional, but she felt safe around Lady Oxley and Lady Roswell.

Caleb's voice came from the doorway. "Dare I hope that you missed me?"

"Oh, were you gone?" Lady Roswell joked, turning towards her brother. "I hardly noticed your absence."

He chuckled. "I love you, too, Sister."

Lady Roswell held up the plate to Caleb. "Biscuit?" she asked.

"Didn't you just have dessert?" he questioned.

"Yes, but there is always room for biscuits," Lady Roswell remarked.

Simone was pleased when Caleb came to sit down on the settee next to her. She enjoyed his nearness since it gave her a sense of comfort.

Caleb turned to face her, concern etched on his features. "What has upset you?"

"Nothing," she lied. "Why do you ask?"

"You have been crying," he remarked.

She forced a smile to her lips, hoping to distract him. "We were just discussing my mother and my emotions got the best of me. But I am well now."

His eyes searched hers. "Are you?" She could hear the compassion in his voice, and it touched her. Greatly.

"I am," she replied.

Caleb leaned closer to her and whispered, "I should have warned you about my sister. She tends to make our guests uncomfortable with her brazen speech."

"I can hear you, Brother," Lady Roswell said.

"Good, because I said it loud enough for you to hear," Caleb bantered back.

Simone laughed, finding the banter between Caleb and Lady Roswell thoroughly amusing.

With a biscuit in her hand, Lady Roswell asked, "Where are Roswell and the rest of the gentlemen?"

"They are coming," Caleb replied. "I snuck out to ensure that you were behaving around Miss Delacourt."

Lady Roswell placed her hand to her chest, feigning outrage. "Of course I was," she declared. "I was on my best behavior."

Caleb narrowed his eyes playfully at his sister. "I doubt that."

"You did call Miss Delacourt boring," Lady Oxley pointed out.

Lady Roswell didn't look the least bit ashamed by what her mother revealed. "Yes, I did, but that is because she tried to pass off poetry as interesting. We all know that it is not."

"Just because you don't like something, doesn't mean everyone else has to," Caleb said.

Lord Roswell entered the room and remarked, "You are wasting your breath, Caleb. Anette has a strange aversion to poetry." He walked over to his wife and kissed her on the cheek. "Hello, my love. Did you miss me?"

Lady Roswell nodded. "You, I missed. My brother, not so much."

Simone's father stepped into the room and sought her gaze out. "Shall we depart?"

"I thought we were staying for some games?" Simone asked, attempting to keep the disappointment off her features.

A look of disapproval came to his face. "I have work that I need to see to, and I don't have time for card games."

Rising, Simone said, "Very well, Father."

Caleb had risen when she had and offered his arm. "Allow me to escort you to the door."

"Thank you," she said, placing her hand on his sleeve.

Lady Oxley rose. "Thank you for coming this evening. I enjoyed getting to know you better."

"Likewise, my lady." Simone shifted her gaze to Lady Roswell. "If you are still interested in learning how to throw daggers…"

"I am."

"… then you must come by tomorrow afternoon for a lesson," Simone said.

Lady Roswell beamed. "I shall be there."

Caleb started leading Simone towards the main door and asked in a hushed voice, "How is my hair? Is the brushing still acceptable?"

Her lips twitched. "It is more than acceptable."

"Good," he replied. "I shall ensure it is brushed forward properly tomorrow when I arrive for our carriage ride."

"I shall be looking forward to it."

Caleb stopped by the door and turned to face her. "Thank you for coming this evening," he said.

"It would have been rude for us to not accept the dinner invitation."

"Dare I hope that you enjoyed yourself?"

Simone pretended to consider his words for a moment, not wishing to give too much away. "It wasn't as unbearable as I thought it would be."

Caleb grinned. "That is high praise coming from you."

Her father cleared his throat. "Shall we, Simone?" he asked, the irritation evident in his tone.

Not wishing to upset her father further, Simone dropped into a curtsy and said, "Good evening, Mr. Bolingbroke."

As her father led her towards the coach, he remarked, "For a man that claims he has no interest in ever marrying, Mr. Bolingbroke seems rather taken with you."

"You are mistaken, Father," Simone said. "Mr. Bolingbroke and I are just friends."

He huffed. "Wonderful," he grumbled.

Once Simone was situated in the coach, she glanced back at Caleb's townhouse and realized that she was saddened to leave at such an early hour. It would have been rather enjoyable to beat Caleb at a game of whist, or two.

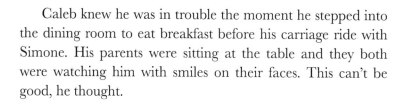

Caleb knew he was in trouble the moment he stepped into the dining room to eat breakfast before his carriage ride with Simone. His parents were sitting at the table and they both were watching him with smiles on their faces. This can't be good, he thought.

"What is it?" he asked as he pulled out a chair to sit. He might as well ask and get this over with. Whatever it was.

His mother spoke up. "You made the Society page."

"Is that all?" Caleb asked, uninterested.

"Yes, apparently the *ton* has taken notice that you have been paying court to Miss Delacourt," his mother continued.

Caleb sighed. "I am not courting her."

"Well, your actions suggest otherwise," his mother responded. "I, for one, would love to have Miss Delacourt as a daughter-in-law. I rather enjoyed our time spent together last night."

He leaned to the side as a footman placed a plate of food in front of him. "Miss Delacourt and I are just friends, and we are enjoying getting to know one another."

His father interjected, "That is a good start to any relationship. First comes friendship, then comes love. It is a simple equation."

Caleb picked up his fork and knife and started eating his food. There was no point in debating this with his parents. He couldn't explain the real reasoning behind why he had been spending so much time around Miss Delacourt.

"You can ignore us all you want..." his mother started.

"Is it so obvious?"

"...but you must proceed cautiously if you don't want to ruin Miss Delacourt's reputation," his mother advised. "The more time you spend with her, the more the *ton* will assume you two have an understanding."

Caleb put down his fork and knife. "I understand. Is this interrogation over?"

"I am only concerned about you," his mother replied.

He lifted his brow. "You are only interested in seeing me wed."

His mother gave him a look that was the epitome of innocence. "There is no shame in that. Look how happy Anette is with Roswell. Those two can't be in the same room without smiling."

"I am happy for Anette, I truly am, but I do not wish to marry," Caleb said.

"You say that now—"

Caleb spoke over her. "I have said that always."

His mother turned towards her husband. "Will you talk some sense into our son?" she asked.

"I have made my thoughts known to him already," his father responded. "Caleb knows his duty to this family."

Duty.

There was that word again. He knew what his duty was. It was to King and Country. Shoving back his chair, he rose and said, "And with that, I am leaving."

His mother gave him a knowing look. "Do you intend to call upon Miss Delacourt?"

With great reluctance, he admitted, "I am taking her on a carriage ride, but do not read anything into it."

"Very well," his mother said. "I will respect your wishes… for now."

With a shake of his head, Caleb departed from the dining room, knowing his mother was trying hard to contain her excitement. He hated to disappoint her but he had no intention of pursuing Miss Delacourt. Or anyone, for that matter. He was a spy, first and foremost. And he would remain as one until his father passed, after which he would inherit his father's title- a day he did not eagerly anticipate.

Caleb exited the townhouse and stepped into the open carriage. Why did his mother believe he needed a wife to be happy? He was content on his own. It was much easier to be a spy without a wife underfoot.

The carriage merged into traffic and drove the short distance to Simone's townhouse. He had been against this partnership at the beginning, but it was growing on him. He found Simone to be rather intriguing. He was slowly breaking down the barriers that she hid behind, and he was starting to see glimpses of who Simone truly was.

He would need to be patient with her. He knew she hated to be vulnerable- with anyone. Which is why he had grown so concerned last night when he had seen her red-lined eyes. The thought that she was hurting greatly upset him.

Caleb stepped out of the carriage and approached Simone's townhouse. He rapped on the door to make his presence known.

The door promptly opened and the butler stood to the side to let him enter. "Welcome, Mr. Bolingbroke," he greeted. "Miss Delacourt is expecting you."

He stepped into the entry hall and waited as the butler closed the door.

The butler gestured towards the drawing room. "Follow me, sir," he directed. "I shall announce you."

Caleb followed the butler into the drawing room and saw Simone was standing in front of the settee, dressed in a pale blue gown. Her whole face seemed to light up when she saw him, or was that him? He wasn't quite sure, but the whole room seemed brighter because of it.

He bowed. "Miss Delacourt."

Simone dropped into a curtsy. "Mr. Bolingbroke," she murmured.

"Shall we go on our carriage ride?" he suggested.

"Yes, please." Simone gestured towards the lady's maid in the corner. "Felicity will be joining us, assuming you have no objections."

"I have none," Caleb replied.

Simone nodded in approval. "Wonderful," she said. "I have been looking forward to our carriage ride all morning."

Caleb approached her and offered his arm. "You are looking particularly lovely today."

She gave him an exasperated look. "You cannot seem to help yourself, can you?"

"It is merely the truth."

"Please keep the *truth* to yourself," Simone said. "We are partners, and you shouldn't notice such things about me."

"Then I would be blind."

Simone placed her hand on his sleeve. "Let's practice thinking about something, but not saying it out loud. Is that even possible for you?" she asked.

"Some women would be flattered by such a compliment," Caleb teased.

"I am not like most women."

Caleb bobbed his head. "No truer words have ever been said," he said. "But surely you know how beautiful you are."

Simone stiffened. "You forget yourself, sir."

"Simone—"

She cut him off. "I want to be defined by my actions, not by my appearance. That is such a small part of who I am."

Caleb started leading her towards the carriage as he replied, "I meant no disrespect."

"I know, but it is nearly impossible to be taken seriously as a woman," Simone said. "I want you to see me as an agent first, a woman second."

"I can respect that, but I will have you know that I already think of you as a proficient agent," Caleb responded.

As he helped Simone into the carriage, she murmured her gratitude.

"I do hear you, but I am trying to be charming," Caleb joked.

"'Trying' would be the key word," she bantered back. "But I do thank you. I haven't felt heard for a long time, at least since my mother was still alive."

Once Simone was situated, Caleb went to sit across from her. "My mother hardly listens to me. She is determined that I marry."

"She just wants you to be happy," Simone attempted.

"I don't need a wife to be happy," Caleb responded.

Simone's eyes held understanding. "I agree with you, and we both know how rarely that happens."

Leaning back in his seat, Caleb asked, "Did you see that we made the Society page this morning?"

"I did, and I was not pleased by it," Simone replied. "And neither was my father. I heard him grumbling about you this morning. He is not pleased that we are just friends."

Caleb nodded. "I know. He made that rather clear last night when we adjourned to the study for a glass of port." He hesitated, not sure how much he should reveal of his conversation with Simone's father. "He did say a few unkind things about you."

Simone grew quiet. "That does not surprise me. He, too, wants me to marry, and quickly," she said. "If I want to continue to be a spy, I must maintain this ruse of being a wallflower. But with each passing day, it is becoming increasingly difficult."

"And us being seen together is not helping," Caleb remarked.

"No, it is not," Simone agreed.

Caleb met her gaze. "What can we do about that?" he asked.

With a determined expression, Simone replied, "After today, we must work hard to avoid being seen with one another."

"How do you propose we do that?"

Simone's lips twitched. "We are spies," she replied. "I am sure we can figure out how we can meet in secret. I have faith in us."

"Us?" Caleb asked.

"Yes, 'us' because we are partners," Simone replied. "And once we finish this assignment, we will both go our own way."

Caleb found those words to be unsettling. Simone was so

quick to get rid of him, but he enjoyed her company. He wasn't ready to say goodbye so easily.

With a glance at the sky, he asked, "What is our plan when we arrive at the boarding house?"

"We will meet with Juliette and determine if she is one of the French spies that we are looking for," Simone said. "As for after that, I am not quite sure."

"Perhaps we should have notified Kendrick before we agreed to meet with Juliette," Caleb said. "A few well-positioned agents outside of the boarding house might have come in handy in case we need to fight our way out."

"You are assuming we cannot handle this assignment on our own," Simone stated.

"Asking for help is not a sign of weakness," Caleb pointed out.

Simone didn't look convinced. "I have learned to make do on my own. It is far easier to go undetected when one doesn't have a partner underfoot."

"I don't know about that. Roswell and I worked well together," Caleb shared. "I never thought having a partner was a hindrance."

"But the one time you did work by yourself, you almost got yourself killed," Simone said, a playfulness to her words.

Caleb crossed his arms over his chest. "When are you ever going to let me live that down?"

Simone seemed to ponder his words before saying, "I don't rightly know. It is so much fun to tease you about it."

"You are a minx."

"I have been called worse," she bantered back.

Caleb chuckled. "I can only imagine, but in all seriousness, Juliette might not be alone. Her brother might be at the meeting and perhaps other French sympathizers." He paused. "Have you considered this might be a trap?"

"I have, but we are spies. We know the risks associated

with doing our jobs, and we can't risk *not* going to meet with Juliette," Simone responded.

As they approached the boarding house, Caleb studied Simone for a long moment. All the humor had left her features, and it was replaced with a fierce determination. And in that moment, he knew the only way to break down her walls was to show her that he cared enough about her to climb over them.

Chapter Seven

Simone exited the coach and came to a stop in front of the boarding house. She didn't know quite what to expect, but she knew she needed to be prepared for anything. She did, however, feel comforted by Caleb's presence, despite her many objections to having him as a partner.

She didn't like being vulnerable around anyone. She had fallen down a thousand times, but she had always gotten back up. She wasn't afraid of breaking, but she was afraid of people knowing it.

Caleb came to stand next to her and asked, "Are you ready?"

"I am always ready," she replied.

With a glance at her, Caleb said, "That is good because we have no idea what we are getting ourselves into."

"It will work out."

"How are you so confident all the time?" Caleb inquired.

Simone shrugged. "I have to be," she said. "I can't very well go in expecting failure."

Caleb offered his arm. "We have each other now. I promise I won't let you get hurt."

"I am not your responsibility," she argued as she placed her hand on his sleeve.

"No, but we are partners, and that means something to me," Caleb said. "It means whatever we do we do together."

Together.

She quite liked the sound of that.

Simone smiled. "All right," she said.

Caleb gave her a curious look. "You aren't going to argue with me?"

"I see no reason to, at least right now," Simone replied. "But I am sure I will think of a reason to argue with you later."

"Ah, I have something to look forward to," Caleb joked.

Simone brought her gaze back towards the boarding house. "If you are ready…" Her words trailed off.

"Let's go save England," Caleb said as he started to lead her into the boarding house.

As they stepped into the entry hall, a desk was positioned in the back and an older man sat behind it. He had white hair and his clothes were noticeably wrinkled.

The attendant glanced up. "Are you two looking to rent a room?"

Simone offered him a polite smile. "No, we are here to meet someone," she replied. "A Miss Juliette."

A look of displeasure came to the older man's face. "What business do you have with a French woman?" he half-asked, half-demanded.

"My business is my own," Simone replied, her smile remaining intact.

With a glance at the corridor, the attendant said, "This is a fine establishment. You best remember that."

Simone didn't dare contradict the man, but it wasn't hard to notice that the building was in a state of disrepair. The paper on the walls was faded and sagging. The floor didn't fare much better. The wood boards were worn and hadn't been polished in quite some time.

Caleb spoke up. "We are just here to visit a friend."

"You should keep better friends," the attendant grumbled. "The French are a lousy, no-good people. I wouldn't have even rented them a room, but my wife saw to them when I was out."

"What room are they in?" Caleb asked.

The attendant scowled. "2B," he responded. "At least my wife had the good sense to put them in a room where I can keep watch on them. I don't want them to sneak out and not pay their bill." He pointed towards the corridor. "The door is on your left."

"Thank you," Simone said. "Do you, by chance, know if Miss Juliette is by herself?"

"Neither her nor her useless brother have left their room since this morning," the attendant responded. "If you were smart, you wouldn't associate with those blasted Frenchmen."

Simone knew she shouldn't contradict the man, but she couldn't seem to help herself. "Not all Frenchmen are bad," she said.

"Show me a good Frenchman, and I will believe you."

Knowing they weren't going to change the attendant's mind, Simone started walking towards the corridor that was just off the entry hall.

They arrived at the door that read "2B" and Caleb knocked.

Simone slipped her hand into the opening in her gown and gripped the hilt of the dagger. She didn't know what to expect, and she needed to be prepared for anything.

After a long moment, the door opened and Juliette stood before them. She was dressed in the same simple gown she wore the day before but her hair was pulled into a loose chignon.

Juliette's eyes landed on Caleb and a broad smile came to her lips. "Well, look who it is," she said in a sultry voice. "Thank you for coming. Do come in."

Caleb put his hand out, indicating Simone should go first.

Juliette took a step back and opened the door wide. "Is that terrible man still out front?" she asked.

Simone assumed Juliette was talking about the grumpy attendant. "He is," she confirmed.

"That man is awful, just awful," Juliette said before she closed the door behind them. "He took an immediate dislike to us because we are French."

"Some people can't see past themselves," Simone attempted.

A tall man stood between the two straw mattresses in the small, rectangular-shaped room. His dark hair framed a thin face, accentuated by a slightly crooked nose. There was no smile on his lips to greet them, but his eyes conveyed a sense of contempt. By all accounts, he did not look happy to see them.

Juliette gestured towards the man. "Allow me to introduce you to my brother, Victor."

Victor crossed his arms over his chest. "It is a pleasure to meet you," he grumbled, his words anything but cordial.

"Be nice to our guests," Juliette chided.

He huffed but remained silent.

Juliette turned back towards Simone. "I see you brought your handsome suitor," she said with a wink.

"He is not my suitor," Simone rushed to say. "We are just friends, friends with a common purpose."

Juliette didn't look convinced but she shifted her gaze towards Caleb. "Mr. Bolingbroke," she said. "Thank you for coming."

Caleb's gaze remained expressionless, giving nothing away. "How is it that you know my name?" he inquired.

"I have my ways." Juliette tsked. "You didn't think we would invite a stranger to meet with us, did you?"

"I'm afraid I am at a disadvantage then since I don't know anything about you, or your brother," Caleb said.

"In due time," Juliette stated. "But we brought you and Simone here for a purpose."

Simone lifted her brow. "Which is?" she asked.

"We need you to secure an invite for us to Lord Pendley's ball," Juliette replied. "It is to be the event of the Season and we don't dare miss it."

"Lord Pendley's ball is in five days," Simone pointed out. "It would be nearly impossible to get you on the guest list now."

Juliette nodded. "True, but surely you can use your connections to help us."

Caleb spoke up. "Why, pray tell, do you wish to go to the ball?"

With a wave of her hand, Juliette said, "Victor and I haven't been to a ball in ages and we think it would be fun to do so."

Simone didn't believe Juliette's innocent act for one moment. There was a reason why Juliette and Victor wanted to attend the ball, and they needed to discover that reason.

Victor crossed his arms over his chest. "If you don't secure us an invite, we can't guarantee we won't kill you."

"Are you truly resorting to threats already, Brother?" Juliette asked lightly. "We haven't even given them a chance to respond. They will do the right thing. I am sure of it."

Juliette smiled at them and continued. "I know we are like-minded individuals and this would truly help support the cause. What do you say?"

"How will it help support the cause?" Simone asked.

"You don't need to worry your pretty little head about that," Juliette remarked. "I knew you would come in handy when I saw you at the pub."

Simone exchanged a glance with Caleb before saying, "We will try our best to secure an invite."

"Trying isn't good enough," Juliette said, her voice growing hard. "You will do as we say or else I can't promise Victor won't make good on his threats."

Caleb looked hesitant, as if he were cowed by Juliette's threats, but Simone knew it was just an act. "We will get you an invite to the ball, but you must promise no harm will befall us," he said.

The smile returned to Juliette's lips. "You have my word," she replied, her words sounding very much like an empty promise. "I knew you were a smart man." She walked to the door and opened it. "This goes without saying, but you would be wise not to discuss this conversation with anyone. It could have dire consequences."

"I understand," Simone said as she approached the door. "How are we to contact you?"

"You don't," Juliette replied. "We will make contact with you."

After they stepped into the corridor, the door was shut behind them. Caleb offered his arm and led her towards the waiting coach. Once they were situated, the coach rolled into traffic, leaving the boarding house behind.

"Why do you suppose they want to go to Lord Pendley's ball?" Caleb asked.

"I don't rightly know, but whatever the reason is, it can't be good," Simone replied. "Victor matches the description of one of the French spies that was given previously, right down to the broken nose. I think it is a reasonable assumption that we have found them."

Caleb nodded in agreement. "We should report our findings to Kendrick at once. He might just arrest them and be done with it."

"Perhaps, or he might want to discover their intent for attending the ball," Simone mused.

"They clearly do not perceive us as a threat," Caleb said. "Which will work in our favor. Although, I can't help but wonder how Juliette knew my name. I suspect Mr. Barnard might have blown my cover."

"We will need to proceed with caution if that is the case," Simone said. "Who knows what else Mr. Barnard told Juliette and Victor?"

Simone shifted her gaze towards the street vendors who were trying to hawk their goods on the pavement, and she was about to turn away, when she saw a familiar face in the crowd. *Lucy.* Her late mother's lady's maid.

Lucy was dressed in a worn blue gown and her silver hair was tucked neatly under a bonnet. She was standing by a cart that was selling loaves of bread.

"Lucy!" Simone shouted, hoping to get her attention.

Lucy turned her head, and their eyes met. Widening with surprise, her eyes took on a hint of panic. She promptly averted her gaze, ducking her head, and briskly walked away without bothering to glance back.

Caleb had followed her gaze and asked, "Who is Lucy?"

"She was my mother's lady's maid," Simone replied as she watched Lucy disappear into the crowd. "After my mother's death, she quit and no one has heard from her since."

"It doesn't appear she was pleased to see you," Caleb said.

"No, which is odd," Simone responded. "Lucy was almost like a second mother to me. She was my mother's lady's maid for as long as I can remember."

"Would you like us to stop the carriage so you can go after her?" Caleb asked.

Simone shook her head. "No, she is gone. I do not believe she wanted to be found."

Shifting in his seat, Caleb asked, "Are you going to let that stop you?"

Her lips twitched. "You know me so well."

"I am starting to," Caleb responded.

Simone didn't understand why Lucy had such a reaction to her, but she was going to find out. She had never understood why Lucy had quit so abruptly. It was so unexpected of her that it had taken Simone by surprise. But a part of her needed to see Lucy again. She needed closure.

Caleb sat in the corner of White's as he relished the time alone. He was biding his time until he needed to meet with Kendrick, but until then, he just wanted a drink and to retreat into his own thoughts.

He was pleased that they had found the French spies, but that meant his time with Simone was coming to an end. And he wasn't quite sure how he felt about that. On one hand, he wouldn't have to work so hard to gain someone's approval, but she had softened towards him. He was sure of that. He could see it in her smile and hear it in her laugh. If he didn't know any better, he'd say she might actually enjoy his company.

But he did know better. Simone was anxious to get rid of him. She preferred to work alone and had told him as much. He just hoped that they could remain friends, even after their assignment was completed.

He couldn't quite explain it but having Simone in his life made it that much better.

As he brought his drink to his lips, he saw Roswell and Fredrick approaching the table with obnoxious smiles on their faces.

"Good afternoon," Roswell greeted as he pulled out a chair. "I didn't think we would find you here, considering you have been spending all of your time with Miss Delacourt." The mirth in his voice was undeniable and rather vexing.

Caleb placed his drink onto the table. "You know precisely why we are spending so much time together."

"I didn't realize that your assignment included having dinner with the lovely Miss Delacourt," Fredrick joked.

"That was not by choice," Caleb argued. "My mother is attempting to play matchmaker."

Roswell nodded. "I can confirm that fact," he said. "Lady Oxley has turned all of her time and energy on ensuring Caleb is wed."

Fredrick shrugged. "That wouldn't be the worst thing."

Caleb looked heavenward. "You are only saying that because you are getting married soon."

"I am, and I am counting down each day in anticipation," Fredrick said. "I cannot wait until Emilia and I can be alone in the same room."

"What a terrible burden you have, my lord," Caleb teased.

Fredrick gave him a pointed look. "Wait until you have fallen madly in love and you have to maintain a proper distance."

"I don't intend to fall in love," Caleb responded. "Falling in love is a liability in our profession."

Roswell spoke up. "I disagree. It has been rather nice to confide in Anette about our assignments. It has helped me see things in a different way."

"That is good for you, but I have made it no small secret that I have no designs to marry," Caleb said. "I can't risk bringing a wife into my complex life."

"Your life is no more complex than ours and we have found happiness," Roswell stated.

Caleb mustered a smile onto his lips. "I am happy."

"Are you?" Fredrick asked. "You don't seem happy."

"What does a happy person look like?" Caleb asked. "Because I can assure you that I am perfectly content with my life."

Fredrick leaned back in his seat and studied Caleb. "You aren't happy," he said matter-of-factly. "I can see it in your eyes."

Caleb huffed. "Do not analyze me."

"I'm not. I am just merely stating the obvious," Fredrick responded. "Happy people don't have to convince others that they are happy. They just are."

Caleb took a sip of his drink before saying, "You are being utterly ridiculous."

"Perhaps I just want everyone to find the joy that I have found with Emilia," Fredrick said. "My fiancée speaks rather highly of Miss Delacourt. She has been teaching Emilia how to throw daggers in her gardens."

"You allow such a thing?" Caleb inquired.

Fredrick gave him a blank look. "Why would I not?" he asked. "Besides, Anette is teaching her how to shoot a pistol. It is no more dangerous than that, and it might come in handy."

"Anette was heading over to Miss Delacourt's townhouse for a lesson as well," Roswell shared. "She was rather excited to learn how to throw daggers."

"That doesn't surprise me," Caleb muttered.

Roswell smirked. "Anette thought Miss Delacourt was a delight when we dined with you. Is she a delight?"

Caleb pushed his drink away from him. "Miss Delacourt is..." His voice trailed off as he tried to think of the right word.

"She is..." Fredrick prodded.

Stubborn. Maddening. Irritatingly beautiful. No, that last one would not do. If he said such a thing, then his friends would think he had fallen for his partner. Which he hadn't. That mere thought was ridiculous.

Knowing they were still waiting for a response, Caleb said, "I suppose Miss Delacourt is tolerable."

"Tolerable?" Fredrick repeated. "I find her to be many things, but tolerable is not one of those things."

"Fine. She is stubborn, almost to a fault," Caleb corrected.

Fredrick grinned. "I concur, but you seem to work well

with her," he remarked. "I read about your carriage rides in the Society page."

Caleb held his hand up at a servant passing by to indicate he needed another drink. He didn't think he could have this conversation sober. But he couldn't drink too much since he needed to keep his wits about him.

Why were his friends being so blasted annoying about Simone? Perhaps it might be best if he just departed and ended this line of questioning.

"I should go," Caleb said, pushing back his seat. "I have work I need to see to."

Roswell grew serious and leaned over the table. "Before you go, have you made any progress in your case?" he asked, his voice hushed.

"We believe we found the French spies, but we are still trying to determine their mission," Caleb revealed. "They want us to secure invitations for them to Lord Pendley's ball."

"Did they give a reason why?" Fredrick asked.

"No, but they did threaten us if we didn't obtain invitations," Caleb replied. "We pretended to be disturbed about it, but the threat fell a little flat."

"Have you spoken to Kendrick?" Roswell inquired.

Caleb shook his head. "No, but Simone and I intend to meet with him in a few hours. We are going to meet at headquarters."

"You aren't going to take her on a carriage ride?" Fredrick asked with a smirk.

Caleb worked to keep the displeasure off his features. "Simone and I are just partners, nothing more."

Fredrick put his hands up in surrender. "I didn't mean to assume otherwise, but you two appear to have gotten rather close."

"That is what happens when you work so closely together," Caleb defended.

Roswell interjected, "We were never that close."

"That is because you are an idiot," Caleb quipped. "Simone is a proficient agent and we do work well together."

"Simone, is it?" Roswell asked.

Caleb frowned. "She gave me leave to call her by her given name. You are just reading into something that isn't there."

"I don't think I am," Roswell remarked. "I saw the way you two interacted over dinner, and you seem to have a cozy relationship."

A server approached the table and placed three glasses onto the table. Caleb reached for one and took a sip. Why was he having to justify his behavior with Simone?

Fredrick pushed his glass towards Roswell and turned towards the server. "Can I get a cup of tea?"

The server tipped his head before he departed to do his bidding.

Roswell retrieved the glass and said, "It is an odd choice to drink tea in a gentlemen's club."

"Whenever I drink alcohol, it gives me a terrible headache," Fredrick shared. "Besides, why would I care what others think of my drink of choice?"

"Good point," Roswell said, holding his glass up.

Fredrick brought his gaze back to Caleb's. "Back to your French spy problem," he said.

"I don't have a problem," Caleb contested.

"You do, and you don't even realize it," Fredrick remarked. "Why would French spies want to attend Lord Pendley's ball? The man is a staunch Tory."

Roswell lowered his glass to the table. "What if they want to gain access to Lord Pendley's townhouse to root around?"

"They wouldn't need an invite for that," Fredrick said. "They could just sneak in at night under the cloak of darkness. I wonder..." He stopped. "General Merrell will be at Lord Pendley's ball, and many consider him to be Wellington's right-hand man."

Roswell shifted in his seat to face Fredrick. "Surely that can't be a coincidence," he remarked. "But what would the French spies hope to obtain by being in the same ballroom as General Merrell?"

"I doubt they wish to plead their case," Fredrick said.

Caleb lowered his voice. "What if their intention is to assassinate General Merrell?" he asked. "That would be a major blow to Wellington and his troops."

"Why did General Merrell return home?" Roswell asked. "After all, I assume he is needed on the Continent."

"Wellington sent him to secure additional funding for the war since the House of Lords balked at his initial request," Fredrick said.

"That is because the poor cannot take another tax increase to fund the war," Caleb stated. "They are barely surviving as it is."

"Regardless, General Merrell won't be left unprotected at the ball," Roswell said.

"True, but his guards won't be as diligent since they are back on English soil, attending a lord's ball," Fredrick pointed out.

"We will just inform General Merrell of the potential threat on his life, and bring the French spies to Newgate," Caleb said. "Then it will all be over."

Roswell bobbed his head. "Yes, and once you complete your assignment, there is no reason for you to work with Miss Delacourt anymore."

"Precisely," Caleb said. "You and I can go back to being partners." That thought did not sit well with him.

"Is that what you want?" Roswell asked, eyeing him closely.

Caleb was tired of defending himself about his partnership with Simone. His business was his own, and he didn't appreciate their meddling.

Shoving back his chair, he rose and said, "If you will excuse me, I need to go speak to Simone about this."

Caleb didn't wait for a response before he headed towards the main door. He knew his friends meant well, but they didn't understand. He may work well together with Simone, but that is where it ended. There could be no future between him and Simone. It was even laughable to think such a thing.

Chapter Eight

Simone stood to the side as Anette brought her hand back and released the dagger, causing it to embed itself at the edge of the target.

"Well done," Simone praised.

Anette gave her a look of disbelief. "You are kind, but we both know that I am awful at throwing daggers."

"You hit the target this time," Simone pointed out.

"This time," Anette said. "But what about the thirty attempts before? No. I think I will stick to shooting a pistol."

Simone walked over to the target and retrieved the dagger. "You just need more practice," she encouraged.

"I don't think that is it," Anette said.

"My mother and I used to practice throwing daggers until the sun went down," Simone shared. "It was so dark that we could hardly see the target, but we kept practicing. It was one of the many things that we did together."

Anette grinned. "Whereas my mother was relentless that I practice my needlework."

"We did that, too, but it wasn't nearly as much fun as throwing daggers," Simone said. "My father was adamant that I grow up civilized."

"What an odd thing to say," Anette remarked.

Simone slipped the dagger into the folds of her gown. "My mother was Scottish and sometimes I wonder if my father was embarrassed by her heritage."

"There is nothing wrong with being Scottish."

"I agree, but my father was furious when my mother gave me a dagger for my eighth birthday," Simone shared. "He didn't think it was an appropriate gift for a genteel young woman."

Anette gave her a knowing look. "He wasn't wrong. It is not commonplace for a lady to know how to throw daggers."

"Perhaps, but it is a skill that has come in rather handy," Simone admitted. "Besides, I like knowing that I can protect myself."

Anette nodded in agreement. "That is precisely why I carry a muff pistol in my reticule."

Simone felt the warmth of the sun's rays as it hung high in the sky, prompting her to adjust the bonnet on her head. "Shall we adjourn to the drawing room for a cup of tea?" she asked.

"That sounds delightful, but I do not wish to overstay my welcome," Anette replied.

"I daresay that is impossible," Simone said as they started down the path. "It has been nice getting to know you a little better."

Anette glanced over at her. "May I ask you a question?"

"It depends."

"On what?" Anette asked.

Simone smirked. "You are not going to ask about Caleb."

Anette gave her a sheepish smile. "Was it so obvious?"

"Only to me," Simone replied.

"Since we are speaking of Caleb..." Anette started.

"We weren't."

"....I was just curious if you two had an understanding."

Simone resisted the urge to laugh at such a ridiculous

notion. A marriage between them would be a disaster, she thought. And she couldn't very well tell Anette that. Instead, she chose to share a partial truth.

"No, we do not have an understanding. Quite frankly, I have no wish to marry," she said.

Anette gave her a thoughtful nod. "I used to think as you did, but it changed when Roswell realized he couldn't live without me."

"I want more out of this life than just being a wife," Simone admitted. "I have an inheritance from my grand-mother that I can live on for the remainder of my days, assuming I live somewhat frugally."

"Then why go through the effort- and expense- of having Seasons if you are so determined not to marry?"

Simone pressed her lips together, knowing she couldn't very well tell Anette the truth. Her cover as a wallflower was extremely useful since it allowed her to overhear conversations that she was never supposed to hear.

They arrived at the rear of the townhouse and a footman opened the door. As they stepped inside, Simone knew that Anette was still waiting for her response. "My father is hopeful that I will settle down and be a good, obedient wife," Simone said. That much was true.

"You might change your mind when you fall in love," Anette remarked.

"Love is not in the cards for me," Simone said. "That would require me to be looking for such a thing, which I am not."

Anette's eyes twinkled with amusement. "Love can be found in the most unexpected places, even when you are not looking for it."

Simone lifted her brow. "Are you a love expert?"

"I am not, but I am a firm believer in it," Anette said. "I didn't always feel this way, especially when I thought there would never be a future between me and Roswell. I was going to be just fine on my own, but can I tell you a secret?"

"Please do."

"Life is hard, but having a companion, a helpmate, by your side makes your burdens seem a little lighter," Anette said. "And isn't that all we can hope for?"

Simone stopped outside of the drawing room and turned to face Anette. "I appreciate what you are trying to do, but I prefer to be alone. It is familiar. Comfortable."

"You don't have to be alone."

"True, but I *choose* to be alone," Simone said. "There is a difference."

Anette opened her mouth to no doubt argue with her when a knock came at the main door. Her butler crossed the entry hall and opened the door, revealing Caleb.

Turning towards her brother, Anette asked, "What are you doing here?"

Caleb stepped into the entry hall. "I would think it is fairly obvious," he replied with a teasing lilt in his voice. "I am here to call upon Miss Delacourt."

Simone smiled at Caleb. "We were just about to have a cup of tea. Would you care to join us?"

"Tea would be lovely," Caleb responded.

Anette brought a hand up to her forehead. "Oh, I just forgot. I have errands that I need to see to before Roswell returns home. I should run along before the day gets away from me."

"Are you sure?" Simone asked.

With a bob of her head, Anette started backing up towards the door. "I enjoyed our time immensely and I will call upon you later."

After Anette had departed from the townhouse, Simone turned her questioning gaze towards Caleb.

Caleb chuckled. "My sister is not so subtle, I'm afraid. She wanted to leave us alone so we would no doubt fall in love and have a bushel of children."

"I assumed as much."

He approached her and lowered his voice. "We need to speak privately." There was an urgency to his words.

"Shall we take a tour of the gardens, then?" Simone asked.

Caleb offered his arm. "Allow me to escort you."

Simone placed her hand on his sleeve and he led her towards the rear of the townhouse. Once they started down a path, she removed her hand and clasped them in front of her.

Caleb's gaze remained straight ahead as he revealed, "I believe the French spies intend to assassinate General Merrell."

Her brow shot up. "Why would you assume such a thing?"

"General Merrell will be at Lord Pendley's ball as an honored guest," Caleb said. "His guards will be distracted and it would be a perfect opportunity to get close to Wellington's right-hand man."

Simone considered Caleb's words before saying, "Then we must tell him at once."

"I agree." Caleb came to a stop on the path and turned to face her. "We need to report our findings to Kendrick first."

With a glance at the back gate, Simone said, "Very well. I will meet you there."

"We could always go together under the ruse of a carriage ride," Caleb suggested.

Simone shook her head. "I would prefer not to be seen with you, at least until the *ton* loses interest in our association."

"That might be some time."

"I know, but it is safer that way," Simone said. "By associating with you, it is drawing unwanted attention towards us."

"Us?" He smirked. "Is there an 'us'?"

Simone pursed her lips. "You are maddening."

"You make it entirely too easy to tease you," Caleb said.

He took a step closer to her, but still maintained a proper distance. "I have noticed that a line between your brow appears when you get frustrated with me."

"It must happen all the time, then," Simone bantered.

Caleb eyed her curiously. "Do you want to know what I think?"

"No, I don't."

His lips curled into a smile. "I think you secretly like me."

"You would be wrong in that assumption."

"Would I?" he asked, his words low, intimate.

Simone locked eyes with him and detected a playful glint in his gaze. Once again, he was teasing her- a delicate interplay of emotions that stirred both excitement and irritation within her. She was uncertain of which emotion to focus on. Annoyance. It felt like the safer option.

Caleb's smile transformed into a devilish grin, drawing her attention to his lips. "You do like me. Just admit it."

"I would never admit such a thing," Simone responded with a stubborn tilt of her chin. "Are you ever serious?"

"I think I have proven I can be serious when the situation warrants it."

"And this situation does not warrant it?"

Caleb took a step closer to her. "I don't think it does," he replied. "It is all right for us to enjoy one another's company."

"How can I enjoy a thorn in my boot?"

He brought a hand to his chest, feigning disappointment. "You wound me," he said. "I shall have to work harder to earn your approval."

"If this ridiculous conversation is over, I need to plan my escape so I can meet you at headquarters."

"I shall count every moment that passes until we see each other again," Caleb said, his hand still over his heart.

Simone made a showing of rolling her eyes. "You should be in the theatre," she joked. "Although, there is such a thing as overacting."

"I save my theatric performances just for you," Caleb responded with a wink.

"Lucky me," Simone muttered.

Simone wanted to continue being annoyed, but with each passing moment, her resolve was softening. She was rather enjoying this playful side of Caleb. But she didn't dare admit that, especially to him. He was already entirely too cocky for his own good, and she had no desire to encourage him. They needed to remain serious.

Taking a step back, Simone said, "I'll be at headquarters as quickly as I am able."

Caleb tipped his head. "I wish you luck but do be careful. It wouldn't be farfetched to assume that you are being followed."

"I shall take extra precautions," Simone declared. "Now if you will excuse me, I need to go tell my companion I am going to my bedchamber to rest and then sneak out the servants' entrance."

"Do you want me to escort you back inside?" Caleb asked, offering his arm.

Simone looked at his arm as she debated what she should do. One part of her wanted to keep him close, while the other urged her to push him away. His ability to break through her defenses unsettled her deeply.

But she had a decision to make.

Propriety won out. With a feigned indifference, she placed her hand on his sleeve, pretending that his nearness wasn't affecting her. "Thank you," she murmured.

As Caleb led Simone down the path, she knew she was in trouble. She couldn't deny it any longer. She liked Caleb, perhaps more than she should.

Caleb sat in the entry hall of the agency's headquarters. He was waiting for Simone to arrive so they could go in together to see Kendrick.

He had pushed her today, knowing she was capable of so much more. He could see it in her eyes. She wasn't completely indifferent towards him. She cared for him. He was sure of that. But he didn't know to what extent. Simone fiercely guarded her emotions, and it was going to take more than his persistent teasing to topple those barriers.

And he did love to tease her.

The door opened, revealing Simone as she entered the entry hall. She was wearing a faded pink gown that bore the marks of time. Atop her head rested a matching bonnet, and her brown shoes, worn and dulled by countless steps, completed the look.

Caleb rose from his seat as she approached him. "Did you walk here?"

"Of course not, I took a hackney. It was much too far to walk, but I did ensure I wasn't followed," she replied.

"You could have ridden with me."

"I could have, but then I would have had to endure your company," Simone said, a teasing lilt gracing her tone.

Caleb offered his arm. "We shouldn't keep Kendrick waiting for much longer."

He was pleased when Simone took his arm without complaint. Perhaps he was making more progress than he thought.

As they walked through the main hall, the other agents didn't pay them much heed as they reviewed documents at their desks.

They arrived at Kendrick's door and he knocked.

"Enter," came the spymaster's gruff reply.

Caleb opened the door and indicated that Simone should go first. He followed her into the room and was mindful to close the door behind him.

Sitting behind his desk, the spymaster, a tall figure with silver hair, studied them with a solemn expression. His eyes, while sharp and alert, also carried a weariness that hinted at the burdens he bore. Kendrick skipped the pleasantries, just as he usually did, by asking, "What have you discovered?"

Simone cast a glance at Caleb, finding encouragement in his nod to speak up. In a resolute voice, she reported, "We made contact with the French spies that we were searching for and we do believe their mission is to assassinate General Merrell."

"You believe?" Kendrick questioned with a furrowed brow. "But you aren't certain? Am I missing something, Agent? Do we not deal in facts here?"

Simone pressed forward, her voice not wavering. "They asked us to secure invitations to Lord Pendley's ball, where General Merrell is to be the guest of honor."

Kendrick leaned back in his seat and let out a sigh. "There could be many reasons why they want to attend that ball. It will be well attended by dignitaries, lords, and all members of high Society. Why do you suppose General Merrell is the target?"

"We just thought—" Simone started.

Kendrick spoke over her. "You are wasting my time here," he declared. "Come back when you know what they are planning."

"Should we not at least warn General Merrell?" Simone asked.

"What would we even say to him?" Kendrick demanded. "We *think* there might be an attack on your life, but we have no proof?"

Caleb was used to Kendrick's abrupt demeanor, but he didn't like it when it was directed at Simone. Before he thought through the repercussions of his actions, he said, "I do not think you are being fair to Simone."

Kendrick's brow shot up. "I beg your pardon?"

Now he had done it. He had stoked Kendrick's anger, and there was no coming back from that. "We located the French spies and we at least know their next move," Caleb attempted.

Kendrick started clapping his hands together. "Do you want me to congratulate you on a job well done when you are missing key components?"

Simone shot Caleb a look of annoyance. No doubt she had figured out that he was trying to defend her and it failed spectacularly.

With a steely look, Kendrick waved his hand over his desk. "These two French spies you have been tracking are not the only ones on English soil. We can't seem to go a moment without a new threat to the Crown popping up. So please excuse me if I don't pat your backs for you doing your job."

Caleb bobbed his head in understanding. "We will report back once we have more proof on what the French spies are planning, but until then, can you assign agents to watch over them?"

"I think that is the first intelligent thing you have said in here. I shall see to it," Kendrick said. "Now off with you two."

Simone barely spared Caleb a glance as she departed from the office. As he went to follow her, Kendrick's voice stopped him.

"Simone doesn't need a caretaker. She needs a partner," Kendrick advised. "She can fight her own battles."

"Yes, sir," Caleb replied.

"She wouldn't be an agent if I didn't think she could handle it," Kendrick said.

Caleb tipped his head in acknowledgement before he went to catch up with Simone. He found her in the entry hall, and noticed the firm set of her jaw. She was angry. At him. And he knew precisely why that was.

"Simone," he started, "I'm sorry."

Keeping her gaze straight ahead, she said, "You had no right to speak up for me."

"I was trying to do the honorable thing."

She arched an eyebrow. "You mean belittle me."

"That was not my intention." He placed his hand on her arm and gently turned her to face him. "I was angry that Kendrick was speaking to you in such a harsh manner and I just reacted."

"He treats me no different than other agents, but apparently, you do," Simone said. "You think I need to be coddled."

Caleb knew that she wasn't entirely wrong. He had a strong desire to keep her safe, but he realized the unfairness of that sentiment. Simone was more than capable of taking care of herself and he needed to trust her to do so.

"I'm sorry," he replied. "I was not acting like a good partner in there, and I hope you can forgive me for my error in judgment."

Simone considered him for a long moment before responding, "I will, but only because I have more pressing matters at the moment."

"Which are?"

"It is not about our case," Simone replied. "I have something I need to see to. A personal matter."

Caleb lifted his brow. "You have piqued my curiosity."

"Good, but it is none of your business," Simone said as she brushed past him.

He followed her out of the building and matched her stride as she hurried down the pavement. "Where are we going?"

"'We' are going nowhere," Simone remarked.

"It appears that we both are going in the same direction," Caleb said. "How fortunate."

Simone emitted a sigh of frustration. "Will you not leave me be?"

"I could, but then I would just follow you and then you would catch me. It would be this whole thing," he said. "I think it is best if you just told me where you are going."

With an exasperated look on her face, she revealed, "Fine. I am going to look for Lucy."

"I can help with that," Caleb asserted.

"No, *you* are going to go home," Simone said.

Caleb tsked. "It would be much more fun to spend time with my partner. Besides, I might be useful to you."

Simone stopped on the pavement and turned to face him. "How can you be helpful to me?" she questioned.

"I am a spy. I will find a way." He smiled.

Annoyance flashed in her eyes. "Do you not have anywhere else to be?" she asked.

"No. I am free as a bird at the moment," he replied.

"Lucky you. Now you don't have to go about this alone."

Emotions played across her face as she pursed her lips. After a long moment, she finally relented. "All right. Don't make me regret this."

"I won't," he replied.

Spinning on her heel, Simone continued down the pavement, not bothering to wait for him to catch up.

As he came to walk beside her, he asked, "What is the plan?"

Barely sparing him a glance, Simone replied, "We return to the vendors where I saw Lucy last and hope we find her again."

"What if she isn't there?"

"Then I will try again tomorrow, and the day after that."

He eyed her curiously. "What will you say when you find her?"

A trace of uncertainty lingered in her eyes as she met his gaze. "I will ask her why she quit so suddenly after my mother died and abandoned me in the process." Her words were spoken plainly enough, yet beneath the surface, a tinge of sadness shone in them.

"I'm sorry," Caleb murmured.

"For what?"

Caleb gave her a look that he hoped conveyed his compassion. "I can hear how much Lucy meant to you."

"Well, I thought she cared about me, as well. But I was wrong," Simone said. "I suppose it was just a job for her. Nothing more."

"You don't know that."

Simone's eyes roamed over the pavement where the vendors were hawking their goods. "It is not what we think or feel but it is what our actions are that define us," she said.

"Then why find her?"

Simone brought her gaze back to meet his. "I need to know the reasons behind her decision to leave. It gnaws at me."

"Perhaps she was dealing with her own grief, and had nothing left to give you," he proposed.

"It can't be as simple as that," Simone argued.

Caleb took a step closer to her. "What do your 'spy senses' tell you?"

"'Spy senses'?"

With a smile, he replied, "That is what Octavia and Anette have been calling it. But I would think it is more instinct."

Simone bit her lower lip as she pondered his words. "I think there is more to the story with Lucy's departure."

"Then we need to find her."

"You believe me?"

Caleb chuckled. "I do not know why you look so surprised. I trust you, and that means I trust your 'spy senses.'"

A smile came to Simone's lips. "Thank you."

"Don't thank me yet," Caleb said. "We haven't found Lucy. She could be anywhere."

Simone turned her head and her eyes went wide. "Not anywhere," she said. "Right over there in front of the cart."

Caleb followed her gaze and saw Lucy as she accepted a loaf of bread from a vendor. "Follow me," he ordered.

He headed over to Lucy and stopped in front of her. "Lucy?" he asked in a hushed voice.

Lucy gave him a baffled look. "Do I know you?"

"No, but you know my friend, Miss Delacourt," he replied.

Lucy's face grew pale. "Do not try to contact me again," she declared as she went to brush past him. "I must go."

Simone stepped out from behind him and blocked her path. "Where are you going?" she asked.

Lucy's mouth dropped open. "Simone," she whispered. "You don't know the danger you are putting us both in. You mustn't be here."

"What danger?" Simone pressed.

Taking a step back, Lucy said, "I swore I would never speak to you again. It had to be this way, for your sake and mine."

"You aren't making any sense," Simone stated. "Who did you promise?"

Lucy brought her hand up to her mouth. "I have said too much."

"But you haven't said anything at all," Simone argued.

Lucy's eyes swiftly scanned the crowd before she lowered her voice. "Whatever you do, don't make the same mistake I did. Don't trust your father."

"My father?" Simone repeated. "Why shouldn't I trust him?"

Regret shadowed Lucy's face as she replied, "Goodbye, Simone. This is for the best. You must trust me on this."

Without waiting for their response, Lucy darted into the crowd, vanishing from view.

Simone's eyes remained on the crowd as she said, "I don't understand. What is she trying to protect me from?"

"It was evident that she is afraid of something, or someone," Caleb stated. "And I think that someone is your father."

"Why would she be afraid of my father?" Simone asked. "He is not the warmest person, but he isn't awful."

Caleb put his hand on her sleeve. "We should get you home before anyone notices your absence," he encouraged.

"You are right," Simone said. "There is no reason to tarry."

He could hear the dejection in her voice, and he wished there was a way that he could fix it. He didn't know how, or when, but he would find a way to help Simone.

Chapter Nine

Simone's mind was in a whirlwind as she tried to make sense of what Lucy had just told her. Why shouldn't she trust her father? None of this made any sense. But it was evident by the panicked look on Lucy's face that she was utterly afraid of something. Or someone.

Could that "someone" truly be her father?

No.

Her father was not a bad man. He may be gruff, and hard around the edges, but he had a kind heart. She had seen it before.

Caleb's voice broke through the silence. "Are you all right?" he asked, the concern evident in his voice.

"Yes… no… I don't rightly know," Simone admitted. And for the first time in a long time, she had no idea where to go from here.

Caleb gently placed his hand on her arm, turning her towards him. "What do you want to do?"

"I don't know."

"Yes, you do," Caleb said. "What are your 'spy senses' telling you to do?"

Simone knew he was just trying to help, but she was at a loss as to what she should do. "It is not that simple."

"It is," he asserted. "What do you want to do?"

As she saw the determination in Caleb's gaze, Simone felt her shoulders slump and she lowered her gaze. Caleb was asking for her to be strong, but she couldn't do it.

Caleb rested his hands on her shoulders and leaned closer. "You must look objectively at this," he urged. "Based upon what Lucy revealed about your father, what would you do next? I want you to think, Simone."

His encouraging words prompted her to take a deep breath. Knowing he believed in her was enough, for now. She brought her gaze up and replied, "I would search his office, and look for any clue as to why Lucy couldn't trust him."

"That is good." Caleb dropped his arms but remained close. "Shall we do so tonight?"

Simone hesitated. Could she truly search her own father's study, as if he were a suspect in one of her cases?

Caleb gave her a knowing look. "You can do hard things, Simone."

"But he is my father."

"More the reason to clear him of any wrongdoing," Caleb responded.

Simone had to admit that Caleb did have a point. She nodded her acknowledgement. "I will search his study tonight."

"*We* will," Caleb corrected.

"That isn't necessary—"

Caleb spoke over her. "We are partners, are we not?"

"But this has nothing to do with our assignment," she argued. "I can handle this on my own."

He smiled, as if he found her stubbornness to be amusing. "I know you can, but I would be a lousy partner if I didn't help you."

Heaven help her, but she did want Caleb's help. She knew

what needed to be done, but she wasn't strong enough to do it on her own.

"Fine," Simone said, feigning exasperation. "You may help me search the study. It will be easier with two people anyways."

Caleb's smile grew. "That wasn't so hard to admit, now was it?"

"It was, actually," Simone said as she fought the smile that was threatening to form on her lips.

He gestured towards a black coach that was further down the street. "Would you like me to escort you home?"

"And risk my reputation by riding in a coach alone with a gentleman?" she asked. "I think not."

Caleb chuckled. "You are right. Taking a hackney is much more respectable for a genteel woman such as you."

Simone ran a hand down her worn gown. "That is why I wore this gown. No one gives me any heed when I wear these simple gowns."

Caleb perused the length of her and asked, "How do you leave the house wearing that gown without causing unwanted attention from the servants?"

"They have just come to accept that I am odd," Simone replied.

"You are not odd," he said. "Stubborn. Maddening. Clever. Those words describe you better than odd."

Simone heard the humor in Caleb's voice and found herself being drawn to him. She couldn't quite believe that she had only known him for a short time, but he had become so important to her. "Thank you," she found herself saying.

"For what?"

She held his gaze steady while she replied, "For helping me."

"That is what any good partner would do," he said, dismissing her praise. "Besides, I didn't do much."

"You did enough."

A smirk came to his lips. "I think you like me."

Simone rolled her eyes. "Not this again," she responded, attempting to be put out.

"It is all right if you admit it," he teased. "I won't tell anyone."

Taking a step back, Simone said, "I feel bad for you that you need such validation."

"Only with you," Caleb remarked, his smirk showing no signs of dimming. "One day, you will admit it. I know it."

"Good day, Caleb."

Caleb's eyes held amusement. "Good day, Simone." He bowed. "I will come to your townhouse at midnight."

"Do ensure you go undetected."

"I am a spy. That goes without saying," Caleb said.

Simone held his gaze a moment longer than would be considered proper before she started down the pavement. Not that there was anything proper about their situation. She would be ruined if anyone from the *ton* saw her, but that was highly unlikely. People in high Society would never frequent a place like this.

She lifted her hand and hailed a hackney. The coach came to a stop in front of her. The heavy-set driver shouted down from his perch, "Where to, little lady?"

"Mayfair," she replied.

"Do ye want to be more specific?"

She reached into the reticule that was around her wrist and removed a few coins. "No. Just drop me off in Mayfair."

After she extended the driver a few coins, she cautiously entered the foul-smelling cab, making a conscious effort to disregard the unpleasant sounds of her boots adhering to the sticky floor.

A short time later, she arrived in Mayfair and exited the coach. She kept her head down as she traveled the few blocks to her townhouse. Once she arrived, she went around to the servants' entrance and opened the door.

Felicity jumped up from the round table in the corner. "Good, you are back."

Simone closed the door behind her as she asked, "Have you been waiting for me this whole time?"

"No, but I started getting worried," Felicity replied. "You aren't normally gone for so long."

"Did Mrs. Fernsby notice my absence?"

Felicity shook her head. "No, I convinced her that you were taking a nap, albeit longer than normal."

Simone sat down at the table and glanced around at the servants who were going about their tasks. In a low voice, she said, "You will never guess who I saw."

Felicity gave her an expectant look. "I don't know. Perhaps you should just tell me."

"Lucy," Simone said.

Her lady's maid sucked in a breath. "Lucy?" she asked. "No one has heard from her since she quit two years ago."

"I know, but I saw her in a disreputable part of Town, appearing down on her luck," Simone shared.

"She isn't working as a lady's maid anymore?"

Simone shrugged. "I don't know," she replied. "She seemed rather unnerved when she saw me and told me not to trust my father."

With a stunned expression, Felicity inquired, "Why not?"

"She wouldn't elaborate, despite my many attempts at getting her to do so," Simone said. "She seemed panicked that we were even speaking to one another."

"Lucy was not one to be frazzled easily," Felicity remarked.

Simone bobbed her head. "I agree, but the whole situation was rather odd."

She had just uttered her words when the short, round cook approached her with a teacup in her hand.

"I heated you up some chocolate," Mrs. Reid said as she placed the cup in front of her. "I thought you could use some, considering you look as if you were up to no good in that worn gown."

Simone smiled up at Mrs. Reid. "Thank you," she acknowledged. "I can always use some chocolate."

Mrs. Reid pulled out a chair and sat down. "So you found Lucy?" she asked. "I couldn't help but overhear. The kitchen is rather small."

"I did," Simone replied. "She was buying bread from a vendor."

Mrs. Reid frowned. "I wish she would come back here. I could always give her a job."

Simone took a sip of her chocolate before saying, "I think this is the last place that she wants to be."

"That is a shame," Mrs. Reid acknowledged. "But you best hurry if you want to change out of your clothes before Mrs. Fernsby comes in search of you."

"You are right, as usual," Simone said, rising. "Fortunately, if Mrs. Fernsby did see me in these clothes, she wouldn't even notice anything is amiss."

Mrs. Reid grimaced. "I saw Mrs. Fernsby talking to a wall yesterday. I suspect she thought she was talking to a maid, but no one was there."

Felicity rose. "Let's get you dressed for dinner."

"For what purpose?" Simone asked. "It is not as if my father even dines with me."

"Regardless, you can't keep parading around the town-house in those clothes," Felicity said.

Simone reached for her teacup and took a long sip. Then she placed the empty teacup onto the table. "Now we can go."

Felicity laughed. "I don't know what you would do without chocolate."

"I hope there never comes a day that I have to find out," Simone joked.

Mrs. Reid remained in her seat as she asked, "Do you

want a tray sent to your room or will you be eating in the dining room?"

Simone hated the two options that were being presented to her. But that was her lot in life. "I suppose I will eat in the dining room."

"I shall see to it, then," Mrs. Reid said.

As she headed towards the servants' stairs, Simone glanced over at Felicity and asked, "Do you know where Mrs. Fernsby is?"

"I saw her last in the library," Felicity replied. "She was sleeping by the fire in the hearth."

Simone walked up the narrow, uneven stairs as she headed towards the second level. She opened the door and stepped into the empty corridor.

In a few strides, she arrived at her bedchamber and stepped inside. Felicity followed her into the room, closing the door behind her.

"What are you going to do about your father?" Felicity asked.

Simone went to sit on the bed. "I'm going to search his study tonight. I can't just rely on Lucy's words."

"Do you think that is wise?"

"What choice do I have?" Simone asked. "The fear was palpable in Lucy's eyes when she spoke of my father."

Felicity walked over to the wardrobe and retrieved a pale yellow gown. "Well, if you are going to engage in espionage, you must at least look good doing it," she said with a smile.

"You are very wise," Simone joked.

"I won't contradict you," Felicity remarked.

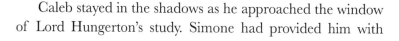

Caleb stayed in the shadows as he approached the window of Lord Hungerton's study. Simone had provided him with instructions on the specific window, assuring him that it would be left unlocked.

He knew that Simone would rather work alone, particularly when it came to investigating her father. However, he felt compelled to help her. He was all too aware of the toll it took on a person to investigate one's own father. It was a path that no one wanted to go down. At least not a sane person.

As he approached the window, he saw that no light came from within. The room was enveloped in darkness. He went to open the window and was met with no resistance. Just as he had expected. Simone had done as she had promised.

He climbed in the window and saw a shadowed figure sitting in the chair.

Simone's voice broke through the silence. "It is about time you arrived."

"It isn't even midnight," Caleb defended.

Rising, Simone closed the distance between them and said, "My father went out earlier and hasn't returned. We must be extra diligent."

The moonlight hit Simone's face, lighting up her eyes, which now gleamed brighter than any star in the night sky. He wondered if she even knew how truly captivating she was. Perhaps what made her so beautiful was not her appearance, but her courage, and the audacity to believe that there was good in people.

Simone arched an eyebrow. "Why are you staring at me?"

"Was I?" he asked, clearing his throat. "I was distracted by something."

Not looking impressed, she said, "That is foolish. Spies are not supposed to be distracted by anyone- or anything."

Caleb couldn't agree more with Simone. Spies had to rise above temptations, especially ones that they were assigned to work with. "Where shall we start looking?"

Simone gestured towards the large desk that sat back in

the square room. "I thought the desk would be a good place to start since my father spends much of his time there."

"I concur," Caleb said as he moved closer to the desk.

Simone reached for one of the drawers and slid it out. "It isn't locked," she said. "Either my father has nothing to hide or…"

"He is overly cocky that no one will come looking," Caleb said, finishing her thought.

With a tip of her head, she responded, "Precisely."

Caleb smirked. "Great minds think alike."

"In this instance, but we do not usually see eye to eye," Simone remarked as she started rifling through the files.

Caleb wasn't sure what he was looking for, but he assumed he would know it when he found it. He started browsing through the papers on the desk until he saw a piece of paper that looked like a contract of some sort. He picked it up and held it towards the moonlight.

Simone glanced over at him. "What do you have?"

"This contract is for the sale of the Earlshall estate," he read. "Does that mean anything to you?"

Simone's voice grew hesitant. "That was my grandmother's estate in Scotland," she revealed. "It boasted the most magnificent castle."

"It lists your name as the seller," Caleb revealed.

"That can't be right," Simone said as she held her hand out. "My grandmother left the estate to my mother, which rightfully became my father's."

"Then why is your name on the contract?" Caleb pressed.

Simone looked up from the paper. "I don't know, but I intend to ask my father."

The sound of a door closing in the distance drew their attention and it was followed by a pair of men's voices.

Placing the contract down onto the desk, Simone's eyes roamed the room as she said, "I think the voices are getting closer. We need to hide."

Caleb's eyes darted to the one place that was big enough to conceal both of them. The drapes. He gently reached for Simone's arm and led her towards the window.

"You cannot be serious—" she started.

He put his finger up to his lips, urging her to be quiet, as the men's voices drifted into the room. Whoever was speaking was coming to the study, and they needed to hurry.

Caleb pulled Simone behind the drapes and ensured they were both hidden. He wrapped his arm around her waist, pulling her closer, and tried to ignore the delightful scent of lavender that drifted off her person.

Simone was tense, not that he blamed her. This situation was not ideal, but they had to manage. If they were caught, the consequences would be dire. No doubt Lord Hungerton would demand that they be married at once.

Their faces were inches apart, but Caleb couldn't think about that right now. He was trying to distinguish the voices that he was hearing. There were definitely two men speaking. One he recognized as Lord Hungerton and the other voice he hadn't heard before.

Lord Hungerton laughed loudly as he entered the study. "Give me a moment. I know the contract is somewhere on my desk," he said. His words were slightly slurred. It would appear that the lord had been drinking before returning home.

The other male voice spoke up. "You need to organize your desk better."

"Why start now?" Lord Hungerton joked.

Caleb could hear the sounds of paper shuffling until Lord Hungerton shouted, "I found it. It is all signed and ready for the buyers' signatures."

"Are you sure you want to sell the Earlshall estate?"

Lord Hungerton huffed. "I hated that place. It is so cold and damp. I cannot see a reason why I would want to ever visit it again."

"It was a castle," the man pointed out.

"Well, it is not my problem anymore," Lord Hungerton said. "Just sell it and be done with it."

There was a silence before the man asked, "Dare I ask if you even asked Miss Delacourt about this? After all, it was her grandmother's estate and has been in their family for generations."

Lord Hungerton clucked his tongue. "She is aware, and she wants it sold as well."

Simone sucked in a breath, but she remained quiet.

"The buyers are on holiday, but when they return, I will finalize the sale," the man said.

"Very good," Lord Hungerton responded. "Shall we celebrate with a drink?"

"No, I have had enough to drink, and I suspect you have as well," the man replied. "I need to be going. It is late, and I have much work to see to in the morning."

"You are right. It is late. Allow me to walk you to the door on my way to bed," Lord Hungerton said.

Caleb stood still, not daring to move, as silence filled the air. It was broken only by the distant closing of a door.

Simone looked up at him and whispered, "I think it is safe. You can release me now."

He dropped his arm but remained close. "Did you recognize the voice of the man who was speaking with your father?"

"No, I did not."

"What did you make of that conversation?" he asked.

She let out a sigh. "My father lied about me knowing about the selling of my grandmother's estate."

"I assumed as much, based upon your reaction."

"Why would he do such a thing?" Simone inquired. "I would have objected since I loved that castle more than anything."

"More importantly, why were you listed as the seller on the

contract?" Caleb asked. "Are you sure your grandmother didn't leave you the estate?"

"I am sure since my mother was still alive when my grandmother died. It would have been left to her since she was the only child."

Caleb furrowed his brow as he thought of something. "When did your grandmother pass away?"

"A few months before my mother drowned," Simone replied. "It was hard losing them both so closely together."

"How did your grandmother die?"

"The doctor said it was cancer," Simone replied. "She was suffering greatly towards the end of her life and she just wanted to die."

"And your mother died a few months later?" Caleb pressed. "Does that timing not seem odd to you?"

Simone shrugged. "It was terrible timing, but death is unexpected. It is not something you can plan."

"Who was with your mother when she drowned?"

"No one," Simone said. "She used to go swimming in a lake near our country estate every morning. When she failed to return, they went in search of her."

Caleb held her gaze. "Who found your mother?"

"Sadly, they never found the body. No doubt it is somewhere in the depths of the lake."

"Simone—"

She put her hand up. "I know what you are going to say, but the coroner did not suspect any foul play. The water was unusually cold for that time of year and it was just a terrible accident," she said. "I once thought as you did, but my investigation yielded no results. I was forced to conclude that my mother did, in fact, drown."

"Where were you when this happened?" he asked.

Simone dropped her gaze. "I went to visit a friend in the next town over and I will always regret not being there."

Caleb could hear the pain in her voice and he wished he

had the power to wipe it away. "It was good that you were not there."

"I doubt that," she replied. "My mother would often invite me to go swimming with her. If I was there, I might have been able to save her."

"You don't know that for certain."

In a shaky voice, Simone said, "The only thing I know for certain is that my mother is gone, and I will never see her again."

Feeling the need to provide her some measure of comfort, Caleb raised his hand and gently cupped her right cheek. "I have heard that 'time heals all wounds,' but I do not agree with that sentiment. The wound remains. But, in time, it will scar over and the pain will lessen. But it is never gone." He stopped, hoping his words were enough.

Simone leaned into his hand. "I just miss her so much."

"That is to be expected, but you are strong enough to go on without her."

"I don't feel strong," Simone sighed.

Even in the dim light, he was able to see the sadness in her eyes, causing his heart to ache. "You are the strongest person that I know," he uttered, his words sincere and low.

"You must not know very many people," Simone joked.

His thumb started caressing her cheek as he replied, "There is no shame in grief. The only way out of the pain is going through it."

Simone's eyes searched his, as if she were looking for the answers to her questions. "I don't think I can."

"Perhaps you can't by yourself, but I can help you," Caleb said. "You just have to trust me and let me in."

Her voice was soft as she admitted, "I do trust you."

Caleb felt elated by her words, knowing he was making progress by tearing down Simone's walls. He had seen the dents and worn edges of her past, but he had no desire to run away. If he had his way, he would never let Simone fight another battle alone. "Then you need not fear. I will be by your side, always."

"Why?" Simone asked.

"Because we are partners."

Simone's eyes held vulnerability as she said, "I will be fine on my own."

"Yes, you would be fine," Caleb agreed, "but you deserve to be more than 'fine.' You deserve to be happy."

"I haven't been happy for so long, not since my mother died," she shared.

Caleb felt a tear slide down Simone's cheek and he wiped it away. "Then *we* must work on that," he said.

They stared at one another, and in that moment, Caleb felt as if time seemed to stop. It was a feeling that he never wanted to end. He didn't know what he was doing with Simone, holding her in his arms, but it felt right.

It felt like he was home.

Simone blinked, as if she had just realized the precariousness of the situation. "I think it is safe to leave our hiding spot."

"Yes, of course," Caleb responded as he reluctantly dropped his hand.

After Simone stepped out from the drapes, Caleb took a deep breath as he tried to gain his composure. He didn't know what had transpired between them, but something had shifted. And he was different because of it.

Caleb tossed back the drapes and approached the window. "It is late," he said. "I shall call upon you tomorrow."

Simone watched him closely. "I have no objections."

"Very well."

After Caleb climbed through the window, he turned back around to Simone and said, "Try to get some sleep tonight."

"I'm not sure if I can, especially after what my father revealed," Simone remarked.

"We will get to the bottom of it," Caleb assured her.

Simone nodded. "I believe you." She hesitated before adding, "I know I was against you helping me, but I am glad that you were here this evening."

"As am I." Caleb smiled. "Goodnight, Simone."

"Goodnight, Caleb."

Knowing that nothing else needed to be said between them, Caleb stepped into the shadows and headed towards the back gate.

Chapter Ten

Simone stared up at the ceiling as she chided herself on how vulnerable she was with Caleb the night before. She wondered what she had been thinking. She was starting to let Caleb in, and that terrified her.

If he ever saw the person she truly was, he would never approve. The way he looked at her was with such compassion, causing her to believe that he might truly care for her. No. He couldn't. That was impossible. How could he care for someone that struggled every day to put one foot in front of the other? Her thoughts, her feelings, everything about her was imperfect.

The only person who had ever understood her was her mother. That is why she still mourned her every single day.

A knock came at the door before it opened, revealing Felicity. "Good morning," she greeted. "Your father has requested that you join him for breakfast."

Simone sat up in bed. "He has?"

Felicity closed the door as she replied, "I was just as surprised as you were when Clarke informed me, but it is a good thing, is it not?"

"I don't rightly know."

Felicity gave her an odd look. "Do you not want to spend time with your father?"

Simone put her feet over the side of the bed and rose. "I searched my father's study last night and I discovered something interesting."

"Which was?" Felicity asked.

"My father intends to sell my grandmother's estate," Simone replied.

Felicity gave her a look that alluded sympathy. "I'm sorry. I know how much you loved visiting that estate as a child," she said. "I can't imagine how difficult that is for you."

"It is, but the contract states that I am the one selling the estate," Simone revealed.

Now Felicity looked baffled. "I thought your grandmother left the estate to your mother."

"I thought so as well."

As she walked over to the wardrobe, Felicity asked, "Have you spoken to your father about this?"

"I have not, but I feel as if he is intentionally trying to keep this from me."

Felicity retrieved a pink afternoon gown and held it up for her inspection. "Why would he do such a thing?"

"I don't know, but I intend to find out."

Walking over to the settee, Felicity placed the gown over the back before asking, "How exactly do you intend to do that?"

Simone blew out a puff of air. "It will come to me. It always does."

"You will find a way," Felicity encouraged. "Until then, let's style your hair. You don't want to keep your father waiting."

"You are right, of course," Simone said as she went to sit down in front of the vanity.

Felicity picked up the brush and removed the cap from

atop her head. "Did Mr. Bolingbroke search your father's study with you?"

"He did."

"Interesting," Felicity murmured.

Simone turned in her seat to face her lady's maid, unsure of her meaning. "Why is that interesting?"

"You two just seem to be spending a lot of time together," Felicity replied.

Not liking where this conversation was headed, Simone responded in a dismissive tone, "That is what partners do."

Felicity didn't look convinced, but rather she appeared amused by Simone's remark. "I just can't help but wonder if you have started to develop feelings for Mr. Bolingbroke."

Simone shook her head, vehemently. "I think not. He is not the type of man that I would fall for."

"Do you take issue with handsome men?" Felicity joked.

"I take issue with men that are entirely too cocky for their own good, which he is. Irritatingly so," Simone defended. "I have not met a more disagreeable man than him."

Felicity placed the brush down and started to style her hair. "Forget I said anything," she said, her lips twitching.

"I will." Simone paused for a long moment before she asked the one question that had kept her up most of the night. "Did you ever find my mother's death to be suspicious?"

With a shake of her head, Felicity replied, "No. Why do you ask?"

"Caleb just put a thought in my head."

"Caleb?"

"Mr. Bolingbroke," Simone corrected.

Felicity lifted her brow. "You two are calling each other by your given names now?"

"We are partners," Simone reminded her, "and it is perfectly acceptable to do so."

Taking a step back, Felicity asked, "Shall we get you

dressed as I try to discover who you are trying to convince? Me or yourself?"

Simone rose from her seat. "I will admit that Caleb and I are friends, but that is all."

"All right."

She continued. "After all, we are both determined not to ever wed because we are agents of the Crown."

Felicity bobbed her head. "I believe you."

Simone took a breath before adding, "If I ever did decide to marry, I would never marry Caleb. He vexes me."

"So you say," Felicity remarked.

"Lastly, Caleb and I would never make each other happy," Simone added. "He makes everything unnecessarily difficult by teasing me. He is relentless at it."

Felicity walked over to the settee and picked up the gown. "How unfortunate you must deal with him then," she said, her voice light.

"It is awful, just awful," Simone remarked.

As Felicity helped her dress, she asked, "Dare I ask why Mr. Bolingbroke thought your mother's death was suspicious?"

"He found the timing to be odd, especially since it was so close to my grandmother's death," Simone explained.

"But your mother drowned, and your grandmother died from cancer," Felicity said. "Those two are in no way connected, and did you not conduct your own investigation?"

"I did." Simone turned to face Felicity. "Besides, my father did not benefit from my mother's death. There was no reason for him to kill her."

Felicity dropped her hands to her sides. "True, but your father might kill *you* if you don't hurry and meet him for breakfast."

Simone laughed. "That was terrible."

"I got the point across, did I not?" Felicity asked.

"You did," Simone replied before she headed into the corridor.

She walked with quick steps towards the dining room on the main level but stopped when she saw Clarke standing in the entry hall.

Clarke tipped his head at her. "Good morning," he greeted.

Stepping closer to him, Simone revealed in a hushed tone, "I saw Lucy yesterday."

"You did?" he asked, surprise etched on his features.

"I did, and she warned me not to trust my father. Do you know why she would say such a thing?" Simone asked.

Clarke gave her a baffled look. "I'm afraid not. Your father may not be an overly affectionate man, but he does love you. I am sure he has your best interests at heart."

"I'm not quite sure if that is true anymore."

"Why do you say that, Miss?" Clarke inquired.

Knowing her father was still waiting on her, Simone gave him a weak smile. "It is just a feeling I am having, but I must run along. My father is waiting for me in the dining room."

Simone headed down the corridor until she arrived at the dining room. She was pleased to discover that her father was still eating his breakfast.

He rose from his seat when he saw her. "Simone," he greeted. "Good, you came."

Simone waved him back down as she went to sit down to the right of him. "Is everything all right?"

Her father gave her a blank stare. "Yes, why wouldn't it be?"

"I was just surprised you wished to dine with me for breakfast," Simone replied. "Not that I am complaining."

"There is something I wish to discuss with you, and it is of a delicate nature," her father said.

Simone assumed he wanted to tell her that he was selling her grandmother's estate, but she couldn't let on that she knew. "What is it?" she asked as a footman placed a plate of food in front of her.

Her father met her gaze. "As you know, it has been almost two years since your mother died and I have been rather lonely," he started. "Which is why I have asked my mistress to move in with us."

Her mouth dropped, but she quickly recovered. "You have a mistress? And you want her to live here, with us?"

"That is right."

Leaning back in her seat, Simone asked, "How long have you had a mistress?"

"Honestly, it is none of your business," her father replied, dismissively. "Miss Laurent and I have been very happy, and I want to include you in that part of my life."

"Then why not marry her?"

Her father stiffened. "My reasons are my own."

"Father, you can't be serious," Simone said. "The *ton* will not be kind to your mistress. She won't be welcome at any social events that we attend."

"You must let me deal with that."

Simone decided to try a different tactic, one that might sway her father. "If you are in earnest about Miss Laurent moving in with us, it might affect the ability for me to pick a suitor. I could very well be ostracized by the *ton* due to the scandal it could cause."

Her father's face grew hard. "You have had your chance to be happy. It is my turn now."

"But, Father—"

He cut her off. "It is done," he shouted. "Miss Laurent will be moving in later today and she will be residing in your mother's old bedchamber."

"*Mother's bedchamber?!* Surely you cannot be serious!" Simone demanded. "How is it that you can replace Mother so easily?"

"I do not see it as her being replaced," her father responded.

Simone shoved back her chair and rose. "I didn't complain when you removed Mother's portrait from the drawing room, but now you have gone too far."

Rising, her father said, "You are emotional. We will continue this conversation when you stop being so hysterical."

"I will never stop fighting for Mother."

"She is gone!" he exclaimed. "It is time for you to accept that and move on. I have."

Simone could feel the tears pricking in the back of her eyes and she knew crying would do her no good. If anything, it would prove her father's point.

While she blinked back her tears, her father's voice turned calm. "I know this is hard to accept, but you have no choice but to learn to live with it."

"Do I not even get a say in this?"

Her father returned to his seat. "I didn't think you would object so heartily."

"You didn't think I would object to a stranger taking over my mother's bedchamber?" she demanded.

"This is my townhouse, and I will do with it as I please," her father replied. "Now, let us finish breakfast before our food grows cold."

Simone shook her head. "I am not hungry."

"You are being stubborn, just as your mother used to be," her father said. "You need sustenance. Sit and eat."

She reluctantly returned to her seat and reached for her fork and knife. As she pushed the food around her plate, Simone felt her emotions whirling inside of her. She felt betrayed by her own father. But was that fair of her? It had been two years since her mother's death, and it wasn't uncommon for a gentleman to take a mistress.

But that didn't mean she had to accept this woman into her home with open arms.

Simone snuck a glance at her father and felt annoyed that he appeared perfectly collected. How could he be so calm with what he had just told her? Her whole life had turned upside down, and she was angry.

However, she did have a question for her father. And she saw no reason to wait any longer. "Whatever happened to Grandmother's estate?"

Her father looked uninterested in her question as he picked up the newssheets. "I'm not quite sure," he said. "A distant cousin inherited the estate. Why do you ask?"

"No reason," Simone replied. Her father was lying to her, but why? She didn't dare press him. At least, not right now.

Clarke entered the room and met her gaze. "Mr. Bolingbroke has come to call," he informed her. "Are you accepting callers?"

Simone turned towards her father. "May I receive Mr. Bolingbroke?" she asked. She wanted to leave, and this was the perfect excuse to escape this conversation with her father.

"You may," her father said as he continued to read the newssheets. "I shall send in Mrs. Fernsby to act as a chaperone."

Simone rose and headed towards the drawing room. She found that she very much wanted to see Caleb. He would understand, and he was very good at making her feel heard. As if she had a voice. Whereas her father was constantly trying to take it away.

Caleb stared out the window as he waited for Simone. He was pleased with the progress that he was making with her, and he found that he was rather eager to see her. Yet, with every passing conversation, every touch, his feelings for her deepened- a disconcerting development considering their partnership. He didn't dare act on them since it would ruin everything between them.

Simone entered the room, and he could tell something was wrong. She smiled, but it didn't quite reach her eyes. "Good morning," she greeted. Her words sounded cordial enough, but there was an underlying sadness to them.

Caleb closed the distance between them and asked, "What is wrong?"

Her eyes grew guarded as she asked, "Why do you suppose something is wrong?"

He lifted his brow. "Do we truly have to do this song and dance?" he asked. "We both know that something has upset you."

It was as if his words allowed Simone to relax because her shoulders slumped. "It is my father. He just informed me that he intends for his mistress to live with us, and she will reside in my mother's bedchamber."

"I'm sorry," Caleb said, unsure of what else he could say.

"I am angry, and frustrated, knowing this stranger is going to take the place of my mother," Simone stated.

Caleb reached for her hand, hoping his touch would comfort her. "No one can replace your mother."

"I should have assumed my father would eventually move on, but it has only been two years," Simone said. "And just think of the scandal that will ensue when the *ton* catches wind of this."

"It will not be ideal," Caleb agreed.

Simone glanced down at their hands. "Am I left to mourn my mother alone?" she asked, her voice soft.

Caleb's heart lurched at the pain that he heard in her voice and he hoped he could find the right words to ease her suffering. "I do believe a part of you will always mourn your mother. It proves that she was a woman worth loving."

Bringing her gaze up, Simone's eyes were moist. "I just wish I could change the past."

"Don't we all?" he asked. "But our past is what defines our future. You are extraordinary because of what you were forced to endure."

"I don't feel extraordinary," she said.

Caleb smiled. "I have never met another person like you. You didn't allow other people to decide who you were. You decided that for yourself," he said.

"You are too kind."

He was pleased that Simone hadn't chided him yet so he continued. "The battles that you have fought, the ones that you have faced alone, make you truly remarkable."

Simone considered his words for a moment before asking, "Why are you so kind to me?"

"You are rather easy to be nice to."

A smile formed on her lips. "We both know that isn't true," she said.

"I listen to you, but I also listen to what you aren't saying," Caleb responded. "And what you aren't saying speaks volumes."

Her expression grew thoughtful. "What am I not saying?"

Caleb held her gaze as he replied, "You don't need to be accepted by others. You need to be accepted by yourself."

Her eyes widened, just a touch, and it was barely discernible. But he knew his words had hit their mark.

Simone slipped her hand out of his. "You are terrible at reading people."

"Am I?" Caleb asked. "I don't trust words. I trust my instincts. People can tell you anything, but my instincts can tell me everything."

"And my instinct is telling me that you are vexing," she said with amusement in her voice. "Regardless, you did not come to discuss my problems. We still have two French spies to contend with."

Caleb nodded. "You are right," he said. "I spoke to Lord

Pendley and I was able to secure two more invitations to the ball."

"Do you think that is wise?"

"What choice do we have?" Caleb asked. "We have to at least play along until we discover what their true purpose is for attending the ball."

Simone grew solemn. "Have they made contact with you?"

"No, they haven't."

"I wonder why that is," Simone questioned. "After all, the ball is only four days away. If securing an invitation was so important to them, why haven't they sought us out?"

Caleb shrugged. "We have been rather occupied with your father."

Simone glanced back at the empty door and lowered her voice. "My father lied to me. He told me that my grandmother's estate was inherited by a distant cousin."

"That is disconcerting."

"Perhaps it is time that I speak with my father's solicitor, Mr. Frickle," Simone said. "He might be able to shed some light on this."

Caleb gave her a pointed look. "What if this Mr. Frickle is loyal only to him?" he asked. "He might very well be the person that your father was speaking to last night."

"I thought about that. I have only spoken to Mr. Frickle on a rare occasion so I am not sure if I could have distinguished his voice, even if I wanted to," Simone admitted. "Which is why there is only one solution. We need to break into Mr. Frickle's office."

"I do enjoy a good break-in, but what purpose will it serve?" Caleb questioned.

"We can look for the contract for my grandmother's estate," Simone replied.

"And if we find it?"

Simone arched an eyebrow. "We take it, of course. I do

not want my grandmother's estate sold if there is even a chance that we can save it."

Caleb tipped his head. "Very well," he said. "Shall we break into Mr. Frickle's office tonight after everyone goes home for the evening?"

"That is a splendid idea," Simone replied.

"I am full of those," Caleb joked.

Simone shook her head. "And you ruined it," she said, but there was a lightness to her words.

Caleb chuckled. "I am just here to entertain you, my dear."

The term of endearment slipped out before he realized what he was doing. He saw Simone grow visibly tense and he wished he could take back his words. What had he been thinking? He should never have said something so bold to Simone.

Before Simone could respond, Mrs. Fernsby entered the room and announced, "You two are entirely too close to one another."

Caleb took a step back. "My apologies."

"What?" Mrs. Fernsby asked, placing a hand to her right ear. "I did not catch that."

He cleared his throat. "My apologies," he said, his voice rising.

Mrs. Fernsby approached him, adjusting the glasses on the top of her nose. "Why do you need a ball of cheese?" she asked.

Simone spoke up. "He didn't say 'ball of cheese,'" she started, "he said 'my apologies.'"

"Oh, that makes much more sense," Mrs. Fernsby said. "Although, I do love a good ball of cheese. Perhaps we shall have the cook make us one."

Caleb knew it was time to leave. "I should be going. I have work to see to," he said, performing a slight bow.

"Must you go so soon?" Simone asked.

"I'm afraid it is for the best," Caleb replied. "I shall be

working late this evening, perhaps even until midnight. Then I shall take my walk, just as I always do."

Caleb was speaking vaguely and hoped that Simone would understand what he was trying to say.

Simone nodded her understanding. "A walk at midnight is not safe. Perhaps you need a walking companion."

"I hope to persuade someone to join me," Caleb said.

Mrs. Fernsby interjected, "The streets of London are a dangerous place. I would not take a walk at such a late hour."

"You are right," Caleb responded with a wink at Simone.

Simone's lips twitched. "Allow me to walk you to the door," she said.

"I would like that very much." He offered his arm.

As they walked towards the main door, Simone lowered her voice and asked, "Could you have been any more obvious?"

"I thought I was being rather devious."

"You thought wrong, but you did get your point across," Simone said. "I shall see you tonight at midnight."

Caleb glanced at her. "We will have to take my coach since no hackneys run that late at night. Will that be an issue?"

Simone pressed her lips together. "I suppose I will survive."

"That is the spirit," he teased.

Lord Hungerton's booming voice came from one of the doorways off the entry hall. "What a pleasant surprise, Mr. Bolingbroke." His words were anything but cordial.

Caleb dropped his arm and bowed. "My lord."

Simone's father walked closer to him. "I see you came to call upon my daughter."

"I did," Caleb said, feeling no need to explain himself.

"That is an odd behavior for someone who wishes to just remain friends," Lord Hungerton growled.

"Father, you are being rude to my guest," Simone chided lightly. "Mr. Bolingbroke and I are friends, nothing more."

Lord Hungerton crossed his arms over his chest. "Very well, but do not even think of compromising my daughter."

Simone blinked, clearly taken aback by her father's accusation. "That was uncalled for. Mr. Bolingbroke has only ever been a gentleman around me," she declared.

Caleb understood Lord Hungerton's enmity for him, considering he did spend time with Simone and they didn't have an understanding. But that was only until this assignment was completed. Then it would go back to normal.

But was that what he wanted? Normal?

Lord Hungerton huffed. "You may go now, Mr. Bolingbroke," he ordered.

Caleb bobbed his head. "Good day, my lord." He turned towards Simone. "Good day, Miss Delacourt."

Simone dropped into a curtsy. "Mr. Bolingbroke."

As he departed from the townhouse, he headed towards his waiting coach. He stepped inside and realized that he wasn't alone.

Kendrick.

Caleb gave the spymaster an expectant look. "I did not realize you made calls to coaches."

"I was in Mayfair and I saw your coach positioned outside of Miss Delacourt's townhouse," Kendrick remarked. "You two are spending an enormous amount of time with one another."

Seeing no reason to deny the truth, Caleb replied, "We are, but that is what partners do."

"I do not recall you spending so much time with Lord Roswell," Kendrick said with a knowing look. "A word of warning- do not hurt Miss Delacourt or you will have me to answer to."

Caleb was surprised by the rare showing of emotion from the spymaster, but his fear was misplaced. He had no desire to hurt Simone, for any reason. She meant far too much to him, and that is what frightened him.

"Yes, sir," Caleb responded.

Kendrick looked pleased by his response. "Good, because we have more important things to discuss," he said. "The agents that were assigned to guard the French spies at the boarding house have reported that they managed to elude them."

"That is not surprising," Caleb muttered.

"They are in the wind again," Kendrick said. "Find them before they wreak any havoc on English soil."

Caleb nodded his understanding. "I secured invitations for them to Lord Pendley's ball. They will reach out to me or Miss Delacourt. I am sure of that."

"Good." Kendrick tapped the top of the coach and it came to a stop. "Report to me once you have something."

"Before you go," Caleb started, "can you look into the death of Lady Hungerton, discreetly, of course?"

Kendrick gave him a baffled look. "Is there a particular reason why?"

"Call it a hunch," Caleb replied.

"Very well, but I do believe you are being foolhardy," Kendrick said. "Miss Delacourt is still struggling with her mother's drowning."

"I know, which is why I am hoping you will keep this between us."

"Secrets?" Kendrick asked, amused. "I am very good at keeping those."

After Kendrick exited the coach, he disappeared into the crowd of people on the pavement.

Caleb leaned his head back against the bench and sighed. He needed to focus on the case, but the image of Simone came to his mind. And he decided to indulge in it. What harm could come from thinking on Simone and her lovely face?

Chapter Eleven

Simone sat in the library as she read a book. She was attempting to distract herself from the fact that her father's mistress was set to arrive at any time.

She wanted to be happy for her father, but she couldn't quite believe he had moved on so quickly. It may have been two years since her mother drowned, but to her, it felt like yesterday. The grief was unrelenting and tormented her thoughts and dreams.

But she did find great comfort in speaking to Caleb about her mother. His words were full of compassion, as if he truly understood her plight. She felt safe in sharing her feelings with him.

Felicity entered the library and met her gaze. "Miss Laurent has arrived," she informed Simone. "She is unpacking her trunks in your mother's... er...her bedchamber."

"Is she truly French?" Simone asked.

Felicity nodded. "Yes, she has a faint accent and she is rather pleasant," she said. "But if you want me to hate her, I will."

"No, I don't want you to hate her on my account."

"It would be easy to do so," Felicity said. "I would even be willing to throw fruit at her and spoil her fancy gown."

Simone giggled. "Thank you, but I do not think throwing fruit will solve this problem."

Felicity walked further into the room. "Why don't you go meet Miss Laurent and decide for yourself if you will like her?" she suggested.

"What if I do?" Simone asked. "I do not want to feel like I am betraying my mother by accepting my father's mistress."

With an understanding look, Felicity said, "Showing kindness to another is never an act of betrayal. Besides, no one will ever replace your mother, you must know that."

Simone sighed, knowing Felicity had spoken true. "All right. I will go meet with this Miss Laurent and I will try to have an open mind."

"Good," Felicity said. "My work here is done."

As Simone rose from her seat, she placed her book down on the table. "Why did my father have to take a French woman as a mistress?"

"Does it matter?"

"I suppose not," Simone replied.

Felicity gestured towards the door. "I think you should stop procrastinating and go greet Miss Laurent yourself."

Simone gave her lady's maid a weak smile. "Was it so obvious?"

"It was, but only to me," Felicity said, returning her smile. "You never know. You might find a friend in Miss Laurent."

"I doubt that, but I will try not to hate her until I have given her a chance," Simone said. "Wish me luck."

"You don't need any luck," Felicity responded. "Just be kind."

Simone tipped her head before she departed from the library. Each step towards her mother's bedchamber felt like a burden, her feet weighed down as if made of lead. Doubt crept in and she wondered if she could truly face Miss Laurent with a smile while her emotions churned within.

Pausing outside the door, she drew in a deep breath. It was time to confront this. Since her mother's passing, she hadn't dared to enter the bedchamber. Now, however, it was time to remedy that.

Simone knocked.

"Enter," a French voice said.

As Simone opened the door, her eyes landed on the last person she expected to see.

Juliette.

Simone closed the door and asked, "What are you doing here?" Her voice was low, accusatory as she debated about reaching for her dagger.

Juliette smiled. "Isn't it obvious?" she asked. "I am moving into my new bedchamber. Although, I will have to redecorate at once."

"No, what are you truly doing here?" Simone repeated.

Juliette's smile grew as she approached Simone. "I can see that you have lots of questions for me, but I have no desire to answer any of them."

Simone remained vigilant as Juliette came to a stop in front of her. "Does my father know you are a spy?" she demanded.

Juliette tsked. "Does your father know how *you* occupy your time?" she asked. "I do not think he would approve of your clandestine outings, as well. When I saw you at the pub, I couldn't quite believe my eyes. You may not have known about me, but I have known about you for quite some time."

"Where is your brother?" Simone asked.

"He is unpacking in one of the guest bedchambers," Juliette replied. "Your father is being most generous in allowing my brother to live here."

Simone narrowed her eyes. "You will leave at once."

"Or what?" Juliette asked. "You will tell your father about

my secret? Go ahead. He won't believe you. But if you did something so foolish, I would be forced to share your little secret, and Mr. Bolingbroke's."

Simone stiffened. "Leave Mr. Bolingbroke out of this."

"How can I?" Juliette asked. "Mr. Barnard warned us about Mr. Bolingbroke being a spy, which is why it wasn't hard to conclude you were one as well."

"I am not a spy."

Juliette gave her a disapproving look. "Do not insult me. I have been doing this for a long time, and I can spot a spy from a distance."

Simone crossed her arms over her chest. "Why are you doing this?"

"Because I love your father," Juliette replied in a lackluster response.

"I don't think you do."

Juliette turned towards her trunks that were opened on the ground. "Regardless, your father has invited me to live with you for the time being."

"Did you even need us to secure you an invitation to Lord Pendley's ball?"

"No, our plans have changed," Juliette replied. "Although, I will admit that it was a brilliant way to distract you and your handsome Mr. Bolingbroke."

"Mr. Bolingbroke is not mine," Simone argued.

Juliette shifted her gaze to meet hers. "He should be," she said. "He is quite handsome, don't you agree?"

"I do not have an opinion on the matter."

"Pity," Juliette said. "Perhaps I should make a go at him."

Simone gave her a look of disbelief. "I thought you were my father's mistress?"

"There is nothing wrong with a little indiscretion here and there," Juliette replied. "It keeps things interesting."

"You are unbelievable."

Juliette removed a gown from one of the trunks. "You are upset, I see," she said. "That will not do."

"I want you to leave."

"That isn't going to happen," Juliette responded, walking the gown over to the bed. "We are going to be one happy family soon."

Simone dropped her arms to her sides. "We are not a family, and we will never be," she asserted. "How did you trick my father? At least, I am assuming that is what you did."

"That was the easiest part. Your father was lonely, and I was more than happy to fill that void. Men are so predictable, so weak," Juliette said.

"You are tricking him, then?" Simone asked. "Pretending to be someone you are not."

Juliette's eyes held amusement. "You are much smarter than I gave you credit for," she said. "Now if you will excuse me, I have a lot to unpack."

"I wouldn't get too comfortable," Simone stated.

A smug smile came to Juliette's lips. "You would be wise to stay out of my way," she warned. "I hold all the power here."

"Not from where I am standing."

"Then you would be wrong," Juliette said. "Whether you like it or not, I am a part of your life for now."

"I won't accept that," Simone remarked.

Juliette closed the distance between them. "Then do it for Mr. Bolingbroke. After all, I wonder what the *ton* would say if it was discovered that he was working as a spy. It is a rather dishonorable position for a man of his standing, is it not?"

"You are threatening me now?"

"I am, and I know you will do the right thing," Juliette said. "After all, I can see the way you look at Mr. Bolingbroke. You care for him."

"Yes, I do, but not in the way you are referring."

"Then you are lying to yourself."

Simone held Juliette's gaze. "You won't get away with this."

Juliette held her hands out wide. "I already have," she declared. "And no one can stop me, or my brother."

"I will stop you."

Juliette's eyes grew hard. "Don't make promises that you can't keep. Just stay out of my way and no one will get hurt." She walked over to the door and opened it. "Good day. I shall see you at dinner where I will expect you to behave."

Simone was fuming but she knew that nothing could be done about this, at least right now. After she walked out of the door, with her head held high, Juliette closed the door behind her.

She needed to see Caleb and she didn't dare to meet with him here. They needed to be able to speak freely.

Once she entered her bedchamber, she saw Felicity organizing the dressing table.

Felicity looked up and asked, "How did it go?"

"Miss Laurent is one of the French spies I was tracking, as is her brother," Simone revealed.

Felicity's eyes grew wide. "Oh, what are they doing here then?"

"Apparently, Miss Laurent is deceiving my father into believing she is something that she is not." Simone walked over to the wardrobe and pulled out her men's clothing from a drawer. "I need to speak to Caleb at once."

"You are going out dressed as a gentleman?" Felicity asked.

"I can't very well call upon him," Simone replied. "This is the only way I can speak to him without causing a scandal."

"It would be a scandal if you were caught in men's clothing," Felicity pointed out.

"That is why I won't get caught," Simone responded.

Felicity approached her and started to help her get

undressed. "I think this plan is foolhardy. You should think on it some more."

"I don't have time," Simone stated. "And I can't wait around and do nothing."

"We could send a footman with an urgent message to his townhouse," Felicity suggested. "That would be less scandalous than what you are attempting to do."

Simone shook her head. "Even if Caleb got the message, it isn't as if we could speak freely here. Two French spies are residing under our roof and they know about me and Caleb."

"What do they know?" Felicity asked.

"That we are spies," Simone replied.

Felicity's hand stilled on the buttons. "What are you going to do?"

"I don't know," Simone said. "But I'm hoping Caleb will have an idea or two." Which was the truth. She needed Caleb, now more than ever. Which was an odd thing to admit to herself because she had never needed anyone before.

Caleb sat in White's as he sipped his drink. He was listening to Roswell and Fredrick converse about something that was utterly boring. Now that they both were happy, they were rather obnoxious, thinking that everyone should fall prey to the parson's mousetrap.

He had his reasons as to why he would never marry, but his resolve was starting to wane the more time he spent with Simone. She was unlike any of the other young women of his acquaintance. And it wasn't just because she was a spy. No. It was more than that. She was fiercely strong, on the inside and out, but she also had a kind heart.

Roswell's voice interrupted his reverie. "Are you even listening to us?"

"No," Caleb admitted. "I stopped a long time ago. I grew tired of your drivel."

"It isn't drivel," Roswell defended. "We were just discussing our plans after the Season ends. I thought we would all return to our country estate."

"Exactly, drivel," Caleb said.

Fredrick chuckled. "Is there something in particular that you would like to discuss?"

"With you, no," Caleb replied. "I am doing just fine on my own."

Roswell reached for his glass as he asked, "How is your assignment going?"

"Not well," Caleb admitted. "The agents that were assigned to watch over the two French spies lost them. So now they are in the wind."

"That is not good," Roswell said.

"No, it isn't," Caleb agreed, "but they will make contact soon enough. They wanted us to secure invitations to Lord Pendley's ball, which I did."

Fredrick grew solemn. "Did you discover why they want to go to the ball?"

A resonant voice came from behind them. "They don't."

Caleb turned his head and could scarcely believe what he was seeing. It was Simone, and she was dressed in gentlemen's clothing. She even had a thick black mustache above her upper lip and a top hat with tufts of hair peeking out.

In a hushed voice, he asked, "What are you doing here?"

"I needed to speak to you," Simone said, dropping the act with her voice.

Caleb gestured towards a chair. "Take a seat before anyone notices you." He glanced around the room to see if anyone was paying them heed. "What were you thinking?"

Simone sat down and shared, "Your butler said you were here."

"And you thought you could just stroll right into a gentlemen's club undetected?" Caleb asked in disbelief.

"It worked, did it not?" she replied, smugly.

Simone turned her attention towards Roswell and Fredrick. "Gentlemen," she greeted. "I am glad that you two are here. You need to hear what I am going to tell Caleb."

Fredrick gave her a curious look. "How is that mustache staying on?"

Simone reached up and gently rubbed the mustache above her top lip. "My cook made a concoction that keeps the mustache on if I am very careful. But it doesn't last long so I don't have much time." She held her hand up to the top hat. "And the wig is attached to the top hat. It is all very clever, if you ask me."

Caleb lifted his brow. "What is so important that you are risking your reputation, and mine?"

"You will never guess who my father's mistress is." She paused before adding, "It is Juliette."

"Juliette?" he repeated in disbelief. "That is your father's mistress?"

"That is what I said, wasn't it?" Simone asked.

Fredrick interjected, "Who is Juliette?"

"That is one of the French spies that we have been tracking," Simone explained.

Turning in his seat to face Simone, Caleb asked, "Where is her brother?"

"In one of the guest bedchambers," Simone replied.

A server approached the table and directed his attention at Simone. "May I get you a drink, sir?"

Simone opened her mouth to respond, but Caleb decided it was best if he spoke for her. "He would just like a cup of tea."

As the server walked away, Simone said, "I can speak for myself."

"Not here you can't," Caleb responded. "One good look

at you and your ruse is exposed. You are far too beautiful to be a man."

Simone visibly tensed. "I will have you know that I have done this ruse many times and I have never been caught."

"I don't know how," Caleb remarked. "They must have been idiots to not be able to see what was right in front of them."

"Regardless, I have come for your help," Simone said, her voice tripping on the last word.

Caleb knew that admission must have cost Simone a great deal so he wasn't about to tease her about it. Instead, he leaned closer and asked, "Did Juliette say what she wanted?"

"No, but she knows that we are spies, and she has threatened to reveal our secret if we do not go along with her charade," Simone shared. "Apparently, Mr. Barnard told her about you and it didn't take much of an assumption on her part to realize I was a spy as well."

"So I was right. My cover has been compromised," Caleb said. "This does complicate things greatly."

"Should we notify Kendrick and have them arrested?" Simone asked.

Caleb shook his head. "We still don't know what their assignment is or how your father plays into all of this."

"I don't think my father is a part of anything nefarious," Simone said. "He lives and breathes for the Crown."

"Yet, he willingly let two French spies into his home?" Caleb questioned.

"I don't think he knows that they are spies, at least that is what Juliette implied," Simone said. "I think she is just using him."

Caleb pushed his drink away from him. "Either way, this is not good. Lord Hungerton is privy to confidential information as a member of the peerage."

"My father wouldn't betray his country," Simone argued.

"You don't know what men are capable of when backed

into a corner," Caleb remarked. "Regardless, he must have some inclination that they are up to no good."

Roswell cleared his throat. "I must agree with Caleb on this. If your father is involved somehow, it will not end well for him."

Simone's shoulders slumped. "That is what I was afraid you would say."

Caleb leaned closer to her. "Keep your shoulders back and your head up," he advised. "A gentleman does not display his emotions in public."

Simone squared her shoulders and the strength returned to her eyes. "I need to find a way to stop Juliette and her brother before they reveal our secrets."

"No, *we* need to find a way to stop them," Caleb corrected. "We will go to Mr. Frickle's office as planned this evening. Perhaps he will have something in his files that will help us discover if Lord Hungerton is involved with Juliette and her brother."

"I hope so because I am out of ideas. I don't like the idea of Juliette and her brother having the upper hand," Simone said.

"Neither do I, but that won't be for long," Caleb stated.

Fredrick's eyes perused Simone and asked, "Dare I ask where you got those clothes?"

"I had my dressmaker make them for me," Simone replied. "She didn't even bat an eye at my request."

"Those clothes are rather fine and could trick the casual bystander, but not anyone that truly takes a moment to look at you," Fredrick said.

In a deep voice, Simone said, "That is why I alter my voice."

Fredrick chuckled. "That was awful," he responded. "That is not what any respectable gentleman sounds like."

"It is good enough," Simone remarked. "But I am not

here for critiques on my disguise. I need to know how to navigate living with French spies."

Caleb had an idea. "I will join you for dinner."

Simone smiled, brightening the whole room with that simple gesture. "That is a grand idea," she said.

"You are smiling too big," Caleb whispered.

Her smile dimmed. "How is that possible?"

"Just trust me on this," Caleb replied.

The server returned and placed the cup of tea in front of Simone. "Will there be anything else?" he asked.

Simone lowered her gaze to the cup as Caleb responded, "Not at this time."

Once the server walked off, Simone reached for the teacup and took a small sip. "This is awful," she said, lowering the cup. "How can anyone drink this tea?"

Fredrick held his teacup up. "You get used to it."

"Gentlemen don't usually request tea, unless you are Fredrick," Roswell explained. "He gets terrible headaches when he drinks alcohol."

Simone pushed the cup of tea away from her. "I would rather not drink another sip of that tea. It is an abomination."

"A true gentleman wouldn't care, or notice, the taste of the tea," Caleb remarked. "They would just drink it without complaint."

"It would have been best if you had ordered me a glass of brandy," Simone said.

Caleb huffed. "I think not."

Simone rose from her seat. "I should be going before my absence is noticed." She shifted her gaze towards Caleb. "I shall see you tonight for supper."

"I will be there," Caleb assured her.

Simone reached up and smoothed down her mustache. "If you will excuse me, gentlemen," she said in the same deep voice that she had first started with.

As she walked off, Caleb sighed. "I shouldn't be surprised

by Simone's antics by now, but I never thought I would see her in White's, dressed as a man."

Fredrick grinned. "I find her utterly fascinating, but only because she has managed not to get herself caught."

"She is good. I will give her that," Roswell said. "Perhaps a little too brazen, though."

"Simone does things her own way, and in her own time," Caleb remarked. "But I am beginning to see cracks in the mask she wears."

"I wish you luck with that." Fredrick gave him a pointed look. "Aren't you going after her to ensure she arrives home safely?"

Caleb put his hand up. "If I did, she would chide me on my impertinence, and I do not think I need another lecture from her."

"Then don't get caught," Fredrick advised.

Rising, Caleb knew that Fredrick was right. He needed to know that she was all right, even if she didn't want him to. He would do anything to keep her safe.

Fredrick gave him an approving nod. "If you need anything, you know where I am."

"Me, too," Roswell added.

Caleb acknowledged their words with a tip of his head before he headed after Simone. With any luck, she wouldn't notice him, and she would return home without incident.

Chapter Twelve

Simone was all too aware that Caleb was following her, but she had no desire to confront him. A part of her was annoyed that he didn't think she could manage on her own, but another part of her, a much larger part, found a certain charm in his concern.

It had been a long time since someone had shown such kindness towards her. She had learned to do things on her own, but Caleb was making it increasingly difficult to do so. He wanted to help her, despite her insistence that she didn't need it. But maybe she did, she thought.

As she approached the servants' entrance of her town-house, she removed her top hat and mustache, holding them in her hand. She opened the door and stepped inside, only to find her father waiting for her. His nostrils flared at the sight of her.

"So it is true?" he demanded. "You dress up as a man and leave the house."

"Yes, but I can explain—" she started, her eyes darting around the empty kitchen. Her father must have sent the servants away so they wouldn't witness this conversation.

He cut her off. "No! I have had enough of your lies!" he

exclaimed. "You have dishonored me by your total lack of regard for propriety."

"Father—"

He put his hand up, stilling her words. "When Juliette told me about what you were doing, I didn't believe her. But now I see it plainly with my own eyes."

Simone should have known that Juliette was behind this, but that was the least of her concerns right now. She needed to find a way out of this mess that she found herself in. Her father's temper was stoked, and she had to come up with a believable lie.

What if she just told him a half-truth, she thought. That could work. In a soft voice, she said, "I dress up so I can attend lectures at university."

"University is for gentlemen. It is not for ladies playing dress up," her father growled.

"Yes, I know, but I want to better myself, just as Mother always encouraged me to do," Simone said, lowering her gaze.

Her father crossed his arms across his chest. "Your mother knew better than to ever dress up as a man. She may have been progressive, but she still operated within the realm of propriety."

"I'm sorry, Father," Simone said.

Some of her father's anger dissipated at her words, but it wasn't entirely gone. "I want you to go upstairs and change. Then bring me all the men's clothing that you have so I can burn them."

Simone's eyes went wide. "You can't be serious," she said.

"I am, and it is time that I take a more active part in your life, at least until you find a husband to watch over you," her father responded.

Now it was her anger that was stoked. Squaring her shoulders, she declared, "I do not need a husband to watch over me."

"I think you do, more than you realize," he said. "I can't

tend to you and accomplish all my other tasks. Which is why I am going to find you a husband."

"I won't marry a stranger," Simone declared.

"Then you may pack your trunks and leave the town-house," her father responded.

Simone reared back, not quite believing her father's words. "You are disowning me?"

Her father uncrossed his arms. "What choice do I have?" he asked. "You act the part of a wallflower, but you are truly a hoyden."

Before she could respond, Juliette appeared at the bottom of the stairs and said, "I apologize for interrupting but perhaps we should continue this conversation in the privacy of your study. The servants are anxious to return to their tasks."

Her father bobbed his head. "I think that is a fine idea. There is much more that needs to be discussed," he said. "Follow me, Simone."

Keeping her head low, she followed her father up the servants' stairs to the main level and into the study.

Once they arrived, Juliette entered the room and closed the door behind her. "I couldn't help but overhear your conversation," she admitted. "But I do not think disowning Simone is the right thing to do."

Her father's face softened, just slightly, as he turned his attention towards Juliette. "And why is that?"

"What would she do?" Juliette asked.

"She has an inheritance from her grandmother that she could live on," her father said. "It is not as if she would be left destitute."

Juliette shifted her gaze towards Simone. "I think the best option is for you to marry, and quickly."

"No, I won't do it," Simone said.

"Think of your future," Juliette urged.

"I am, and that is why I refuse to be tied down to a man that I don't love," Simone pressed.

Her father huffed. "Not this again," he declared. "Love has no place in a marriage. It is a pure fantasy on your part."

Juliette's eyes feigned compassion. "Listen to your father," she said. "He knows what is best for you."

"Does he?" Simone asked. Why was Juliette even here, attempting to help her? She didn't need or want her help.

Her father's eyes narrowed. "Watch your tone, Child," he stated.

"I am not a child anymore," Simone retorted.

"You are acting like one," her father said. "Everything I have done has been for you. Yet you are too ungrateful to see that."

Simone knew that she should bite her tongue, and to consider her next words carefully, but she was angry. "What have you done for me?" she demanded. "You ignore me for days on end, and when we speak, it is usually in passing."

Juliette interjected, "You are not being fair to your father. He is an important man and he has work that he needs to see to."

"Precisely," her father said. "You do not understand the pressures that I am up against."

Simone resisted the urge to roll her eyes. Juliette was good. She would give her that. If she wasn't a spy, she could have had a career in the theatre.

Her father walked over to the drink cart and poured himself a drink. "So we are decided, then?" he asked. "You will marry a man of my choosing or you will leave this town-house at once."

Juliette walked over to her father and placed a hand on his sleeve. "It might be best to give Simone some time to think on such an important decision. You don't want to do anything that you might come to regret later."

Her father took a sip of his drink before lowering it to his side. "Fine. I will give her three days to allow her to carefully consider her options."

"That is very generous of you," Juliette said. "Isn't it, Simone?"

Simone frowned. "It is," she replied. Why was Juliette trying so hard to help her, when it was her fault that she was in this situation? What game was she playing?

Her father walked over to his desk and sat down on the chair. "Bring me your men's clothing so I can burn them, and I do not want you to leave this townhouse without my approval. Do we understand one another?"

Simone took a step closer to the desk as she tried to plead her case. "But I use the trousers on occasion to ride my horse."

"Not anymore. Those days are behind you," her father said. "I tire of this conversation. You are dismissed."

Simone held her father's gaze for a moment before she spun on her heel and departed from the study. As she walked down the corridor, she heard Juliette call out after her. What now, she thought.

She stopped and turned around to face her nemesis. "What do you want?"

Juliette smirked. "What? No thank you for helping you?"

Simone's brow shot up. "Help me?" she asked. "You were the one who ratted me out to my father in the first place."

"It had to be done," Juliette said.

"Did it?"

Juliette took a step closer to her. "You may try to dabble in the spy world, but you are no match for me," she replied. "I can take everything from you by just a few choice words to your father. You would be wise to remember that."

Simone wasn't about to be cowed by Juliette. "You don't know me or what I am capable of."

Juliette patted her arm. "You are sweet, and under different circumstances, we might have been friends. But there can only be one victor here, and it will be me."

"I will not go away quietly. I can promise you that," Simone assured her.

"I am counting on that," Juliette said.

Simone knew that there was nothing else that needed to be said between them, and she was tired of looking upon Juliette's smug expression.

Without saying a word, Simone turned and hurried up the stairs to her bedchamber on the second level. She stepped inside and saw Felicity fluffing her pillows.

She slammed the door closed and leaned back against it.

Felicity put the pillow down. "What is wrong?"

"It is Juliette," Simone revealed. "She told my father that I dress up as a man to leave the house and he caught me coming back in through the servants' entrance."

Felicity gasped. "What did he say?"

"I am to marry a man of his choosing, or I can pack my trunks and leave, forever," Simone replied. "He has given me three days to decide."

Her lady's maid came to stand next to her. "What are you going to do?"

"Well, I refuse to marry a stranger so the only option is for me to leave," Simone said.

"Where will you go?"

Simone shrugged. "I could rent out a room at a boarding house until I decide what to do next," she said. "I am not sure if I would be able to continue working as a spy. I might just have to retire to the countryside and live a quiet life."

Felicity gave her a curious look. "You are just going to give up, then?"

"Give up?" Simone asked. "That is not what I am doing. I am just trying to be practical."

With a laugh, Felicity inquired, "Since when have you been practical? Your entire life you have defied the rules of polite Society. Why start now?"

Simone bit her lower lip, not sure what to say. She agreed with Felicity, but she was at a loss for what she should do.

Felicity continued. "Furthermore, are you going to let Juliette win?" she asked.

"She outplayed me," Simone admitted, dejectedly.

"This time," Felicity said. "What about next time?"

Simone met her lady's maid's gaze, and she knew that she spoke true. This was just a hiccup in her plan. She would find a way to beat Juliette. She had to.

She straightened up from the wall, and with determination in her voice, she said, "You are right. Everyone has a weakness, and I just have to find hers and exploit it."

"That is what any good spy would do," Felicity stated.

Simone glanced down at her clothing. "The first thing I must do is change into a gown and bring my men's clothing down to my father. He intends to burn them."

"All of them?"

A small smile came to her lips. "It might be best if I keep a pair of trousers for when something unexpected arises."

"I can easily hide the trousers in a place that no one will find them," Felicity said.

Simone removed the jacket and dropped it to the floor. "I can always ask the dressmaker to make me more clothing in the future."

While she changed out of her clothing, Simone felt in her gut that this game with Juliette was far from over. She may have the upper hand now, but that would change. It had to.

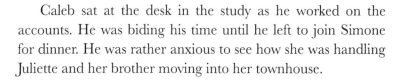

Caleb sat at the desk in the study as he worked on the accounts. He was biding his time until he left to join Simone for dinner. He was rather anxious to see how she was handling Juliette and her brother moving into her townhouse.

A knock came at the window, drawing his attention. He turned his head and saw Kendrick on the other side of the window.

Caleb rose and went to open the window. "You do realize that we have a main door," he joked.

Kendrick extended him a file. "The fewer people that know I am here, the better," he said. "This is everything I could find on Lady Hungerton's death. It isn't much, though."

Opening the file, he saw newssheet clippings and a report from the coroner. He perused the report and saw that the coroner determined the drowning was accidental and no foul play was suspected.

Glancing up, Caleb said, "It seems odd that Lady Hungerton's body was never found."

"It is, but the lake near her country estate was deep," Kendrick remarked. "The body could have sunk to the bottom, never to return."

"I think I need to speak to Lady Hungerton's lady's maid again and see if she can shed any light on this," Caleb said.

Kendrick tipped his head. "Very good," he said as he turned to leave.

Caleb called out to him. "Before you go, you should know that Juliette and Victor are now residing with Lord Hungerton in his townhouse."

The spymaster's brow shot up. "Whatever are they doing there?"

"Supposedly, Juliette is the baron's mistress," Caleb replied.

"You have your doubts?"

Caleb shrugged. "I am not quite sure what to believe, but I suspect Lord Hungerton knows more than he is letting on. I will investigate him on my end, but would you delve into his finances?"

"I will, but what do you think we might find?"

"I'm not sure, but my gut is telling me that Lord

Hungerton is not who he claims to be," Caleb said. "I think it would be best if we stationed two guards outside of Simone's townhouse, just as a precaution."

Kendrick gave him a knowing look. "Have you spoken to Simone about this?"

"Not yet, but I worry that she might be too close to the situation."

"I would proceed cautiously, then. You two are supposed to be working together, not against one another."

Caleb bobbed his head. "I understand, but I assure you that I am only thinking of Simone's best interests."

His mother's voice came from the doorway of the study. "Who are you talking to?" she asked as she stepped further into the room.

Turning towards her, Caleb replied, "No one." He closed the file in his hand. "I was just talking to myself."

"That is a habit that you should rid yourself of."

"I would agree," Caleb said, placing the file down onto the desk. He glanced at the window and saw Kendrick was gone. "Is there something that you need, Mother?"

His mother smiled, and he knew he was in trouble. "I just heard that you will not be joining us for dinner this evening."

"That is true," he replied. "I am dining with Miss Delacourt this evening."

"For someone that is adamant that he will never wed, you are spending an enormous amount of time with Miss Delacourt."

"We are just friends, Mother," Caleb said. "Do not read anything more into this."

His mother's smile grew broader. "How can I not?" she asked.

Caleb sighed. "I just fear that you will be left disappointed once Miss Delacourt and I go our separate ways."

"But I thought you were friends."

"We are—"

She spoke over him. "So why wouldn't you just continue down the path you are both on?" she asked. "It seems to be working well for both of you."

His mother was good at manipulating his words, but he had no desire to debate this point with her. "I should be going."

"Yes, you should," his mother agreed. "You wouldn't want to be late."

Caleb walked over to his mother and kissed her cheek. "Good evening, Mother," he said. "Do not wait up for me."

"I hardly do anymore," his mother responded. "Please tell Miss Delacourt that I said hello."

"I will."

His mother gave him a thoughtful look. "You don't get to choose who you fall in love with. It just happens on its own."

Caleb lifted his brow. "I never said anything about love."

"I know, but love is confusing. It is not something that we understand or know. We are just meant to follow our hearts."

"Are you implying that I love Miss Delacourt?"

His mother's eyes went wide, looking entirely too innocent. "I would never dare to presume you had such strong emotions for Miss Delacourt," she said. "I was just merely offering some advice."

"Unsolicited advice," Caleb muttered.

"That is what any good mother would do," his mother declared with a wave of her hand. "I just want you to be happy."

Caleb frowned. He questioned why everyone was so concerned with his happiness. He was doing just fine on his own. "I am happy," he said.

"Are you?" his mother asked. "Because I can't help but notice that your smile grows whenever you are around Miss Delacourt."

"Why can't you just be happy that Anette is married?"

His mother grew somber. "You are sad. I can see it in your eyes."

Caleb mustered up a smile to his lips. "I am perfectly happy." He wondered who he was trying to convince. His mother or himself?

"If you want Miss Delacourt in your life, you must let her know with words and actions, and all those little things will make her want to stay," his mother advised.

"Are you even listening to me?" he asked. "I have no intention of taking a wife, now or ever. That is not the path that I am on."

"Then get off that path."

"It isn't that simple, Mother," Caleb argued. "My life is not conducive to having a wife."

"Everyone needs a companion, a helpmate, to make the journey bearable," his mother remarked. "You just need to trust the direction that your heart is telling you to go."

Caleb placed a hand on his mother's shoulder. "I love you, but my mind is made up. I do not see a future that includes a wife for me."

His mother opened her mouth to respond, so he continued. "I need to go. I do not wish to be late."

"Very well," his mother sighed. "I will just remain in this large townhouse without any grandchildren to keep me company."

"I do think you will survive," he teased.

"Just barely," his mother said.

As he departed from the study, Caleb had to admit that he was lonely. But that didn't mean he would take a wife to entertain him. That would be terribly unfair to her, and to him. He wasn't entirely unhappy at the moment. He had plenty of things to occupy his time, including this blasted assignment that was getting more and more complicated with each passing day.

He exited the townhouse and stepped into the waiting

coach. It merged into traffic and Caleb closed his eyes for a moment. An image of Simone came to his mind, and he smiled. He was glad that they were friends, but he didn't dare to hope for anything more. Once this assignment was over, they would go their separate ways.

That thought did not sit well with him.

His feelings for her had deepened over time, and now he found he wasn't quite ready to say goodbye to her. He wanted her in his life. No, he *needed* her in his life. She challenged him, making him want to be a better spy and a better person.

The coach came to a stop in front of Simone's townhouse and he stepped down on the pavement, not bothering to wait for the footman to step off his perch.

He approached the main door and knocked.

The door was promptly opened and the butler stood to the side. "Welcome, Mr. Bolingbroke," he greeted. "Do come in."

Caleb stepped into the entry hall and his breath caught when he saw Simone descending the stairs. She was dressed in a pale pink gown and her hair was piled atop of her head, with two long curls framing her face.

It wasn't her comely figure or hairstyle that was drawing his attention. It was the smile that played on her lips. Her perfectly formed lips, filling him with such longing to kiss her that it was only a lifetime of good manners that kept him from doing so.

Simone came to a stop in front of him. "Good evening," she greeted.

"You look…" His words trailed off as he tried to find the right word. "Tolerable."

Her smile grew. "Tolerable?" she repeated. "I suppose that will do."

Caleb offered his arm. "May I escort you into the drawing room?" he asked.

"You may," she replied as she placed her hand on his sleeve.

As they walked the short distance to the drawing room, Caleb leaned in and asked, "How are Juliette and Victor?"

Simone let out a puff of air. "Juliette has managed to make a nuisance out of herself, and I don't think Victor has even left his bedchamber," she revealed. "My father caught me when I came home from White's. Juliette tipped him off."

"Why would she do that?"

"She wants me to know that she has all the power," Simone said. "It is all about control with her, and I need to rise up and beat her at this game."

Caleb glanced over at her. "This isn't a game."

"I fear that Juliette has made it into one."

"Yes, but one small misstep and it could be your last," Caleb said. "I would be cautious."

Simone nodded her head. "I have every intention of being diligent."

"Good," he said.

A line between Simone's brow appeared before saying, "We do have a problem, though."

"Another one?"

His attempt at humor fell flat as she held his gaze. "My father was irate when he saw me dressed as a man. He has given me three days to agree to an arranged marriage or else he will disown me."

Caleb's brow shot up. "Three days?"

"Yes, and I refuse to marry a stranger, or anyone, for that matter," Simone said. "I wouldn't be able to work as a spy if I was wed."

An idea struck him. One that would benefit both of them. "What if we wed, in name only?" he asked.

Simone slipped her hand off his sleeve and said, "That is a terrible idea."

"Why?" he asked, turning to face her. "We both get along, for the most part, and you need a husband."

"But you don't need a wife," she countered.

Caleb bobbed his head. "True, but I am willing to make an exception."

Simone's brow furrowed. "You don't want to marry me," she asserted.

"I think I do."

Reaching up, she tucked one of her curls behind her ears. "I know you mean well, but I do not want to get married."

"That is why this would be a perfect arrangement for us," Caleb said. "You go your way, and I'll go mine, but you will have the protection of my name."

Simone grew quiet. "Your offer is quite generous, but I must say no."

Caleb felt a stab of disappointment at her words, but he wasn't about to grovel. Not yet, at least. He thought it was a brilliant idea, but he needed to give her time to realize that it was her best option. "What will you do, then?" he asked.

"I'm not quite sure, but I will figure it out," Simone replied.

Feeling a need to tease her, he asked, "Am I not handsome enough to tempt you?"

"No, sir, you are more than handsome," Simone rushed out as a blush formed on her cheeks. "I mean… you are tolerable, I suppose."

Caleb chuckled. "It is all right if you think I am handsome," he said. "There is no shame in admitting it."

"I do not wish for you to become more cocky than you already are," Simone remarked, tilting her chin.

"Marry me, Simone," he said. "It is the perfect solution to your problems and you will never have to be lonely again."

Simone pressed her lips together before admitting, "Loneliness is familiar. It is what I am comfortable with. More importantly, I do not need you to come in and save me. I can save myself."

"I have no doubt, but I can't very well have my partner living on the streets," Caleb said. "Now can I?"

"I wouldn't live on the streets. I would find a respectable boarding house where I could rent a room until I figure out my next step."

Caleb decided to try a different tactic, one that he knew Simone couldn't refute so easily. "Do you want to continue working as a spy?"

"I do, more than anything," Simone admitted.

"By marrying me, you would have the freedom to do so," Caleb said. He could see the doubts in her eyes, but he also saw vulnerability. She wasn't completely turned off by the idea.

He took a step closer to her and continued to press his suit. "Taking chances can be scary, but I do believe that there is something that should scare you far worse than anything."

"What is that?" she asked.

Leaning closer, he responded, "Missing out on something truly wonderful because you were scared."

Simone searched his eyes, and he hoped she found what she was seeking. He was laying himself bare for her. It was something he had never done before with a young woman. Despite his previous resolve against marriage, being with Simone in this moment made him certain that offering for her was the right decision. He desired to marry Simone not as a means of protection but because of the genuine care he felt for her.

Someone cleared their throat and Caleb turned his head to see Juliette and Victor standing in the doorway.

"My, my, what do we have here?" Juliette asked, a smirk playing on her lips. "It seems that you two are alone, completely unchaperoned. That is entirely inappropriate, is it not?"

Foregoing the pleasantries, Caleb narrowed his eyes and asked, "Juliette, what is your plan here?"

"Dinner first," Juliette replied. "Then we shall talk."

Chapter Thirteen

Simone didn't know what was more awkward: dining with two French spies or sitting next to Caleb, who had just offered for her.

She was listening to the polite conversation that was going on around her, but she noticed Caleb had yet to say a word. He was staring intensely at Juliette and Victor. His body was tense, indicating a readiness to act, though Simone couldn't decipher his intentions.

As she moved the food around her plate with her fork, Simone couldn't quite believe that Caleb had proposed the idea of a marriage between them. The worst part was that she wasn't turned off by it. The idea had seemed ludicrous at first, yet she couldn't dismiss it entirely.

Caleb wanted to marry her, in name only. Such an arrangement would allow her to maintain her role as a spy, coming and going as she pleased. And they got along, at least for the most part. They would just have to pretend to hold some affection for one another when they entered the world of high Society.

Truth be told, she held Caleb in high regard, but she didn't want to dwell upon that too much. If she did, she would have to face the fact that her feelings for Caleb were much deeper than she wanted them to be. Which was absurd. A spy did not have the luxury of falling for one's partner. It was too dangerous to ever blur that line.

Her father spoke up from the head of the table, drawing her attention. "Are you in agreement, Simone?"

Simone brought her head up and saw that her father was staring at her. "I do apologize, but I'm afraid I was woolgathering."

With a disapproving look, her father said, "You have been awfully quiet this evening and you have been neglecting your duties as hostess to Mr. Bolingbroke."

"That was not my intention," Simone said, her eyes shifting towards Juliette and Victor.

Juliette flashed her a smile. "You are looking lovely this evening, Simone," she praised.

"Thank you," Simone responded, her words holding no warmth to them. She was not going to make this easy on them.

Not appearing concerned by her lackluster response, Juliette announced, "I have unpacked all my belongings."

Her father reached for Juliette's hand and brought it up to his lips. "I am glad that you are here."

"As am I," Juliette said. "And thank you for allowing my brother to reside with us."

Victor tipped his head in response. "It was a most generous offer on your part, my lord."

Her father acknowledged Victor's words with a smile. "It was the least I could do, considering you both do not have a home to return to."

Juliette turned her attention towards Simone and explained, "We lost our country estate in the war."

"Did you now?" Caleb asked, his words curt.

"Yes, Napoleon's forces set our estate on fire and we were lucky to escape with our lives," Juliette replied.

Caleb leaned back in his seat. "I was under the assumption you just returned from France."

"That is correct," Juliette replied. "We were able to visit the few family members that we had to leave behind. Bless their souls, they are enduring the terrible effects of war. I'm afraid God only knows what they have been through."

"How were you able to get past the blockade of English warships?" Caleb inquired.

Her father interjected, "They were fortunate enough to find a merchant that was willing to make the journey in the cover of darkness."

"How fortunate," Caleb muttered.

"It was," Victor agreed. "We were nervous about making the trip, but we are grateful for the sacrifices of the brave merchant." He reached for his glass and held it up. "And for your father who encouraged us to go and funded our trip."

Simone glanced at her father and wondered if he truly believed this utter nonsense. Juliette and Victor were playing the victims, but they were anything but. They were calculating and would toss her father aside the moment he was of no use to them. Or was her father more involved than she realized? She wasn't sure what his role was in all of this, so until then, she needed to be cautious around him. Around all of them.

Her father released Juliette's hand and reached for his fork. "It was the least I could do for Juliette."

Juliette smiled at her father, and it looked genuine. But Simone was not so easily fooled. Juliette didn't care for him. She couldn't. She was just using him. But for what purpose?

Victor took a sip of his drink and returned the glass to the table. "How are you enjoying the Season, Simone…" He hesitated. "May I call you Simone? I feel as if we are already family."

"We are not family, nor will we ever be," Simone responded.

Her father cleared his throat. "That was uncalled for, and

I am disappointed in you for speaking so harshly to our guest."

"But he isn't a guest, is he, Father?" Simone asked. "He is the brother of your mistress, who now resides in Mother's bedchamber."

Her father's face went slack. "We discussed this—"

Simone spoke over him. "No, we did not. There was no discussion. You just told me how it was going to be from now on."

"Regardless, Juliette and Victor will be living with us for the foreseeable future, and it would be in your best interest to get on board with that," her father said firmly. "At least until you are wed."

The way that her father spoke his words grated on Simone's nerves. And she was tired of her father having any control over her life. She wanted to be in charge of her own destiny. To do so, she would need to marry Caleb.

"About that," Simone started, "I think you are right. It is time for me to wed."

Her father's brow shot up. "It is?"

"Yes, and I have decided that I will be marrying Mr. Bolingbroke," Simone announced.

Caleb turned in his seat to face her. "You have?" he asked with astonishment on his features.

"Yes, assuming the offer is still on the table," Simone said.

"It is," Caleb confirmed.

Simone bobbed her head. "Good. We shall post the banns and be married in three weeks' time." She shifted her gaze back towards her father. "Then you won't need to worry about 'taking care of me' any longer."

Her father studied Caleb for a long moment before saying, "I think this will be an advantageous marriage for both of you."

"Yes, that is precisely why we are doing this," Simone said.

A broad smile came to her father's face as he shoved back

his chair. "This calls for a celebration. I will go get my finest port to celebrate. If you will excuse me," he said before he walked out of the dining room.

In a hushed voice, Caleb directed his comments towards Juliette and Victor. "Why are you doing this?"

Juliette gave him an innocent look. "Whatever do you mean?"

"Cut the act, Juliette," Caleb replied. "We don't have time for that. Lord Hungerton will be returning shortly. I am just wondering why I haven't arrested you yet."

"You wouldn't do anything so foolish or else everything you have worked for will be gone," Juliette said. "I know all about you. You and Lord Roswell." A smirk came to her face. "I even know about Lord Chatsworth, the great war hero, turned spy by Wellington."

Juliette kept her voice low as she continued, "If anything happens to me or Victor, all the newssheets will be informed of your nefarious actions. You and your friends will be ostracized. After all, spying is rather dishonorable, especially for a man of your station."

Caleb narrowed his eyes. "Being ousted is not the worst thing that could happen to me. I knew the risks going into this profession."

"What about your parents?" Juliette asked. "They would be forced to leave London, never to return. What a sad existence for such distinguished families."

Caleb's expression gave nothing away, but Simone knew that he was considering Juliette's words. How could he not? If Juliette made good on her threat, many lives would be ruined. Innocent lives.

Simone met Juliette's eyes. "What is your plan?"

Juliette let out a laugh. "You expect me to tell you?" she asked. "No. That is not how it works. You two will just stay out of my way, and your secret will be safe."

"And if we don't stay out of your way?" Caleb asked.

All humor left Juliette's face. "Threatening to ruin you is not the only way to ensure you stay quiet. I can think of a more permanent solution for you and your fiancée."

"And there is the rub," Caleb remarked.

"Just remember who holds the power," Juliette responded with a smug smile on her lips.

Before anything else could be said between them, her father stepped back into the room with a decanter in his hand. "Shall we celebrate?" he asked.

Caleb shoved back his chair and rose. "I'm afraid I don't feel much like celebrating this evening," he announced. "Perhaps another time."

Rising, Simone said, "Allow me to walk you to the door."

"Thank you," Caleb responded, offering his arm.

After they departed from the dining room, Simone asked, "What are we to do? We can't let Juliette make good on her promise and ruin us all."

"That won't happen," Caleb assured her. "We will find a way to stop her and Victor."

"We don't even know what they are planning," Simone sighed.

Caleb stopped by the main door and turned to face her. "Don't give up hope. Hopefully, our search of Mr. Frickle's office will yield us some clues."

"I hope so."

Caleb's eyes held questions as he held her gaze. "Do you truly want to marry me or were you just saying so to goad your father?"

"A little of both," Simone admitted.

"I will take that, for now," Caleb said. "But before I post the banns, I need you to be sure because I am."

Simone stared up at him, the doubt creeping in. "How can you be sure of anything?"

Caleb took a step closer to her. "Whatever life throws at

us, whatever obstacles we have to overcome, I know that we will be stronger together."

"But we will fight incessantly."

"There is no one else that I would rather fight with," Caleb responded with a smile.

Simone found herself returning his smile. "I do think I would like to be married to you, assuming you honor your word that it is in name only."

"You need not fear. I keep my promises," Caleb said.

"Then, yes, I am sure," Simone responded. "You should post the banns at once."

Caleb reached down and tucked her hair behind her ear, his fingers grazing her skin. "You won't have any regrets."

"I hope not," she said, pleased that she found her voice.

He moved closer and whispered, "I do not want to leave you here with Juliette and her brother. I do not trust them."

"I can handle them," Simone assured him.

"I know you can, but be sure to lock your door at night," Caleb said. "I think they would just as easily kill you as continue this ruse."

Simone nodded. "I agree. I will be vigilant."

Caleb looked as if he had more to say, but instead, he took a step back, albeit reluctantly. "I shall see you tonight."

"I will be waiting."

With indecisiveness in his eyes, he said, "Promise me that you will be safe."

"I promise," Simone said. "You need not worry about me."

"But that is where you are wrong," he started. "I will always worry about you, Simone. That is the job of any dutiful husband."

Simone didn't dare admit that she found his concern about her to be endearing. Before, it would have irritated her to no end, but now she was different. Because of him.

Caleb leaned closer and kissed her cheek. "Until later, my dear," he said before he departed the townhouse.

Simone brought her hand up to her cheek and closed her eyes. That one simple, quick kiss shouldn't have changed anything, but it did. It changed everything.

***

Caleb held a drink in his hand as he watched the fire in the hearth. He was biding his time until he could retrieve Simone and search Mr. Frickle's office. He felt rather anxious at leaving Simone alone with Juliette and Victor. He knew that she could take care of herself, but that didn't mean it stopped him from worrying, especially if she was to be his wife.

He still couldn't quite believe that he had managed to convince her to marry him. Although, he was in disbelief that he had even offered for her in the first place. Not that he didn't want to marry her. He did. It was the perfect cover, for both of them. At least that is what he kept telling himself. This marriage was practical, and in name only. Nothing more.

So why had he kissed her on the cheek, he wondered. And why had it felt so right to do so?

Botheration.

The feelings that he felt for Simone were discombobulated, but one thing was for certain, he did care for her. Greatly. He had never felt this way about a young woman before, and that is what scared him the most.

He was a spy, and falling in love was the last thing he could afford to do. Feelings were weaknesses.

A knock came at the door, breaking him out of his musings. He turned his head and saw Fredrick standing in the doorway.

"What brings you by at this late hour?" Caleb asked.

Fredrick walked further into the room. "Kendrick sent me," he replied.

"You are Kendrick's messenger now?"

As Fredrick sat down on the settee, he replied, "I was meeting with him on another matter, and he asked me to relay a message to you."

"It must have been important if he had sent you."

"Not really," Fredrick said. "He just wanted to inform you that he has placed two agents to guard Miss Delacourt's townhouse, per your request."

Caleb took a sip of his drink before saying, "Not that it matters much. The real threat is inside of Simone's townhouse."

"Kendrick is aware, but he doesn't want to make a move until he knows what they are planning," Fredrick said.

"I figured as much," Caleb muttered. "I just do not like the thought of Simone being alone with them. I wish I was there to protect her."

"I daresay that Simone doesn't need- or want- your protection," Fredrick reasoned.

"That is what she keeps saying, as well."

A smile came to Fredrick's lips. "I hear that congratulations are in order."

Caleb gave him a bemused look. "Whatever for?"

"You are engaged to Miss Delacourt, are you not?" Fredrick asked. "At least that is what my housekeeper told me."

He furrowed his brow. "How in the blazes did your housekeeper know about my engagement already?"

"Apparently, one of your footmen fancies one of my scullery maids and couldn't wait to share the news with her," Fredrick explained.

"Yes, well, it is true. I am engaged to Simone," Caleb said. "I shall post the banns at once and we will be married in three weeks' time."

Fredrick eyed him curiously. "Pardon me for saying so, but you don't seem too excited about the prospect of marrying Miss Delacourt."

"The marriage will be in name only," Caleb explained.

"And Miss Delacourt agreed to this… willingly?"

Caleb nodded. "It will allow her to continue working as a spy, and my mother will finally leave me alone about getting married."

"Ah, so you both get what you want," Fredrick said. "It is practical."

"Exactly," Caleb responded.

Fredrick frowned. "But is that what you truly want- a marriage of convenience?"

Caleb tightened his hold on his glass. "Yes, that is why I proposed the idea."

"Interesting," Fredrick muttered.

"There is nothing 'interesting' about this arrangement," Caleb stated. "Simone's father was pressing her to get married and I came up with a solution that would benefit both of us. That is all it was."

Fredrick leaned back in his chair. "But you care for Miss Delacourt." His words weren't phrased as a question, but more of a statement.

"No more than I would care for a partner," Caleb lied.

His friend chuckled. "You are in denial, I see," he said. "Anyone with eyes can see that you have developed true affection for Miss Delacourt."

"They would be wrong."

"Would they?" Fredrick questioned.

Caleb took a sip of his drink, hoping to end this line of questioning. He didn't want to discuss his feelings for Simone. Not to Fredrick. Not to anyone.

But he was not so lucky.

"There is nothing wrong with admitting that you are happy to be marrying Miss Delacourt," Fredrick said.

"If I did admit it, would you leave me alone?" Caleb muttered.

"No, but it would be a start," Fredrick responded.

Caleb leaned forward and placed his glass onto the table. "I have made peace with the fact that I will never marry for love. My duty is to King and Country."

Fredrick sighed. "I used to feel as you did, but everything changed when I met Emilia. She showed me another way- a better way."

"For you, perhaps," Caleb said. "I do not have the luxury of falling in love. Someone has to keep England safe."

"And it has to be you?"

Caleb lifted his brow. "Why wouldn't it be me?" he asked. "I am not going to give up being a spy just because I developed pesky feelings for Simone."

"Those pesky feelings will have a way of revealing themselves, one way or another," Fredrick advised. "You shouldn't discount them so easily."

"Regardless, Simone and I will wed, and we will go on as we have always been."

Fredrick considered him for a moment before saying, "Marriage between you will change everything."

"It will change nothing."

"So say you," Fredrick started, "but how can it not? You will be responsible for Miss Delacourt, and you will have to play the part of devoted newlyweds."

Caleb shrugged. "That shouldn't be a problem. I have pretended to be someone that I am not for many years now."

"This is different. You will have to look upon Miss Delacourt as if you two are desperately in love," Fredrick counseled. "After all, you wouldn't want to give the *ton* anything to gossip about."

"I can do that."

Fredrick's eyes grew reflective as he shared, "I used to think as you did- King and Country were the only things that mattered. But it all changed when I killed a child on the battlefield."

"I'm sorry," Caleb said, unsure of what else to say.

"I didn't think I was worthy of anything, especially love," Fredrick stated. "I was determined to be alone, miserable, and make it on my own. I thought it was my penance for what I had done."

Fredrick continued. "Fortunately, Emilia helped me see past all of that and gave me something back that I had thought I had lost years ago."

"What was that?"

"Hope," Fredrick replied. "Life without hope is not a life worth living."

Caleb shook his head. "What do I need hope for?"

"A hope for a brighter future," Fredrick replied. "Isn't that what everyone wants? A future that doesn't look as bleak."

"I have a good life," Caleb said. It was a true statement, but even he knew that something was missing from it. Was it hope?

Fredrick nodded in agreement. "You do, but you deserve to be happy, as well. You just need to believe that."

"I don't have time to worry about whether or not I am happy."

"But what of Miss Delacourt's happiness?" Fredrick asked. "Do you have time to ensure that she is happy?"

Caleb shifted his focus to the flickering flames of the fire. Fredrick's words resonated with him. He might be indifferent to his own happiness, but Simone's well-being mattered deeply. He would do whatever it took for her to be happy.

Rising, Fredrick said, "I have done enough preaching for one evening. I will leave you to it, whatever it is that you are doing."

"I do appreciate what you are trying to do, but I know what I am getting myself into."

Fredrick looked amused. "You are marrying Miss Delacourt, a young woman who has managed to fool the *ton* into believing she is something she is not."

"Haven't we all done that?"

"Yes, but Miss Delacourt can throw daggers," Fredrick joked. "I would not want to get on her bad side."

"I can handle Simone."

Fredrick grinned. "I wish you luck with that." He walked over to the door and stopped. "Having the courage to reveal one's heart is one of the most daunting and rewarding experiences in life."

After his friend departed, Caleb leaned his head back and stared up at the ceiling. He knew his friend meant well, but his situation was different. He was marrying Simone, knowing it was not a love match.

They were helping one another. Nothing more, nothing less. So why couldn't he believe his own words? He knew he had fallen for Simone. She had been an unexpected surprise. He had never expected it to be her. But it was her. It was all her. And now there was no turning back.

Chapter Fourteen

Simone sat in the darkened coach as it traveled down the deserted street. No one was out this late at night- unless they were up to no good.

She sat across from Caleb and tried to pretend that his nearness didn't affect her. But it did. Quite frankly, she couldn't stop thinking about that kiss. He may have only kissed her cheek, but that one simple gesture touched her deeply.

The worst part was that she wanted him to kiss her again.

It didn't matter to her that they were so different. All that mattered was the way that he made her feel. She laughed more freely when he was around, and she even noticed her smile felt more genuine. Not the forced smile that she showed the world.

Simone resisted the urge to groan. This would not do. They were supposed to be married, in name only. She couldn't risk falling in love and pining after her husband for the remainder of her days.

Caleb's voice interrupted her thoughts. "You are rather quiet," he observed.

"I am thinking."

"Anything you would wish to share?"

No.

She didn't dare reveal what she was truly thinking on. So instead, she said, "I was just thinking about Juliette and Victor."

"We will figure out their plan and stop them," Caleb encouraged.

"I know, but I do not like that they included my father in it," Simone said. "He may be brash and inattentive, but he is still my father."

Caleb bobbed his head. "I understand that, more than you know."

Simone smoothed down her simple blue gown. "I know you do, which is why I feel comfortable sharing such things."

"I hope you are comfortable sharing everything with me since we will soon be married," Caleb said.

"Not in every sense," Simone corrected.

A playful smirk came to Caleb's lips. "I would be willing to make an exception."

Simone's back went rigid at his insinuation. "You gave me your word."

"I am just teasing you, Simone," Caleb said. "I would never do anything that would make you feel uncomfortable."

She felt herself relax and she even returned his smile. "I wish you wouldn't tease me so much."

"You'd think you would be used to it by now," Caleb joked. "Besides, I do not think I can stop. It is too much fun."

"You are incorrigible."

Caleb chuckled. "I have been called far worse- by you, actually."

She laughed. "It seems so long ago that we were at odds with one another," she said. "You are not as awful as I once thought."

Placing a hand over his heart, Caleb said, "Your words mean the world to me."

"I doubt that."

Caleb lowered his hand to his side and perused the length of her. "I half-expected you to wear trousers this evening."

"I debated about it, but I thought a dress would do just fine for sneaking into Mr. Frickle's office," Simone said. "I'm hoping this is not a waste of time."

"It won't be."

Simone's lips twitched. "Since when did you become so optimistic?"

"I was recently told that I need more hope in my life," Caleb shared. "I thought I would try it out on you."

"Who told you this?"

"Fredrick." Caleb hesitated before saying, "He expressed some concern about us marrying."

Simone frowned. "Why would he be concerned?"

"He worries that we won't be able to separate our personal lives from being spies, but I assured him that won't be the case," Caleb said.

She bit her lower lip, knowing she had a similar concern. "Do you think we are making a mistake?"

"No," he quickly replied. "Do you?"

Simone grew quiet. "I know I am not the easiest person to get along with, and I worry that you might come to regret marrying me."

Caleb leaned forward in his seat and held her gaze. "You are fierce, compassionate, and unapologetically authentic. What would I ever come to regret?" he asked.

"But you will never fall in love."

A solemnness marked his features. "I am a spy, and my duty is to King and Country. Nothing else is as important to me."

Simone felt a stab of disappointment at his words, but she didn't disagree with him. She felt the same way. She couldn't let emotions get in the way of their assignments.

The coach came to a stop in front of a two-level brick

building and Caleb opened the door. After he stepped onto the pavement, he reached back and assisted her out.

Once her feet were on solid ground, she withdrew her hand and looked up at the darkened structure.

"Shall we?" Caleb asked.

They bypassed the main door and went to find a side entrance. Once they located one in the alleyway, Simone removed two slender metal pins from the pocket of her gown and maneuvered them into the lock. The soft click signaling the door's surrender echoed in the quiet alley moments later.

Simone rose and reached for the door handle. "Mr. Frickle's office is 2C," she revealed before she slipped inside. As she headed up the narrow flight of stairs to the second level, she saw that Caleb remained close behind.

Upon reaching 2C, Simone crouched down and retrieved the metal pins. Her second attempt at opening the door proved successful. The door creaked open, granting them access to Mr. Frickle's office.

The small room was laid out with a desk at its center. A lone window adorned the back wall, while bookshelves lined the remaining space.

Simone headed for the desk and started methodically opening its drawers. She needed to find that contract, but beyond that, she wasn't quite sure what she was looking for.

Caleb pulled out the bottom drawer and ran his fingers along the files. His finger stopped on one and he pulled it out. "This file has your name on it," he informed her.

Simone accepted the file and opened it. She saw the contract for her grandmother's estate was on the top of the pile, but she couldn't make out anything. It was too dark, and not even the moon shining through the windows cast enough light to read the small print.

"I can't read anything," she admitted.

Caleb reached for the candle on the table and lit it. Then, he brought it close to the paper in her hand.

"Thank you," Simone murmured.

As she reviewed the contract, she didn't see anything that they didn't already know. The contract was in her name and it had been signed on her behalf. Most likely by her father.

Simone placed the contract down onto the desk and rifled through the other papers in the file. Her hand stilled on her grandmother's will.

"It is my grandmother's will," Simone said.

Caleb gave her an expectant look. "Are you going to read it?"

"Yes," Simone said as she brought it closer to the light.

As she read it, she could scarcely believe what she was reading. This paper proved everything that her father had told her about her grandmother's estate was a lie.

Lowering the paper, she shared, "My father lied to me. He told me that my grandmother only left me fifteen thousand pounds, but that wasn't true. My grandmother left me every-thing- the estate, her money, and all of her land."

Simone handed Caleb the will and continued. "My grand-mother's estate is worth over forty thousand pounds, and that doesn't include the twenty thousand pounds in the bank."

Caleb's brow shot up. "You are an heiress."

"Yes, but my father kept this from me," she said. "Why?"

"Greed," Caleb replied.

Simone placed a hand up to her forehead. "My father may be many things, but I never thought he would cheat me out of my inheritance."

Caleb reviewed the will before asking, "What do you intend to do?"

"First, to start with, I am going to stop the sale of my grandmother's estate, and claim my inheritance," Simone replied.

"I have a solicitor that can help with that," Caleb said. "He is trustworthy and has been employed by my family for many years."

Simone shook her head. "This won't be an easy feat. I suspect that my father will try to fight me on this."

"Legally, he has no footing," Caleb said.

"It is a large sum of money that he stands to lose."

Caleb placed the will down onto the table. "It was never his money to have," he pointed out. "We will take your grandmother's will so Mr. Frickle nor your father have a chance of destroying it."

Simone was curious about something. "Why do you suppose my grandmother didn't leave her estate to my mother?"

"Does it matter as to the reason?" Caleb asked.

"I suppose not, but my mother shared a close relationship with my grandmother," Simone revealed. "I don't know why she would have been left out of the will."

Caleb gathered the papers and placed them into the file. "That doesn't matter now. We just need to ensure you receive what is rightfully yours."

"You are right," Simone said.

Keeping a tight hold on the file, Caleb blew out the candle and headed towards the door. Simone followed him, being mindful of locking the door behind her.

Neither of them spoke as they returned to the coach. Once the door was closed, Caleb held up the file. "Do you want me to hold on to these until I give them to my solicitor?"

"I think that is wise," Simone said.

Caleb brought the file down and asked, "Are you all right?"

Simone didn't know what to feel, knowing what she knew now. "I had no idea my father would treat me so unjustly. He would have stolen my inheritance had I not searched his office and overheard his conversation."

"It was a good thing that you ran into your mother's lady's maid," Caleb said.

"Do you think she knew what my father had planned?" Simone asked.

Caleb shrugged. "I don't know, but she did warn you not to trust your father. Apparently, she was right in doing so."

Simone acknowledged his words with a nod, then shifted her gaze towards the window. Her father was not the man that she thought he was. She wondered what else he was keeping from her. Was he working with Juliette and Victor?

So many emotions whirled in her head and she wasn't sure what she should feel. Anger. Betrayal. Despite all of this, she still loved her father, but now she knew she couldn't trust him. Not anymore.

As an heiress, did this change anything? Would Caleb still want to marry her? She hoped so because she still very much wanted to marry him.

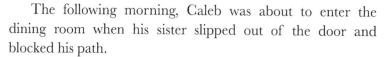

The following morning, Caleb was about to enter the dining room when his sister slipped out of the door and blocked his path.

"I'm sorry," Anette said with a weak smile on her lips.

Unsure of why she would utter an apology, he asked, "For what?"

Anette stepped out of his way. "You will see soon enough."

Caleb entered the dining room to find his mother and father seated at the table, both wearing broad smiles. His heart dropped. They knew of his engagement to Simone, and now he was dreading this upcoming conversation.

His mother jumped up from her chair when she saw him. "Caleb, come sit and join us for breakfast," she said in a far too exuberant voice for such an early hour. "Anette just told us the wonderful news."

With a glance over his shoulder at Anette, Caleb muttered, "Did she now?"

Anette winced, having the decency to look ashamed. "Roswell told me this morning," she shared. "I had come over to congratulate you and I had wrongly assumed that you told them about Simone."

"I had not," Caleb said.

"Sorry," Anette mouthed.

His mother spoke up, drawing back his attention. "Have you posted the banns yet?" she asked.

"Not yet," Caleb replied. "I only just asked Simone to marry me last night. But I hope to do it soon."

"I will start planning the wedding luncheon at once," his mother said. "Do you know what Simone's favorite flower is? We will decorate the townhouse with an abundance of fresh flowers."

Caleb shrugged. "I do not know what her favorite flower is."

His mother gave him a disapproving look. "You will have to ask her. A man should always know his wife's favorite flower." She paused. "Is she commissioning a gown for the wedding? If so, she needs to meet with the dressmaker at once. That is not something that she can wait until the last minute for."

"I don't know what dress she intends to wear," Caleb said. "Does it matter?"

Her eyes went wide. "Of course it matters!" she exclaimed. "The gown a woman wears at her wedding sets the tone for the whole marriage."

"Breathe, Elizabeth. It is just a gown," his father's calm voice interjected.

Anette approached the table and suggested, "I think it might be best if we do not bombard Caleb with questions since he only just got engaged."

Caleb offered his sister a grateful look, but it was short-lived. His mother was many things, but being patient was not one of them.

His mother waved her hand in front of her. "Unfortunately, that is impossible. We have a limited time to plan the wedding of the Season."

"I just want a simple wedding," Caleb said.

"But is that what Simone wants?" his mother asked. "Her mother had an extravagant wedding and even the queen was in attendance."

The last thing Caleb wanted was such an elaborate wedding, but he would do whatever Simone wanted. "I will ask her."

His mother bobbed her head in approval. "Will you go now?"

"Now?" Caleb asked, glancing at the plate of food in front of him. "I haven't even had breakfast yet."

"Let the boy eat," his father said.

His mother sighed. "Fine. Eat some bread and..."

"Elizabeth, you need to pace yourself," his father counseled, speaking over her. "You can't wear yourself out planning this wedding."

"I won't, I promise," his mother said. "I just want everything to be perfect."

Caleb reached for his fork and knife. "All I want is Simone to stand up with me in the front of the chapel. Nothing else matters to me."

His mother snapped her fingers. "I should go speak to our cook now about the menu for the luncheon," she stated. "Anette, would you care to join me? I could use your opinion."

"As you wish, Mother," Anette said.

After his mother and sister departed from the dining room, his father leaned closer to him and asked, "Why are you truly marrying Simone?"

Caleb furrowed his brow. "I beg your pardon?"

His father gave him a pointed look. "You have been telling

us for years that you have no desire to marry and suddenly you get engaged. With no warning. Why is that?"

"It was unexpected, but not unwanted, I assure you," Caleb said.

"Why Simone?"

Caleb placed his fork and knife down and turned towards his father. "Does the reason really matter?"

"I suppose not, but you better be sure," his father replied. "Taking a wife is not a decision to be taken lightly."

"I am aware."

His father reached for his glass and took a sip. As he placed the glass back onto the table, he asked, "Do you love her?"

"Father—"

He cut Caleb off. "Do you love her?" he repeated.

Caleb clenched his jaw, knowing he didn't have a straightforward answer for his father. "I can't explain precisely what I feel for Simone, but I do care for her. Is that not enough?"

"Marriage is hard enough, even when you like the person," his father said. "But love binds you two together. Without it, you both will go in different directions."

"I understand."

His father lowered his voice. "I don't pretend to know how you spend your time, or what you got yourself into, but I do believe it is honorable. You saved me, and this family, from ruination when you helped me out of my predicament." He paused. "I can't help but wonder if Simone is involved in what you do."

"I can't say—"

His father put his hand up, stilling his words. "I just hope you aren't going about this alone. You deserve someone to love you, and help you, in whatever it is that you are doing."

Caleb leaned forward and said, "I like being alone. I prefer it, actually. But that is how I knew Simone was different, because for the first time, I wanted someone else's company more than my own."

"If that is the case, I am happy for you, Son."

"Thank you," Caleb said, leaning back. "Now about Mother..." His voice intentionally trailed off.

His father chuckled. "I will see what I can do, but you know how she gets."

"I do, and that is what concerns me."

The butler stepped into the room and met Caleb's gaze. "Mr. Morrish has arrived. I have shown him to the study."

Caleb pushed back his seat. "Thank you."

His father gave him a curious look. "Why is our solicitor here?" he asked. "Did I miss a meeting?"

"I had an issue arise with Simone and I was hoping for Mr. Morrish's expertise on the matter," Caleb said, rising. "If you will excuse me, I will return shortly."

Caleb left the dining room, making his way towards the study located at the rear of the townhouse. Upon entering, he saw Mr. Morrish was standing near the hearth. The solicitor was tall, thin, and had a head full of white hair. His sharp eyes held a keen intelligence as they focused on Caleb's entrance.

"Mr. Morrish," Caleb greeted. "Thank you for coming so quickly."

"Your note said that it was urgent," Mr. Morrish said, adjusting the rounded spectacles on his nose.

Caleb walked over to the desk and retrieved Simone's file. "I need your advice on something," he said. "My fiancée, Miss Simone Delacourt, has found herself in an unusual spot."

"I hadn't realized you were engaged, sir," Mr. Morrish stated. "Congratulations are in order."

"It is a recent development." Caleb retrieved the will and extended it towards Mr. Morrish. "Miss Delacourt came across this will and needs help to ensure her grandmother's wishes are honored."

Mr. Morrish studied the will for a long moment. "Everything appears to be in order. What is the problem?"

"Her father did not tell her about her inheritance and tried to claim it for himself," Caleb said.

"Is your fiancée of age?"

Caleb nodded. "She is, and I do believe her father's intentions were dishonorable," he replied.

Mr. Morrish's eyes held understanding. "With your permission, I will take this will to probate court and we will get this figured out," he said. "I see no reason why the judge won't decide in Miss Delacourt's favor."

"That is what we are hoping for," Caleb responded.

The solicitor pulled out his pocket watch. "I will go to court at once, but I should warn you that it could take a few weeks until the judge hears the case."

"That is not unexpected," Caleb said. "I would ask that you use discretion in this matter, considering Miss Delacourt stands to inherit a large estate."

Mr. Morrish bowed. "Yes, sir. I would have it no other way."

"Thank you," Caleb said.

After the solicitor walked out of the study, it was only a moment later before Anette stepped into the room.

"Have you recovered?" she asked.

"From what?"

Anette grinned. "Mother's inquisition," she said.

Caleb returned his sister's smile. "I do not think Mother can help herself," he said. "I just hope she will let Simone have a say."

Anette approached the desk and sat down. "I am happy for you, Brother. Simone is a good choice and will make a fine addition to this family."

"You are just saying that because you think she is a spy."

"Isn't she?"

Caleb shook his head. "I won't ever say," he said.

Anette tilted her head, scrutinizing him for a prolonged moment. "I thought you were against marriage," she remarked. "Which makes all of this so much more confusing."

"Am I not allowed to change my mind?"

"You are," Anette replied. "Once we are both wed, I fear that Mother won't have a purpose anymore."

"But she will. It will be her grandchildren."

Anette let out a sigh. "Let's hope that won't be for a long time. I am just enjoying being married to Roswell."

The clock in the corner chimed, signaling the time for Caleb to depart. "If you will excuse me, I have an errand that I must see to before I call upon Simone."

Rising, Anette said, "Make sure you ask her what her favorite flower is. If not, Mother is likely to show up on her doorstep and ask her herself."

"Most likely." Caleb walked over to his sister and kissed her on the cheek. "You are lucky that I like you, Sister, or else I would be furious you told Mother and Father about my engagement."

"I am sorry."

Caleb took a step back. "It was a conversation that had to happen. I suppose I should be happy that it is over now."

"So I did you a favor, then?" Anette asked, perking up.

Caleb chuckled. "I think not." He walked over to the door and stopped. "If I had my way, I would acquire a special license and marry Simone today."

Anette's eyes grew wide. "You wouldn't dare," she said. "Mother would never forgive you if you did such a thing."

"I care more for what Simone thinks," he responded.

As Caleb headed towards the main door, he realized that he had meant his words. He would marry Simone today, tomorrow, or any day that she was willing to do so. It didn't matter to him when they were wed, as long as they *were* wed.

Chapter Fifteen

Simone wasn't quite sure what to feel. Her father had tried to steal her rightful inheritance and she was residing with two French spies. She felt conflicted about so many things. The only thing that she knew for certain was that she felt something for Caleb, something she didn't quite understand. And those feelings only seemed to intensify with each passing day.

She had so many questions, but very few answers.

Emilia's voice pierced through her thoughts, bringing her back into the present. "Was that better?" she asked.

Simone glanced at the target and saw that Emilia's dagger was embedded in it, albeit slightly off center. "Yes, that is much better than your last attempt."

Emilia studied her for a moment before asking, "Are you all right? You just seem rather preoccupied at the moment."

"I suppose I am," Simone admitted.

Lowering her voice, Emilia inquired, "Is it spy related?"

"It is," Simone confirmed.

"Can I help?"

Simone shook her head. "I don't think you can, but I do thank you for the offer," she said. "I just have to work through a few things on my own."

Emilia glanced at the townhouse before saying, "I read in the Society page that your father's mistress now resides with you."

With a slight wince, Simone said, "I had assumed it wouldn't take long before word got out."

"How are you coping with that change?"

Simone decided to be honest with Emilia, at least, somewhat. "It has been quite the adjustment, to say the least."

"I can only imagine."

She decided to change subjects and she knew one topic that would bring a smile to Emilia's face. "How are the wedding preparations going?"

Just as she'd predicted, a bright smile came to her friend's face. "They are going well," she gushed. "I can scarcely wait until I marry Fredrick. Every day seems to move excruciatingly slow."

Simone laughed. "Your wedding day will come before you know it."

"Speaking of which, I understand you are to be married, as well," Emilia said. "I hope you don't mind but Fredrick told me."

"No, I do not mind. It is only a matter of time before the *ton* catches wind of it," Simone remarked.

Emilia gave her a curious look. "Are you not excited about the prospect of marrying Mr. Bolingbroke?"

Simone brought a smile to her lips, and hoped it was convincing enough. She was still conflicted about how she felt about marrying Caleb. But she didn't dare reveal that to Emilia so she decided to tell a half-truth. "I am excited, but I have a lot of things going on right now that take precedence."

"What could be more important than getting married?" Emilia hesitated before adding, "I suppose you are busy keeping England safe."

"I am, among other things."

Emilia walked over to the target and removed the dagger.

"I do not know Mr. Bolingbroke very well. Is he anything like his sister?"

"No, they are quite different, but in a good way," Simone replied. "Caleb is much more serious than Anette. Although, he does spend a great deal of time teasing me."

"Does that bother you?"

"At first, it did, but now I know it is his way of showing he cares," Simone shared. "Bantering with him is one of my favorite things to do."

Emilia approached her and extended the dagger. "Not everyone is lucky enough to marry for love. We are both so fortunate to do so."

Simone blinked. "You are mistaken. I do not love Caleb."

"Don't you?" Emilia asked.

"No, it is a marriage of practicality. We both thought we would benefit from being married to one another," Simone explained.

Emilia furrowed her brow. "Then why do you smile when you say his name?"

"Do I?"

"You do, which is why I worry that you are setting yourself up for heartbreak," Emilia replied.

Simone slipped the dagger into the folds of her gown. "That won't happen," she rushed to assure her. "By marrying Caleb, I will be able to maintain my cover as a spy, and my heart won't even come into play."

Emilia didn't look convinced. "If you say so…," her words trailing off.

"I do," Simone said. "I thank you for your concern, but it is unfounded."

"And Mr. Bolingbroke feels the same as you?" Emilia questioned.

As they started down the path, Simone replied, "He does, considering it was his idea."

Emilia looked as if she had much more that she wanted to

say on the subject, but thankfully she changed topics. "It is a fine day we are having."

"It is," Simone agreed.

"Fredrick is taking me on a carriage ride to Hyde Park during the fashionable hour," Emilia shared. "You are more than welcome to join us."

Simone made a face. "I could not think of anything worse to do with my time."

Emilia laughed. "It is not that bad."

"Hyde Park is terribly crowded during the fashionable hour and there are far too many busybodies that are milling about," Simone said.

"You aren't wrong about that, but it is the time to be seen," Emilia responded.

A footman opened the back door and they stepped inside. While they were making their way towards the entry hall, Simone said, "I prefer to be in the shadows of Society."

"That will all change when you marry Mr. Bolingbroke," Emilia pointed out. "You will one day be a viscountess."

"Not for a long time."

Emilia glanced over at her. "I still can't quite believe this is my life," she admitted. "Just a short time ago, I was a lonely teacher, destined for spinsterhood, and now I am marrying an earl. It is rather surreal."

"I am truly happy for you."

Coming to a stop in the entry hall, Emilia turned to face her. "And I'm happy for you, albeit slightly concerned."

"I assure you that I know what I am doing."

Emilia sighed. "That is the problem," she said. "You think you can control your heart, but that is impossible. You will love who you are meant to love."

Simone smiled at her friend, knowing she was just trying to help. But it was not necessary. She may care for Caleb, but love… no, neither one of them were foolish enough to fall in love. "Love will have no place in our marriage."

"Then why marry him at all?" Emilia asked.

For once, Simone was at a loss for words. She didn't dare reveal that she wanted to marry Caleb, more than she had ever wanted anything before. He was her future. She was sure of that. But how did she explain such a thing without expressing the depths of her feelings?

Emilia must have taken pity on her because she continued. "Thank you for the lesson today. I rather enjoyed myself."

"You are progressing nicely," Simone said.

With a disbelieving huff, Emilia responded, "We both know that isn't true, but at least I hit the target today."

"It just takes practice."

Emilia offered her a grateful look before she headed out the main door and stepped into her waiting coach.

Once the door was closed, Simone debated about what she should do with her time until Caleb came to call upon her. The townhouse was quiet, almost too quiet, making her wonder what Juliette and Victor were up to.

Perhaps her father would be able to enlighten her. Most likely, he would be in his office at this early hour.

Coming to a decision, she headed towards the study in the rear of the townhouse but her steps faltered as she heard her father's gruff voice drifting out into the corridor.

"That isn't what we planned," her father growled.

"I know, but plans change," Juliette said. "You, of all people, should know that."

Simone crept closer to the door, being mindful to avoid the floorboards that were prone to creaking. She needed to hear this conversation.

Juliette's voice grew more persuasive. "It is just one night."

A silence ensued before her father said in a resigned voice, "Very well, but I will be the one that will tell Simone."

"I assumed as much," Juliette responded.

Simone risked the opportunity to peek into the study and saw her father and Juliette were sitting next to one another on the settee. What did her father have to tell her, and why did it seem as if the decision weighed upon him?

Her father rose from his seat. "I suppose I will tell her now."

It was time for her to leave, and quickly. Simone didn't want to be caught eavesdropping on their conversation.

In quick steps, she headed towards the drawing room and dropped down onto the settee. She reached for her needle-work and started working on the handkerchief.

It wasn't long before her father stepped into the drawing room. "Ah, there you are," he said. "I need to speak to you."

"Oh," Simone responded, lowering the needlework to her lap. "Is everything all right?"

Her father stepped further into the room. "We will be attending Lord Pendley's ball in two days' time and Juliette will be accompanying us."

Simone's mouth dropped. "You are bringing your mistress to Lord Pendley's ball?"

Rather than looking ashamed, he buckled down. "I am, and I expect you to be cordial with her," he said. "Do not think I haven't noticed that you go out of your way to avoid Juliette."

"She should not be residing with us, Father."

With a swipe of his hand, her father responded, "It won't matter soon enough. Once you are wed, it will no longer be a concern."

Feeling hurt well up inside of her, she asked, "Are you so quick to get rid of me?" She held her breath, fearful of his response. It was not the first time she had asked the question, but her father always seemed to skirt around the answer. Why wouldn't he just tell her the truth?

His eyes softened, but his body remained rigid, almost as if he were fighting a battle within himself. "That has nothing to do with this. You should have been married years ago."

"I am only in my third Season," she argued.

"Regardless, I need to speak to Caleb about your dowry," he said. "Will you inform him of this when he calls upon you?"

"I will."

Her father took a step back. "You should give Juliette a chance. You may discover that she has more in common with your mother than you realize."

Simone didn't say anything in response. What could she say? Her mother was good and kind, and Juliette was conniving. No. There was no comparing them, and she refused to even think on it.

Finding herself curious, Simone asked, "How long have you known Juliette?"

Her father's face blanched. "Why does that matter?"

The way he spoke his words made Simone think Juliette had been around longer than she had realized. "Did Mother know about her?"

In a hard voice, her father replied, "It is none of your business."

Placing her needlework down on the settee, Simone rose. "I thought you loved Mother," she said. "How could you have kept a mistress on the side?"

Her father's eyes narrowed. "You know not what you speak of."

"Then enlighten me."

"No," he replied flatly. "You have no right to be asking me such questions."

Rather than back down, she stood her ground, knowing she was going to stoke her father's ire even more. But she didn't care. "Do you even miss Mother?"

Her father took a commanding step towards her. "I demand that you stop speaking."

"I am not a servant you can order about," Simone said. "I am your daughter, and I deserve to know the truth."

"The truth?" her father huffed. "You deserve nothing. It is

only because of my generosity that you are allowed to live here. You would be wise to remember that."

Simone pressed her lips together as she stopped herself from confronting her father about her inheritance. As much as she wanted to reveal his deceit, she knew there was a time and a place for such things. She would bide her time, but she knew he would have his comeuppance, one way or another.

Her father took her silence as acceptance. "Good," he muttered. "I do not want to hear you speak of this nonsense again. Do I make myself clear?"

He didn't bother to wait for her response before he departed from the drawing room.

Simone let out a deep breath as she returned to her seat. Her father was impossible. She already knew he was a liar, but she didn't know how far his treachery went. Was he a traitor to the Crown or was he being forced to aid Juliette? As much as she wanted to believe there was some good in her father, she had to admit that the odds were not in his favor.

Caleb's coach came to a stop outside of his agency's head-quarters and he opened the door, not bothering to wait for the footman to come around. He looked up at the dilapidated building and realized that he missed when their headquarters were situated below a bakery. The smell of freshly baked bread was much more welcoming than the pungent odor that hung in the air in this part of Town.

He headed into the building and tipped his head at the agent who was stationed along the back wall. "Good morning," he greeted.

The agent moved to the side and opened the door, allowing him entry. "Kendrick was asking about you earlier."

"Was he in a good mood?"

"Is he ever?" the agent joked.

"You make a good point," Caleb replied as he stepped into the main hall.

He passed all the agents that were stationed at their desks, no one giving him any heed. Once he arrived at Kendrick's office, he knocked and waited to be acknowledged.

"Enter," Kendrick ordered.

Caleb opened the door and stepped into the small, square room. "I received your message," he said, closing the door behind him.

Kendrick shuffled the papers on his desk before giving him his full attention. "I made some more inquiries into Lady Hungerton's death and I discovered a few odd discrepancies."

"Such as?" Caleb asked as he sat on a chair that faced the desk.

"The coroner that was sent to investigate her death turned up dead a few weeks later," Kendrick replied. "Someone broke into his home and shot him."

"Did they find the killer?"

Kendrick shook his head. "They had no leads, no witnesses, and the case eventually went cold," he said.

"Do you think the coroner's death was related to Lady Hungerton's case?"

"I don't know, but shortly after Lady Hungerton's death, the baron let go all of the household staff at his country estate and boarded it up," Kendrick replied.

Caleb frowned. "Did he at least provide them references?"

"Some, but others, he let fend for themselves," Kendrick shared. "According to the villagers, Lord Hungerton never has come back to his country estate."

"You could make a case that he is grieving the loss of his wife."

Kendrick bobbed his head. "You could, but that is where it gets a little more interesting." He leaned back in his seat. "When we looked into Lord Hungerton's finances, per your suggestion, we discovered he has been sending Mr. Underwood fifty pounds a month for the past two years."

"Who is Mr. Underwood?"

"He is one of the Bedlam's Governors," Kendrick said. "Also, I should note that right before Lady Hungerton supposedly drowned, a large donation was given to Bedlam by her husband."

Caleb furrowed his brow. "Why the sudden interest in Bedlam?"

"Why, indeed?" Kendrick asked. "The Court of Governors has been pleading for donations to fund the asylum for years but Lord Hungerton doesn't strike me as a kindhearted donor."

"No, he doesn't," Caleb agreed.

"There is only one explanation that I can come up with, and I don't think you are going to like it," Kendrick said.

It was easy to deduce what Kendrick was going to say but he hoped it wasn't true. If Lord Hungerton truly had his wife admitted to Bedlam, then her fate was worse than death. Many sections of the hospital were deemed uninhabitable, and the cruel, unusual treatment of the patients had been under investigation for years.

Kendrick met his gaze. "If he hid her away in Bedlam, it would explain why her body was never found."

"But why lie?" Caleb asked. "Why not just have her admitted?"

"Because it would cause too many questions and Lady Hungerton was well-liked amongst the *ton*," Kendrick replied. "No doubt the news of her admittance would have made its way to the queen and she might have interceded on Lady Hungerton's behalf."

Caleb jumped up from his seat. "If this is true, we have to do something to help Lady Hungerton."

Kendrick gave him a knowing look. "Lord Hungerton has

every right to admit his wife to Bedlam. It isn't right, but it is the law."

He pressed his lips together before musing, "What if we circulated news that Lady Hungerton is still alive, and it will force Lord Hungerton to retrieve her."

"Or he could just have her killed," Kendrick said. "Patients die all the time at Bedlam and no one asks any questions. Quite frankly, no one cares what happens to them."

Caleb balled his hands into tight fists. "That doesn't make it right."

"I never said that it does, but the hospital has been understaffed, underfunded and overcrowded for years," Kendrick remarked. "It would be easy to slip someone like Lady Hungerton into the hospital, especially if Lord Hungerton was lining their pockets."

Caleb refused to accept that there was nothing that they could do to help Lady Hungerton. He would find a way to help her. He had to. He couldn't let her continue to suffer horrific conditions through no fault of her own.

"I know that look," Kendrick said. "You intend to go half-cocked on me. Don't you?"

He took a step closer to the desk. "I am going to free Lady Hungerton one way or another, and no one is going to stop me."

Kendrick studied him for a moment. "Good," he said. "Once you have retrieved her, I have a cottage just outside of London that could be used to house her for the time being."

"You aren't going to stop me?"

"Stop you?" Kendrick asked. "No, I am going to help you. But I want you to understand that there are risks associated with rescuing Lady Hungerton."

Caleb bobbed his head. "I understand."

Kendrick leaned back in his seat. "Do you intend to tell Miss Delacourt?"

"I think she has a right to know about her mother," Caleb replied.

"Yes, but she might do something drastic. We both know that Miss Delacourt doesn't always think through the repercussions of her actions," Kendrick remarked.

Caleb had to acknowledge that Kendrick had a point, but he also knew that Simone would never forgive him if he kept something like this from her. He had just gotten her to trust him and he didn't want to do anything that would jeopardize that.

Kendrick grinned. "You are going to tell her straightaway, aren't you?"

"I see no other way," Caleb replied. "Besides, we are partners, and Simone would do the same for me."

"Speaking of which, when you two are married, do you want to continue working cases together?" Kendrick asked.

"I do."

Kendrick leaned forward in his seat. "It is quite unusual for spies to marry one another, but I suppose it will be for the best."

"You have no objections?"

With a huff, Kendrick replied, "I have many, but I shall keep them to myself. I just want to ensure that your intentions are honorable when it comes to Miss Delacourt."

"They are," Caleb assured him. "This marriage will be in name only, giving Simone the freedom to do as she pleases."

"Very good, but before you go, we must discuss the French spies that are residing at Miss Delacourt's townhouse." Kendrick grew somber. "Has any progress been made on discovering their intentions?"

"Not yet."

Kendrick reached for a stack of papers on his desk and brought them in front of him. "My agents scoured Lord Hungerton's office but found nothing that would indicate he was working with the French. But how could he not know his mistress is a French spy?" he asked. "I'm going to give you two more days to investigate and then I'm going to arrest them, including Lord Hungerton."

"What if Lord Hungerton is not involved?" Caleb asked. "Do you truly want to risk arresting a baron, especially one as influential as him?"

"I don't, but unless you can convince me otherwise, I am going to assume he is guilty by association," Kendrick replied. "Inform Miss Delacourt of my decision."

"She won't be happy."

"Perhaps not, but she will understand," Kendrick said. "I am just left to wonder if a man is capable of hiding his wife away in Bedlam, and faking her death, where do his loyalties lie? Does he even have any?"

Caleb nodded his agreement. "Furthermore, we found proof that Lord Hungerton tried to cheat Simone out of her inheritance."

"That doesn't surprise me. The more I am learning about the baron, the less I like him," Kendrick said. "Now off with you. I have work that I need to see to."

Caleb walked over to the door and stepped into the main hall. As he exited the building, a feeling of dread settled over him. He was not looking forward to the upcoming conversation with Simone. He would have to tell her some hard truths and he hoped she was in the right frame of mind to hear them.

Once he was situated in the coach, it started making its way down the street and he knew it would only be a short drive until he arrived at Simone's townhouse.

He leaned his head against the back of the coach and closed his eyes. Simone would no doubt be angry and hurt by her father's actions, but that might be the least of their concerns. He might be aiding the French, an offense that is punishable by death.

Caleb knew that Simone was strong, but even she had her limits. Could she handle what needed to be done?

It wasn't long before the coach came to a stop in front of Simone's townhouse and Caleb stepped down onto the pavement. He approached the main door and knocked. It was promptly opened by the butler and he stood to the side to grant him entry.

After he was in the entry hall, the butler ordered, "Wait here, sir. I will inform Miss Delacourt of your arrival."

The butler walked away and disappeared into the drawing room. A moment later he stepped out and gestured towards the door. "Miss Delacourt will see you now."

Caleb didn't need to be told twice. He headed into the drawing room and saw Simone seated on the settee, adorned in a pale green gown. Her hair was styled in a loose chignon at the nape of her neck. To say she looked beautiful would have been an understatement.

Rising, Simone took one look at him and asked, "Whatever is the matter?"

"I need to speak to you."

"We are speaking."

With a glance at the maid in the corner, Caleb responded, "Privately, if you don't mind."

Simone's eyes held understanding. "Would you like to take a tour of the gardens?" she asked. "We have the most magnificent roses this time of year."

"That would be wonderful." Caleb stepped forward and offered his arm. "Shall we?"

She placed her hand on his sleeve and allowed him to escort her to the rear of the gardens. Once they started walking down the path, Simone removed her hand and asked, "Now what has you so bothered?"

Caleb knew there was a time and a place to be light-hearted and this was not one of those times. He would just tell her the truth and be done with it.

"I just came from Kendrick's office," he revealed.

A line between her brow appeared. "Is it about my father?" she asked, her words hesitant.

"Yes, in a way, but something came up, something much more pressing, that I need to discuss with you," Caleb said.

Not appearing convinced, Simone asked, "More pressing than my father possibly being a traitor?"

Caleb stopped and turned to face her, his boots grinding on the gravel. He met her gaze and replied, "It is about your mother."

Simone gave him a bemused look. "What about my mother?"

He took a deep breath, knowing what he was about to reveal would change everything. In a voice that betrayed his emotions, he said, "We have reason to believe she might be alive."

Chapter Sixteen

Simone stared at Caleb, unable- or unwilling- to comprehend what he was saying. The only sound she could hear was the pounding of her heart in her chest. Why would he say something so awful? Her mother was dead and it was painful to think otherwise.

Caleb took a step closer to her, concern etched on his features. "Did you hear what I said?"

"I did, but you are surely mistaken," Simone replied. "My mother drowned, and it is rather cruel of you—"

He spoke over her. "That is what your father wanted everyone to believe but we suspect she is at Bedlam."

"*We?*"

"Kendrick and I."

Now Simone knew this was utter nonsense. Her mother was many things, but being mad was not one of them. "What would possibly make you think such a thing?" she asked in a harsh tone.

In a calm, collected voice, Caleb replied, "Kendrick discovered that your father made a large donation to Bedlam right before your mother died and he has been paying one of the Bedlam Governors every month."

This was all starting to make sense, at least, somewhat. "My father was one of the lords that toured Bedlam when they requested funds from Parliament and he was heartbroken over what he saw," Simone said. "That could easily explain the large donation."

"What about the monthly payment to one of the Bedlam Governors?" he asked.

Simone sighed. "Are you referring to Mr. Underwood?"

"I am."

"That is the Bedlam Governor who gave the tour of the facility to the members of Parliament," Simone said. "I am sure my father is just donating to whatever cause he believes in."

Caleb looked skeptical. "Why wouldn't your father just donate to Bedlam?"

"I can't answer that, but my mother is not hidden away at Bedlam," Simone replied. "My father may be a liar, amongst other things, but it is ludicrous to even think my father would subject my mother to such abuse."

"But your mother's body was never found. Is that not suspicious, in and of itself?" Caleb pressed.

"It is a deep lake, and her body might have become tangled in the weeds that sat below the surface, at least that is what the coroner had suggested," Simone said. "I told you that I looked into her death and found nothing of note."

Caleb held her gaze as he replied, "I asked Kendrick to look into her death because the timing of it just never sat well with me, especially so close to when your grandmother died."

"It was just a coincidence."

"Surely you don't believe in coincidences, do you?" Caleb asked. "You are a spy and should know better."

Simone frowned. "You are looking into something that you have no business in. My mother is dead."

"What if she isn't?" he asked. "Do you not want to know for certain?"

"I do!" she said, her voice rising.

Caleb's eyes held compassion. "I know this is hard on you, but if there is even a chance that she could be alive, wouldn't you risk everything to find her?"

"I have spent the past two years trying to move on from my mother's death. What you are asking of me is not an easy feat," she said. "In all this time, I never found time to be happy because I was trying too hard to be strong."

"You don't have to be strong all the time," Caleb said. "Let me help you."

With a tilt of her chin, Simone remarked, "I can do it on my own."

"I know you can, but seeking assistance isn't a display of weakness; it's a testament to one's strength."

"If I ask for help, everyone will know I can't handle something."

With a shake of his head, he said, "No, it just means that you know what you can and can't handle. There is great strength in that. Trust me, Simone."

"I do," Simone said. "Surely, you must know that."

Caleb reached for her gloved hand. "I know I am asking you to take a leap of faith with me, but I suspect your mother is in Bedlam. I won't rest until I know the truth."

"It just seems so unbelievable." She wanted to believe his words, but could she risk the heartache if he was wrong? It would almost be as if her mother died all over again.

He watched her with a tenderness that tugged on her heartstrings. "I won't ask you to come with me, but you are welcome to accompany me to Bedlam."

In a soft voice, she asked, "What if you are wrong?"

"Then I will have a lot to apologize for."

Simone glanced down at their hands as she considered his words. Truth be told, a part of her had always held out hope that her mother was alive since they hadn't found the body, but time had a way of killing that dream.

However, she would always wonder if she didn't go to Bedlam with Caleb. Could she live with that uncertainty?

Coming to a decision, Simone said, "I will go with you."

"If I didn't think it was a real possibility, I wouldn't have come to you." Caleb grew uncharacteristically solemn. "I want you to know that I will be there for you where others have failed you."

"You say that now…"

Caleb intertwined their fingers, causing her words to catch on her breath. "I say that now and always. I am not going to let you down."

Simone truly did not expect Caleb to have such an effect on her, her heart, her mind, or her feelings. He accepted her for who she truly was. Something that no one had ever done before. How could she not care for this man?

Knowing he was still waiting for a response, she said, "I believe you."

A smile came to his lips. "You are going to like being married to me. We are going to have such fun."

"That is not why I am marrying you."

"I know, but it will be an added benefit," Caleb said with a wink.

A laugh escaped her lips before she could stop it.

Caleb took a step closer to her. "You have the most beautiful laugh and I daresay that it is my favorite sound."

Simone tried to ignore the blush that was warming her cheeks. "It is no different than any other laugh."

"But you are wrong. It is uniquely yours, and I could never get tired of it."

With a glance back at the townhouse, Simone asked, "As much as I tire of your vain attempt at flattery…"

"It isn't vain."

"…how do you suppose we get into Bedlam to search for my mother?"

Caleb released her hand and took a step back. "I will have a plan soon enough, and it will be a good plan, I assure you."

"I hope so because we can no longer tour the facility without an escort," Simone said. "The days that the public could poke the patients with sticks are long over."

"My father plays cards with one of the Bedlam Governors. I might ask him for a favor."

"Be careful of who you owe favors to," Simone advised.

Caleb bobbed his head. "It is not something that I take lightly, but the rewards outweigh the risks in this case," he said. "How are you handling Juliette and Victor?"

Simone let out a slight groan. "My father intends to take Juliette to Lord Pendley's ball on his arm."

"What about Victor?"

"There was no mention of him," Simone said. "But I wouldn't discount him too easily. Victor spends much of his time in his bedchamber. Whereas Juliette walks around the townhouse as if she owns it."

"Why did Juliette have us secure invitations to Lord Pendley's ball if she had been planning to go with your father all along?" Caleb mused.

Simone shrugged one shoulder. "The intention was to distract us and keep us busy, which they succeeded. But Juliette said that their plans had changed. What if she had been referring to their mission?"

Caleb looked displeased by her remark. "Have you been able to search Juliette's bedchamber?"

"I have, multiple times, but I found nothing of interest," Simone replied. "Not that I was expecting anything. Juliette is much too clever to leave things out in the open."

"Kendrick is only giving us two more days before he arrests them, including your father," Caleb revealed.

Simone kept the emotion off her expression. "I want to say that I am surprised, but I am not. I have no idea what my father is involved in. Quite frankly, I don't know what my father is capable of anymore. He is a stranger to me."

"We both know if your father is arrested, he won't live much longer."

She had a thought. "If my mother is at Bedlam, I do hope that is the case," she said. "For she would never be free as long as my father is alive."

"Kendrick has offered the use of his cottage to house your mother until we sort out the details," Caleb said.

"That was kind of him."

"I do believe that Kendrick has a fondness for you," Caleb teased.

With a disbelieving huff, Simone said, "I doubt that. Frankly, I don't think he has a fondness for anyone."

"No, it is true," Caleb stated. "He threatened me if I hurt you in any way."

As Simone went to reply, Juliette's voice came from down the path. "There you two are," she said. "I have been looking for you."

Caleb visibly stiffened. "What do you want, Juliette?"

Juliette came to a stop in front of them and smiled. "Nothing but the pleasure of your company, Mr. Bolingbroke." Her voice was cordial, too cordial. It was evident that she knew the effect that she had on Caleb.

While Caleb narrowed his eyes at Juliette, Simone spoke up. "Unfortunately, Mr. Bolingbroke was just leaving. Weren't you?"

"I was, but now I think my presence is required," he replied, his eyes not straying from Juliette.

Simone gestured towards the gate. "That won't be necessary," she assured him. "Why don't you leave by the gate rather than the main entrance?"

When Caleb didn't make a motion to move, Simone placed her hand on his sleeve. "Mr. Bolingbroke, I will be all right. Juliette will play nicely."

"I will," Juliette said.

Simone's words seemed to appease Caleb. He turned towards her, and his eyes softened. "If you are sure..." His words trailed off.

She offered him an encouraging smile. "I am. You don't need to worry about me."

"Very well, but send word if something goes awry," Caleb said before his gaze returned to Juliette. "I will kill you if you hurt Simone."

Juliette tsked. "Threats are uncalled for, Mr. Bolingbroke."

Caleb's jaw tensed and Simone was worried that he might reach for the pistol that was in the waistband of his trousers. She needed to do something to contain the situation, and quickly. "It is time for you to go, Caleb." Her voice was firm.

"I will go, but only because you asked it of me," Caleb said before he proceeded to the back gate.

Juliette's eyes followed his retreating figure. "I don't think Mr. Bolingbroke likes me very much."

"I don't like you very much," Simone muttered.

Feigning innocence, Juliette asked, "Should we go enjoy a cup of tea together?"

"You can drop the act," Simone replied. "We both know that this will end when I figure out what it is that you are up to."

Juliette offered her a condescending smile. "That won't happen. You may be clever, but you can't stop what is coming."

Glancing at the window of Victor's bedchamber, Simone asked, "Why don't you ask your brother to have tea with you?"

"He is busy. No doubt he is tinkering with something," Juliette replied. "He gets a little engrossed by his little projects."

"What projects are those?"

Juliette waved her hand dismissively in front of her.

"Nothing that would interest you," she said, taking a step back. "I believe I have earned a rest."

After Juliette headed down the path, Simone returned her gaze towards Victor's bedchamber. She would need to discover what he was working on, especially since he spent nearly all his time in his room.

Simone found herself conflicted. She should focus on her assignment, but her mind kept straying towards what Caleb had revealed. Could her mother truly be alive? He believed so, making her have hope. And that was something she hadn't had in quite some time.

But if her mother was alive, her father was more awful than she could have ever imagined. That did not sit well with her. Had she been living with a monster this whole time and not know it?

The moon was high in the sky as Caleb stood in the shadows of the alleyway. The lights had been extinguished long ago in Simone's townhouse, but he couldn't quite convince himself to leave. He needed to know she was all right. Not that staring at her townhouse would give him the answers that he sought.

He wanted to protect Simone, at all costs, but he also wanted her to know that he trusted her enough to protect herself. It was a balancing act, one that he wasn't very good at. Which is why he was staring at her darkened townhouse at such a late hour.

Simone was inside with French spies and there was nothing he could do to help her. He understood Kendrick's reluctance to arrest Lord Hungerton, but he hated waiting around, hoping the French spies would make a mistake and reveal something. Anything. Perhaps if he had learned to play nice with Juliette, but he couldn't do it. She was the enemy and he would never trust a word out of her mouth. He would rather shoot her than carry on a polite conversation with her.

And that was the problem.

He had to admire Simone for the way she was handling Juliette, and her father. It couldn't be easy to be in her shoes at the moment. Her father was not the man that she had thought he was. He had lied to her and tried to cheat her out of her inheritance. And now, he might have done the unthinkable by faking his wife's death and placing her in Bedlam.

But that all was relative if he was a traitor to the Crown. Had he betrayed his countrymen and the King? Lord Hungerton had been born into privilege, and with that came certain responsibilities. Would he truly turn his back on what mattered the most?

A familiar voice came from behind him. "What, pray tell, do you think you are doing?" Fredrick asked.

Caleb turned around and saw Fredrick and Roswell, both with curious expressions on their faces. "Is it not obvious?" he asked. "I am ensuring Simone is protected."

"By loitering outside her townhouse?" Roswell asked with mirth in his voice.

Caleb knew how ridiculous he sounded. "It is the only thing I can think of doing," he said. "I thought about obtaining a special license and marrying her tomorrow. But I do not think Simone would be agreeable to that plan."

"Not until she finishes her assignment, considering she is in the perfect position to spy on Juliette and Victor," Fredrick remarked.

"Don't forget her father," Caleb muttered.

Roswell's eyes held understanding. "Have you made any progress on the case?"

"Not really," Caleb admitted. "Juliette will be attending

Lord Pendley's ball on Lord Hungerton's arm, but not her brother."

"That is odd, and entirely too suspicious," Roswell said.

Caleb nodded. "They are up to something, and time is running out. Kendrick gave us two days to figure out their plan before he swoops in and arrests the lot of them, including Lord Hungerton."

"Do you truly think he is involved?" Fredrick asked.

With a slight shrug, Caleb replied, "I don't rightly know, but his association with them is suspect. How could he not know that Juliette is a French spy?"

"He may know, but he might not be involved," Roswell pointed out.

"Is that any better?" Caleb asked.

Roswell frowned. "Good point," he said. "What is your plan, exactly? Do you intend to remain out here until dawn?"

Caleb shook his head. "I haven't thought that through yet. I suppose I just need to be close to Simone, even if she has no idea that I am here."

Fredrick exchanged a glance with Roswell before asking, "Have you come to terms with your feelings for Simone?"

"No… yes… I don't know what I feel," Caleb said. Which was a lie. He was already halfway in love with Simone, but he didn't dare admit that to his friends. Quite frankly, he couldn't believe he had done something so stupid and fallen for his partner. That was a line that he wasn't supposed to cross. But how could he not love Simone?

Simone would always be enough for him, and no one could ever convince him that there was more to life than loving her. It was rather unfortunate that he had promised to marry her in name only, but he couldn't change the terms now.

Roswell placed his hand on Caleb's shoulder. "Be patient with yourself, and your feelings. It is all right to be conflicted."

"No, it isn't," Caleb said. "I offered Simone a marriage of convenience. That is what she agreed to."

"Plans can change," Roswell encouraged, dropping his hand to his side.

"Not these," Caleb asserted. "I would never do that to Simone."

Roswell lifted his brow. "Is your intention to just pine after your wife for the remainder of your days?"

Caleb winced, knowing how miserable that sounded. "If that is what it takes." He paused. "But we have much more important things that we have to address first."

Fredrick spoke up. "Anything we can help with?"

"Not unless you want to help us break Lady Hungerton out from Bedlam," Caleb said.

With stunned expressions, Fredrick and Roswell stared back at him. Fredrick recovered first and asked, "Lady Hungerton is alive?"

Caleb bobbed his head. "It is likely. Kendrick discovered some proof that makes us suspect that Lord Hungerton faked his wife's death and placed her in Bedlam."

"Poor Lady Hungerton," Roswell muttered.

Fredrick grew somber. "I have toured Bedlam, alongside my father, and it is not a place that I would ever want to linger in. The floors are terribly uneven, the walls are buckled and the roof continuously leaks whenever it rains. The pungent odor of unwashed bodies seeps through your nose, making it entirely unbearable."

"Is the women's wing any better than the men's?" Caleb asked.

"No. If anything, it is worse," Fredrick replied. "The patients are locked in their cells, for there is no other word for it, and the lucky ones are not chained to the walls."

The picture that Fredrick painted was bleak, urging Caleb to act, and quickly. "My father has arranged a meeting with one of the Bedlam Governors tomorrow," he revealed. "I am hoping it will give us access to the women's wing."

Fredrick's eyes grew pained. "Upon reaching the gate, you are met by two statues, similar to gargoyles. They are positioned at the entrance welcoming everyone to Bedlam, symbolizing the dual nature of madness- Raving and Melancholic," he revealed. "It is a sight that I will never forget, and for most of the patients, it is the last thing they see before they enter the hospital."

"It sounds awful," Caleb acknowledged.

"Very few patients are ever released from Bedlam," Fredrick shared. "Once they arrive, the lives that they knew before are stripped away, and they are forced to endure such squalor that many take their own lives."

Roswell interjected, posing the question, "Are you sure that Lady Hungerton is at Bedlam? Many of the patients were moved to other hospitals due to the deteriorating conditions there."

"I had that same thought, but Lord Hungerton still pays a Bedlam Governor once a month," Caleb replied. "Surely that can't be a coincidence."

Fredrick met Caleb's gaze. "We will assist you in any way that you see fit. I am not acquainted with Lady Hungerton, but I cannot allow her to remain in Bedlam, through no fault of her own."

"Thank you," Caleb acknowledged.

The sound of a door closing drew their attention and Caleb turned his head to see Simone approaching them.

Simone gave them an expectant look. "Why are you all huddled in the alleyway?" she asked, adjusting the blue spencer over her gown.

"Did you see us?" Caleb questioned.

"How could I not?" she responded. "I knew agents were guarding the place, but I had not expected to see all of you."

Caleb offered her a smile. "I came to ensure you were protected."

"How were you going to protect me from here?" Simone asked.

"I hadn't thought that through yet," Caleb replied.

Simone glanced over her shoulder at her townhouse. "Everyone is asleep, except for Victor. I saw the light was on in his room."

"Why is he up so late?" Caleb asked.

"I know not, but Juliette said he is tinkering with something," Simone responded. "I intend to find out what that is."

Caleb had to admit that didn't sit well with him. "By going into his bedchamber?" he asked. "What if you are caught?"

Simone smirked. "Why do you assume I would get caught?" she asked.

"Perhaps I should investigate his bedchamber," Caleb suggested.

"That is a terrible idea. It makes much more sense for me to do it," Simone declared. "After all, it is my home."

Caleb knew that Simone had a point but he still wasn't comfortable with her entering another man's bedchamber. "I can climb through the window and be out before anyone sees me."

"It is on the second level," Simone shared.

"I can climb the wall," Caleb asserted. "The bricks jut out and make excellent footholds. It would only take me mere moments to scale it."

Simone arched an eyebrow. "What if one of the servants sees you scaling the wall?" she asked. "They no doubt will sound the alarm."

"You are assuming I will be caught," Caleb remarked, using her own words against her.

Turning her attention towards Fredrick and Roswell, Simone said, "Please talk some sense into your friend."

Fredrick put his hands up in front of him. "Caleb is on his own on this one. But, for the record, I side with Simone."

"As do I," Roswell said.

"Traitors," Caleb muttered.

Simone gave Caleb a smug smile. "It is three to one. I will search Victor's bedchamber and you can wait in the alleyway to protect me."

Caleb said his next words without thinking them through. "I just worry about you."

Rather than grow defensive, just as she always did, Simone's eyes softened a tad bit. "That is sweet of you, but I can handle searching a bedchamber."

"You are right. I am sorry," Caleb said.

Simone took a step closer to him. "There is no reason to apologize. We are partners and we look out for one another." She turned her head. "I should get back. I do not want my absence to be noticed."

Caleb watched as Simone hurried back to her townhouse and disappeared within. She was safe, for now, and he could return home.

Fredrick followed his gaze. "Simone seems different," he observed.

"Different, how?" Caleb asked.

"I don't know, but different," Fredrick replied. "A good different, though."

Caleb stepped out of the alleyway and said, "It is late. I am going to retire for the evening. Will you do the same?"

As they followed him out, Roswell said, "We were on our way home from Kendrick's office when we saw you."

"I am glad that you stopped," Caleb remarked.

"As am I," Fredrick said. "It allowed us to see you make a complete fool of yourself with Simone. Why were you so adamant that you search Victor's bedchamber?"

Caleb didn't want to have this conversation, but he did

owe his friend an explanation. "It just didn't sit right with me that she was searching a man's bedchamber."

Fredrick chuckled. "She is a spy."

"I know," Caleb said. "I never said that it made sense. I just said I didn't like it."

They continued down the pavement as they retreated to their thoughts. Tomorrow would no doubt be a difficult day for Simone. But he would be there for her. If she let him, he would never leave her side again.

Chapter Seventeen

Simone stepped into the dining room and saw her father and Juliette speaking cordially to one another as they ate their breakfast.

She came to an abrupt halt since she had no desire to eat with Juliette. Perhaps they wouldn't notice her if she left now. With light steps, she slowly started to back out of the room.

Just as she thought she might have succeeded, Juliette looked over and said, "Simone, you must join us for breakfast."

Drats. She had not been able to escape without notice. "I do not wish to be a bother," she attempted.

"Nonsense," Juliette said. "This is your home, after all."

"I would rather take a tray in my room—"

Her father cut her off. "Sit, Simone," he ordered. His tone brokered no argument.

Knowing she had little choice in the matter, Simone approached the table and waited as the footman pulled a chair out for her. She murmured her thanks as she sat down. Why had she thought coming down for breakfast was a good idea?

Juliette picked up a piece of toast from her plate and took

a bite. Once she finished chewing, she wiped her hands together to brush away the crumbs.

Simone watched Juliette, an uneasy feeling coming over her. How could she dine with a French spy so easily? She was tired of playing by Juliette's rules. It was time that she took back the power. But it was proving to be much more difficult than she had first anticipated.

"Is something amiss?" Juliette asked.

Realizing she had been caught staring, Simone replied, "No, I was just woolgathering."

"A terrible habit for a young woman to engage in," her father remarked.

Simone reached for the cup of chocolate the moment the footman placed it onto the table. As she took a sip, she wondered how she was going to search Victor's bedchamber. He hardly left it, and when he did, he locked it, giving strict orders to the servants that no one was to enter the room. Why all the secrecy unless he had something to hide?

Her father's voice broke through her musings. "How do you intend to occupy your time today?" he asked her.

"Caleb is coming to call upon me so we can take a carriage ride through Hyde Park," Simone lied, not wishing to reveal they were going to travel to Bedlam.

He nodded in approval. "The Society page mentioned your engagement," he informed her.

"How wonderful," Juliette acknowledged. "Although, I do not think Mr. Bolingbroke likes me very much."

Her father shook his head. "That is preposterous. What possible reason could he give as to not like you?"

"I am just your mistress," Juliette pointed out.

"Regardless, soon Simone will be his responsibility," her father declared.

Simone stiffened. "Is that what I am to you- a responsibility?" she asked as she tried to keep the hurt out of her voice.

"What do you want me to say, Simone?" her father asked.

"You have proven time and time again to be a disappointment to me."

His words had just left his lips when Juliette reached over and placed her hand on his sleeve. "That was not very nice," she said. "You shouldn't say such cruel things to your daughter."

Now Juliette was defending her? Could this conversation get any worse, she thought. One thing was for certain, she wished that she had never come downstairs for breakfast.

Her father had the decency to look ashamed. "My apologies. My words came out much harsher than I had intended."

"But you said them, none the less," Simone argued.

"Yes, but I could have said it differently," her father said.

Simone stared at her father in disbelief. She knew that people always had a way of revealing who they were. You just had to give them enough space and time to do so. Why did she think the best in her father? He just kept disappointing her, over and over, proving to her that he was not the man she thought he was. It was time to stop seeing the good in him and start seeing what he showed her.

Her father turned his attention towards Juliette, for which Simone was most grateful. She was done with this conversation. "How do you intend to spend your day today?"

Juliette smiled, one that she seemed to reserve only for her father. "I have loads to do today, including the final fitting for my ballgown," she said.

"Why doesn't the dressmaker just come to the townhouse?" her father asked.

"I have a few other errands that I must see to and it only made sense for me to go to the dressmaker's shop," Juliette replied.

"Perhaps Simone can go with you," her father suggested.

Simone went to object but Juliette spoke first. "I do not think that is a good idea. She would no doubt get bored with everything I must accomplish today."

Now Simone's curiosity was piqued. "What errands must you see to?" she asked.

"This and that," Juliette remarked dismissively.

Her father reached for Juliette's hand and kissed her knuckles. "I am needed at the House of Lords today, but I shall return home for dinner."

"Wonderful," Juliette said. "I shall have the cook prepare your favorites."

He shoved back his chair and rose. "Simone," he muttered before he walked out of the room.

Juliette's eyes trailed after her father as she remarked, "Your father does not seem pleased with you."

"He never is." And that was the truth. With every passing day, her father seemed to look at her with more and more contempt. How would he treat her when he discovered that she had claimed her inheritance?

Leaning back in her seat, Juliette shared, "I didn't have a close relationship with my father either. He was always disappointed that I was born a useless female."

"But he did have a son."

Juliette waved her hand in front of her. "Yes, he did have Victor, but he believed I would become an utter drain on his finances," she said. "The moment I was able to leave his household, I seized the opportunity to make it on my own."

"What of your mother?"

Looking unimpressed by her question, Juliette replied, "My mother was weak. She looked at my father like he was God's gift to her, but he was just a drunk. He would beat her relentlessly."

"I'm sorry to hear that," Simone said.

"He beat me, too, but it wasn't as much fun when I fought back," Juliette admitted. "Before I left, I told my father that if he ever hit my mother again, I would kill him." She paused. "It was his last mistake that he didn't believe me."

Fearing she misunderstood Juliette, Simone asked, "You killed your own father?"

Juliette shrugged. "I killed a monster, who happened to be my father," she said. "I don't regret what I did, and I freed my mother from the prison she was in."

Simone didn't think it was possible but she felt a twinge of sympathy for Juliette. She had protected her mother from a fate that was far worse than death. She questioned if she would have done the same.

With a glance at the footmen standing guard, Juliette ordered, "Leave us."

The footmen promptly stepped out of the dining room and closed the door behind them.

"Finally, we are alone," Juliette said. "I do not know how to deal with servants constantly being underfoot."

"Did you not grow up with servants?"

Juliette nodded. "We had servants, but you seem to have servants to tend to servants. I can't seem to find a moment alone in this household."

"Your brother doesn't seem to have that same issue since he spends plenty of time alone in his bedchamber," Simone remarked.

"Yes, he is quite busy."

"Doing what, exactly?" Simone pressed.

Juliette smiled, as if she were privy to a secret. "I cannot say, but you will find out soon enough."

Simone held her gaze and asked, "What is my father's involvement in all of this?"

Her smile grew smug, much too smug for Simone's liking. "Do you truly expect me to answer that question?" Juliette inquired. "I have a feeling that is why I have not been arrested yet. Your father is an influential man and it is not as if he could just disappear. Now could he?"

"If my father is involved, he will pay for his crimes..." Simone started.

Juliette laughed. "I can't quite tell if you are truly as naive as you appear," she said. "How is it that someone like you became a spy?"

"Someone like me?" Simone asked. She wasn't quite sure if she should be insulted or not. But since it came from Juliette, she doubted it was a compliment.

"You are sweet, but you are not clever enough to compete with me," Juliette stated. "You, or your handsome Mr. Bolingbroke."

Simone pursed her lips together. "Caleb is not mine."

"Isn't he, though?" Juliette asked. "You two appeared rather familiar with one another in the gardens yesterday."

"Looks can be deceiving."

"Yes, they can be," Juliette agreed. "Which is why I propose we come to a truce."

Simone's brow shot up. "A truce?" she asked. "Surely you can't be serious."

Reaching for her teacup, Juliette took a sip and placed it back onto the table. "I see you out in the gardens, practicing with your dagger. You are quite good," she said. "It is an unusual pastime for a woman of your position, no?"

"It is, but my mother taught me how."

Juliette gave her a thoughtful look. "I met your mother once," she informed her. "She was a lovely woman."

Simone did not want to talk about her mother, especially to Juliette. "You mentioned a truce," she said.

"I did," Juliette responded. "I have spent too much time in England. It is time that I return home."

"That is unlikely to happen."

Juliette looked amused. "No one paid me any heed until I went home to retrieve my brother and smuggled a ride on Lord Drycott's ship," she said.

"If what you are saying is true, why did you risk returning to England with your brother?" Simone asked. "Why not just stay in France?"

"Why, indeed?" Juliette asked. "I suppose it was because I couldn't leave well enough alone. I needed to finish my assignment. You understand that, do you not?"

Simone leaned forward in her seat. "If you are asking me to understand why you are working as a French spy, then no. I do not understand that."

Juliette wore an expression of discontent. "I thought we could be civil about this, but you are being entirely too stubborn."

"It is just a matter of time until you are in Newgate."

Shoving back her chair, Juliette said, "You seem to forget that I hold all the power. I know about your secret, Mr. Bolingbroke's secret and many others. Do you want them all to be rejected from the *ton* because of your mistake?"

"There are worse things," Simone stated.

"To me, perhaps, but your whole world revolves around high Society," Juliette said. "Furthermore, what happens if your father discovers your secret?"

"You haven't told him?"

Juliette looked the epitome of innocence as she rose from her seat. "A promise is a promise, is it not?" she asked. "I told you that I wouldn't tell him and I meant it. Spies have a code."

Simone wanted to believe Juliette, but, quite frankly, she knew she couldn't trust a word out of the French spy's mouth. Juliette would tell her father that she was a spy when it benefited her; she was sure of that.

Coming around the table, Juliette came to a stop near Simone. Her voice seemed to lack any emotion as she said, "If you interfere with me or my brother, I will kill your precious Mr. Bolingbroke."

"If anything happens to Caleb—"

Juliette cut her off. "It is cute how much you care," she said. "But you made one crucial error."

Simone was sure she was going to regret asking, but she did so anyways. "Which was?"

In a low voice, Juliette said, "You fell in love."

Before she could respond, Juliette walked swiftly out of the dining room, leaving her all alone in the expansive room.

Love.

She was not in love with Caleb. She couldn't be. But the more she thought on it, the more she realized that Juliette was right. She loved Caleb. It was so easy for her to love him that it frightened her.

She contemplated what she should do. She was a spy. Love was a weakness. And Juliette was exploiting that weakness.

The long clock in the corner chimed. It was time for her to start getting ready for her carriage ride with Caleb. The worst part was that she was looking forward to it. Every moment she spent with him, she was starting to cherish.

Caleb sat across from Simone in the carriage and he watched as she fidgeted with her hands in her lap. She had hardly spoken a word to him since they had departed from her townhouse, not even to chide him when he told her how lovely she looked.

Perhaps she was just growing anxious as they were approaching Bedlam. With every rotation of the wheels, he hoped that this was not a fool's errand. He truly believed that Lady Hungerton was one of the patients at Bedlam. But what if he was wrong? He had no doubt that it would devastate Simone. He didn't want to do one thing that would cause Simone pain.

"It will be all right," he assured her.

A line appeared between Simone's brow. "A part of me hopes my mother is there, but another part hopes she isn't."

She paused. "If she is there, my father is a monster and I didn't even know. What kind of spy would I be?"

"The kind that sees the best in people," he encouraged.

She let out a puff of air. "A spy is supposed to be objective. Yet I am fooled by the people that I am closest to."

"No mask can be worn forever," Caleb said. "Besides, there were already starting to be cracks in your father's mask."

"Is there any word on my inheritance?"

Caleb nodded. "Mr. Morrish has drawn up all the required paperwork and is just waiting for my word to have it delivered to your father's solicitor."

"Once that happens, all hell will break loose," Simone said. "I am not quite sure what my father will do. Do you think he would disown me?"

"Even if he does, we will be wed soon and you will have a home with me," Caleb remarked.

Simone grew thoughtful. "I haven't felt at home since my mother died."

Leaning forward in his seat, he revealed, "My mother is thrilled to be gaining a daughter. She barely can contain herself at the prospect."

"Will she be terribly disappointed when she learns that our marriage is in name only?" Simone asked.

Caleb worked hard to keep the emotion off his face. He wanted so much more out of this marriage, but he didn't want to scare Simone off. He would honor his word, but that didn't mean he wouldn't at least attempt to woo her.

"No," he responded. "She is just happy that I am getting married."

Simone looked unconvinced but thankfully she didn't press him. "My father is anxious to get me off his hands. Apparently, I am just a burden to him."

"He said that?"

"Not quite," she replied. "The word he used for me was 'responsibility,' amongst other things."

Caleb didn't like that Lord Hungerton was saying such hurtful things to Simone. "He was wrong to say that of you."

Simone grew quiet, and he feared that he had said something that might have upset her. Finally, she spoke, "I had an interesting conversation with Juliette this morning."

"Did you discover anything new?"

"She wanted to have a truce with me."

Caleb thought that was the most ridiculous thing he had ever heard. "A truce?" he asked. "Is she mad?"

Simone pressed her lips together before replying, "If we don't leave her be, she threatened to kill you."

"I would like to see her try," Caleb declared.

"I'm serious."

"So am I."

Simone sighed. "Juliette is a terrible person, but she isn't completely incompetent. She has managed to live in England for years, undetected. She was only discovered when she went back to retrieve her brother."

"You can't trust her," Caleb admonished.

"I don't," Simone said. "She even had the absurd notion that I…" Her words came to an abrupt stop.

Caleb gave her a curious look. "That you, what?" he prodded.

Simone looked hesitant as she replied, "Juliette is under the impression that I care for you, more so than just a friend. Which is ludicrous, is it not?"

Caleb felt a stab of disappointment at her words. He did care for her but it was evident that she didn't feel the same. Before he could reply, they approached the gate for Bedlam and they both seemed to retreat into their own thoughts.

The carriage came to a stop in front of the large, three-story building. Despite the palatial pretensions, Caleb saw the exterior was faded and starting to crumble in many areas.

As he exited the carriage, a man with a bald head and protruding belly exited the hospital and approached him.

"Mr. Bolingbroke," he greeted. "Your father mentioned you would be coming today. I am Mr. Stephen Radcliffe, one of the Bedlam Governors."

Caleb reached back and assisted Simone onto the graveled courtyard. "Thank you for agreeing to meet with us."

"Your father said the matter was most urgent, and I know he is not a man prone to exaggeration," Mr. Radcliffe said in a hushed voice.

"You are right," Caleb agreed as he moved Simone's hand to the crook of his arm. "Perhaps we could discuss this inside."

Mr. Radcliffe tipped his head. "That is a fine idea."

Caleb led Simone into Bedlam and it wasn't long before they arrived at Mr. Radcliffe's office. They stepped inside the small, square room and Mr. Radcliffe closed the door behind them.

Mr. Radcliffe came around his desk and gestured towards the two chairs. "Please have a seat," he encouraged.

Once Simone was situated, Caleb sat down next to her and said, "Allow me to introduce you to my fiancée, Miss Delacourt."

"It is a pleasure to meet you, Miss Delacourt," Mr. Radcliffe said. "I read about your upcoming nuptials in the Society page."

Simone smiled politely. "Thank you, Mr. Radcliffe."

Mr. Radcliffe turned his attention back to Caleb. "I must assume introducing me to your fiancée is not why you are here."

"You would be correct," Caleb replied. "The reason why we are here is of a delicate nature and I hope for your discretion."

"You have it, considering how your father helped raise funds to build the new hospital," Mr. Radcliffe said. "I owe him that much."

Caleb decided to say what needed to be said and be done

with it. With any luck, Mr. Radcliffe would be reasonable about it. "We are here because we have reason to suspect that Lady Hungerton is one of your patients."

Mr. Radcliffe blinked. "Surely you can't be serious?" he asked, glancing between them.

Knowing how unbelievable it sounded, Caleb continued. "We believe that Lord Hungerton paid off Mr. Underwood to hide his wife away in Bedlam."

Jumping up from his seat, Mr. Radcliffe shouted, "That is an outlandish accusation. I have known Mr. Underwood for many years and he would never do something so dishonorable."

Caleb put his hand up. "It sounds unlikely but—"

Mr. Radcliffe scoffed. "No, it is impossible," he declared, cutting him off. "I know every patient here and not one of them is Lady Hungerton. I am not saying that we don't have a few genteel ladies, but none of them are a baroness."

"Mr. Radcliffe, if you would just allow us to tour the facility—" Caleb attempted.

"Absolutely not!" Mr. Radcliffe exclaimed.

Caleb glanced at Simone, wondering why she hadn't said anything. It wasn't like her to remain silent.

Mr. Radcliffe gestured towards the door. "I think it is time that you both leave."

In a steady voice, Simone said, "I have come into a great deal of money and I am considering donating a thousand pounds to your building fund." She held Mr. Radcliffe's gaze. "At least I assume you are still looking for donors."

"We are," Mr. Radcliffe admitted.

"I would be happy to donate the money, assuming I can have a tour of your lovely facility," Simone said, holding the Governor's gaze.

Mr. Radcliffe returned to his seat and his eyes held a look of regret. "I know precisely why you want the tour, but I am afraid that you will leave disappointed. Your mother is not here. I can promise you that."

"Is there any harm giving us the tour then?" Simone asked.

With a defeated sigh, Mr. Radcliffe said, "I suppose not."

Simone awarded him a bright smile. "Thank you, Mr. Radcliffe. This tour will go a long way with easing my conscience."

Mr. Radcliffe rose. "I suppose we should get this over with," he muttered before he walked towards the door.

Simone rose and Caleb offered his arm to her. They followed Mr. Radcliffe out of his office and down a long corridor.

Upon reaching a door flanked by two guards, Mr. Radcliffe came to a stop and said, "This wing is where most of the women patients are housed."

"Most of them?" Caleb inquired.

Mr. Radcliffe nodded. "Yes, the other patients have been deemed unstable and a danger to themselves. They are chained to the wall for their own protection, and the workers'."

"I understand," Caleb said.

As Mr. Radcliffe went to open the door, he explained, "I'm afraid the rooms that the women were housed in before were deemed uninhabitable so we had to make do until the new hospital is built. I do hope you understand."

Simone entered the hall first but turned back around towards Mr. Radcliffe with disbelief on her features. "I daresay that it very much appears as if the patients are in prison."

Mr. Radcliffe looked apologetic. "It is the best we could do for them, considering the lack of funding we have available to us."

Turning her attention towards the patients, Simone waited for Caleb to join her before they slowly walked down the central aisle surrounded by the cells where the patients were confined. Some of the unkempt women turned their heads to glance at them, their sunken eyes and thin shoulders visible through tattered clothing.

Most of the patients gave them little heed, as if their presence was merely an imposition to them. The smell of unwashed bodies permeated the air, leaving Caleb to wonder how Simone managed to endure such a pungent odor.

They continued down the hall and Simone would occasionally step closer to the bars to examine a patient. Once they arrived at the end of the long hall, her eyes held disappointment. "I do not see my mother," she admitted, her voice resigned.

"There are still more patients," Caleb said in an attempt to encourage her.

Mr. Radcliffe spoke up from behind them. "I assure you that is a waste of your time. Those patients are not the type of people you want to trifle with. There is a reason they are not with the general population."

"Be that as it may, I would like to see them," Caleb said.

"Mr. Bolingbroke, you are wasting my time and—"

Caleb spoke over him. "I will match Miss Delacourt's donation, assuming you will take us to the other patients."

In a hushed voice, Mr. Radcliffe said, "I think you are making a grave mistake. You are only going to disappoint your fiancée even more."

"She can handle it," Caleb admonished.

Mr. Radcliffe's eyes shifted towards Simone and they held compassion. "Are you sure, Miss?" he asked. "I only ask for the sake of your delicate constitution."

Simone nodded. "Mr. Bolingbroke is right. I can handle whatever, come what may."

Mr. Radcliffe's lips formed a thin line before he grumbled, "Follow me, then." He proceeded out the door and down another long corridor.

As they followed behind Mr. Radcliffe, Caleb asked, "How are you faring?"

"Those poor people," Simone said in a hushed voice. No other words were needed. He knew precisely what she was saying, and not saying. The patients were suffering and no one seemed to care about their plights.

Mr. Radcliffe approached a door and removed a key from his jacket pocket. "I will have to lock the door behind us for everyone's sake."

Once they stepped into the darkened hall, Mr. Radcliffe made good on his promise and locked the door, remaining by it. The only light came from the small, dirtied windows along one of the side walls.

Simone proceeded down the dimly lit corridor with an air of unyielding determination. Alongside her, men and women were confined in adjacent cells, their hands bound and shackled to the cold walls. The straw strewn on the aged, misshapen floor provided little comfort, and the rats scurried around the floor, as if the patients were the unwanted intruders.

The horrific stench that lingered in the air failed to deter Simone, who scrutinized each suffering soul with a somber countenance. Her expression remained stoic, yet Caleb could see the anguish in her eyes. How these people were able to survive such horrific conditions was beyond him. This was a place that people came to die, and he suspected they knew it, too.

As Simone came to the last cell, she stopped and cocked her head. A woman sat in the shadows of the cell, her back against the wall. Her long, dark hair covered her face as her eyes were downcast.

"Mother?" Simone asked.

Chapter Eighteen

Simone stared at the woman in the cell, hoping that maybe, just maybe, this was her mother. But she couldn't quite tell. The woman kept her gaze fixated on the ground, her long hair partially covering her face.

Simone wondered why she wouldn't look up. The woman was dressed in a tattered gown that did little to hide her frail state. Her skin had layers of grime on it, and her dark hair was terribly disheveled. If this was her mother, it was a far cry from how Simone remembered her.

As she took a step closer to the cell, Mr. Radcliffe spoke up. "Don't get too close, Miss," he warned. "That patient is particularly dangerous."

"She doesn't look dangerous to me," Simone said.

"Looks can be deceiving," Mr. Radcliffe responded from his position by the door. "Jane arrived nearly two years ago."

Simone's eyes darted towards Caleb, who stood a few paces back from her. Surely, that could not be a coincidence that this woman arrived around the same time her mother supposedly died.

Caleb gave her the briefest nod, as if to acknowledge what she was feeling. She hoped she wasn't wrong on this.

Turning back towards the cell, Simone asked, "Mother, is that you?"

Slowly, ever so slowly, the woman brought her gaze up. Her face was smeared with dirt but it was her green eyes that confirmed her identity. It was her mother!

"Simone?" the woman asked in a weak voice. "Are you truly here?"

Simone could hardly contain herself as she grasped the iron bars. "I am, Mother. I'm here, and I am going to get you out of there."

Mr. Radcliffe interjected, "Miss Delacourt, that is not your mother—"

She cut him off. "Open this cell," she commanded.

"I know you want to believe it is your mother, but—"

Simone turned to face Mr. Radcliffe, stilling his words. "You will open this door and release my mother," she ordered.

Mr. Radcliffe pressed his lips together. "I'm afraid I cannot do that," he said. "There are protocols in place—"

"If you do not give me the key, I will come and take it from you," Simone stated, her voice holding a warning.

Looking unsure, Mr. Radcliffe said, "You wouldn't dare." His eyes darted towards Caleb. "Would she?"

Caleb nodded. "She would. You best do as she says."

"But I can't," Mr. Radcliffe rushed out. "Besides, Jane is not Lady Hungerton. She couldn't be. Lady Hungerton is dead."

Simone shook her head. "No, my mother is still right there. Do you not think I would recognize my own mother?" she asked. "Give me the key."

Mr. Radcliffe drew himself up to his full height. "I cannot do that," he said firmly.

In a swift motion, Simone retrieved her dagger and brought it up. "This is your last warning, Mr. Radcliffe. I do not want to hurt you, but I cannot stand by and do nothing while my mother is suffering."

Mr. Radcliffe's eyes went wide at the sight of the dagger. "You wouldn't dare," he said, his voice betraying his fear.

"Give her the key," Caleb urged.

"But the protocols—" Mr. Radcliffe started.

Speaking over him, Caleb shouted, "Forget the protocols! You are holding Lady Hungerton without just cause."

"She is mad, and dangerous," Mr. Radcliffe attempted. "That is why she is in this wing with the other patients."

Simone narrowed her eyes. "Does she look dangerous to you?" she asked, pointing at her mother's frail body. "In fact, do any of these patients look dangerous?"

Mr. Radcliffe's eyes scanned over the patients as he replied, "They must be. Why else would they be here?" His words were spoken with uncertainty, as if he were beginning to question what he was seeing.

"The key?" Simone asked, holding out her hand.

As Mr. Radcliffe opened his mouth to no doubt object again, Caleb said, "Do the right thing here. We both know what that is."

Mr. Radcliffe's shoulders sagged slightly. "Fine, but you have five minutes." He retrieved the key from his jacket pocket and approached Simone. "Understood?"

Simone glared at him. "No, Mr. Radcliffe. I do not understand," she said. "Help me understand why you are keeping my mother prisoner here."

"I still contend that is not your mother," Mr. Radcliffe attempted, holding up the key. "I think you want to believe it is her."

She reached out and retrieved the key. "Go stand by Mr. Bolingbroke and do exactly as we say."

With a glance at the dagger, Mr. Radcliffe remarked, "There really is no need for threats. We could have discussed this civilly."

Not bothering to respond to Mr. Radcliffe's idiotic remark, Simone unlocked the cell door and opened it. She entered the cell and ignored the way her feet seemed to slip along the grime-coated floor.

Her mother attempted to stand but she wobbled on her feet.

Simone rushed over to steady her. "I have you, Mother," she said as she held her tight. "It will be all right."

Her mother's eyes filled with tears. "I always hoped that you would find me."

"I am embarrassed that it took me so long," Simone said. "Had I known you were alive…" Her voice trailed off. "I would have come sooner."

"You are here now and that is all that matters," her mother stated. "Does your father know that you are here?"

"No, he doesn't," Simone replied.

"Good. He is the one who put me in this horrid place," her mother shared. "He promised me that he wouldn't hurt you if I never revealed who I truly was."

Simone felt anger course through her. Her mother had been trying to protect her, even from Bedlam. Her father would pay for this. That was the only thing she was sure of at the moment.

Her mother tried to lift her hands but the chains prevented her from doing so. "Just seeing you has lifted my spirits. Thank you for coming."

"We are going to get you out of here," Simone said as she went to unlock the shackles.

Mr. Radcliffe's shrill voice came from behind her. "You can't unchain her!" he exclaimed. "There are protocols—"

"Stop with the protocols," Simone said, matching his tone. "I do not care about your blasted protocols."

"Mr. Bolingbroke, you must talk some sense into your fiancée," Mr. Radcliffe said, his voice frantic.

"I think she is making perfect sense," Caleb stated.

As the shackles dropped to the floor, her mother wrapped Simone up in her arms. "I love you, Child," she murmured.

Simone closed her eyes as she tightly embraced her mother, not quite believing that she was truly alive. All this time had been wasted. And it was her father that had robbed her of that time with her mother.

After she released her mother, Simone faced Mr. Radcliffe. "I am leaving with my mother," she said in an unwavering voice.

Mr. Radcliffe's face blanched. "You can't just walk out of here with her. She is a patient here and there are—"

"Don't you dare say 'protocols'!" Simone exclaimed.

"I will admit that this is an unusual circumstance," Mr. Radcliffe started, "and I intend to look into it. But I can't just let Lady Hungerton go free. Not now. Even if I wanted to, she is still under the care of a doctor, who believes she should be here."

Caleb turned towards Mr. Radcliffe. "Mr. Underwood brought Lady Hungerton here under false pretenses. She is not mad, but her husband wanted her hidden away."

"That may be true, but only her husband can petition for her release," Mr. Radcliffe said. "I'm sorry but my hands are tied on this one."

Simone didn't know how but she refused to leave here without her mother. She would fight through anyone that stood in her way.

Fortunately, Caleb must have known that, as he stated, "I am going to make this very simple for you. We are going to leave with Lady Hungerton right now, and you better not stand in our way. Or there will be consequences for you- dire consequences."

"Mr. Bolingbroke—"

Caleb took a commanding step towards him, silencing Mr. Radcliffe's words. "You do not want to make me angry, Mr. Radcliffe. The people I associate with can make you disappear. Is that what you want?" he asked. "I suggest you think of your family at this time. Would they be able to survive without you?"

Emotions flickered across Mr. Radcliffe's face as he understood the danger he was in. After a long moment, Mr. Radcliffe said, "It is a shame that Jane escaped."

"Yes, it is," Caleb agreed, taking a step back.

Mr. Radcliffe waved them forward. "I will show you to the back door and I will inform your driver to come around to retrieve you. But I will sound the alarm in an hour's time."

"That should give us enough time to be far away from here," Caleb mused.

"I won't say that you took her, but I can't promise Lord Hungerton won't learn about his wife's escape," Mr. Radcliffe said. "Furthermore, I intend to look into how it was possible Lady Hungerton arrived in such distasteful circumstances."

Simone helped her mother as she took steps to leave the cell. Her legs were shaky and she didn't seem sure-footed.

Caleb hurried to her mother's side. "Allow me, my lady," he said as he slipped his arm around her shoulders. "I won't let you fall."

Her mother smiled at him. "Thank you."

"My name is Caleb, by the way," he said. "My mother is Lady Oxley, and I have no doubt she will be happy to see you."

"But not like this," her mother joked.

Mr. Radcliffe cleared his throat. "Keep your voices down and follow closely behind me," he ordered. "No one can be privy to what we are about to do."

While they followed Mr. Radcliffe down a dark, narrow hall, Simone noticed that her mother was leaning heavily into Caleb for support. She found herself growing increasingly angry for her mother's sake. How could she have received such poor treatment?

Mr. Radcliffe stopped by a door. "Wait here. I will send your carriage around," he said. "If you are discovered, I can't promise anything. But no one comes to this wing anymore. It has remained vacant since the prisoners were moved to another hospital."

With quick steps, Mr. Radcliffe hurried down the hall, disappearing around a corner.

"Do you trust him?" Simone asked.

Caleb nodded. "I do," he replied. "I meant what I said to Mr. Radcliffe. If he even utters a word of what happened here today, it will not end well for him."

Simone's mother looked at her. "Is this really happening?" she asked, her voice soft.

"Yes, Mother," Simone replied. "We are going to get you out of here and somewhere safe."

"I am not safe as long as your father is alive," her mother responded. "He put me in here and he is the only one with the power to release me."

Simone reached for her hand and squeezed it. "We will find a way to keep you safe. You need not fear."

Her mother grimaced. "You don't know what your father is capable of."

"He doesn't know what *I* am capable of," Simone responded. "I promise you that Father will answer for what he has done to you."

"Your father is a spy for France," her mother revealed.

Simone's heart dropped upon hearing the unexpected news. Why had she tried to believe that there was good in her father when he showed her time and time again that he was not the man she thought he was?

Caleb clenched his jaw but maintained his firm hold on her mother. "We suspected as much," he said.

"How could you suspect such a thing?" her mother asked. "He fooled me for so many years, but it wasn't until I met Juliette that I discovered the truth."

Simone went to respond but a knock came at the door, drawing their attention.

Caleb opened it up, revealing a liveried footman. "The carriage is ready, sir." He held up a blanket. "I thought this might prove useful."

"That is very thoughtful of you," Caleb acknowledged as he accepted the blanket. "We will need to be quick about this."

Her mother's eyes held understanding. "Cover me with the blanket and I will lay on the carriage floor as we depart."

In a swift motion, Caleb placed the blanket over her mother's head, and he returned his arm to her shoulder, supporting her weight.

Simone followed them out to the carriage and waited until her mother was resting on the floor before she sat on the bench.

Caleb sat across from her and reached for her hand. "You did it," he praised. "You rescued your mother."

"No, *we* did it, together," she corrected. "I daresay that we make a great team."

He smiled. "That is what I have been saying all along."

"Well, now I am starting to believe it," she said, returning his smile. How could she not love this man? He had done the impossible. He had returned her mother to her.

Any joy that Caleb felt that Lady Hungerton was alive and well was short-lived when he looked upon her disheveled state. He couldn't quite imagine what she had gone through these past two years, but he made a silent vow to himself that she would never go back to Bedlam. He would protect her, for Simone's sake.

As the carriage left the tall gates of Bedlam behind, Lady Hungerton removed the blanket from over her but remained in her crouched position.

"It is best that I remain hidden from view," Lady Hungerton said. "I wouldn't want anyone to see me, for obvious reasons."

Caleb nodded. "There is a cottage on the outskirts of Town that you will be safe in," he informed her. "Our friend has graciously offered to let you use it and has stocked it with food and other provisions."

"That was most thoughtful of him." Lady Hungerton glanced at him with a curious expression. "May I ask why you are helping me?"

"Aside from it being the right thing to do, it is because I am engaged to your lovely daughter," Caleb revealed.

A smile came to Lady Hungerton's lips. "I had hoped that was the case. I can only imagine how elated your mother must be."

"That is an understatement," Caleb remarked. "She is thrilled to have Simone as a daughter and is spending far too much time planning the luncheon."

"As well she should be," Lady Hungerton said.

Simone spoke up, drawing her mother's attention. "How was it that you ended up in Bedlam?" she asked.

The light from Lady Hungerton's eyes faded, and she grew pensive. "I went for my morning swim, just as I always do, and someone abducted me from behind. I tried to fight them off, but I was too weak," she revealed. "Once I woke up, I was in a coach with your father and that is when he threatened you. I couldn't risk anything happening to you so I remained quiet all these years."

She continued. "The day before, I overheard a conversation between him and a woman named Juliette. They were discussing a plan to bomb a rally in Granary Square," she shared. "When I confronted them, your father dismissed my concerns and tried to convince me that I misheard the conversation. But I knew what I heard, and *they* knew what I heard."

Simone spoke up. "About two years ago, there was a bomb

that went off in Granary Square and it killed twenty people. I can't believe Father was involved in that."

"Me either," Lady Hungerton said. "Theodore is not the same man that I married all those years ago."

Simone leaned forward. "You mentioned that Father was a spy. How did you know that?" she asked.

"He told me as much in the coach on the way to Bedlam," Lady Hungerton shared. "He informed me that no one would believe me anyways and it felt refreshing to tell the truth, for once."

Caleb shook his head. "He just admitted it to you?"

"Theodore was always too cocky for his own good, but I never expected him to betray his country," Lady Hungerton replied. "His ideas were radical, but I thought he kept them to himself. He wanted to liberate England from King George's oppressive rule and he idolized Napoleon. He always has."

"Was Juliette his mistress when he sent you to Bedlam?" Caleb asked.

Lady Hungerton shrugged her thin shoulders. "I suspect as much, but he denied it. He claimed that Juliette was a family friend."

With a frown on her lips, Simone shared, "Father is introducing Juliette as his mistress, and she even moved into the townhouse with us. He intends to take her to Lord Pendley's ball this evening on his arm."

Caleb grew thoughtful. "There have been many bombings at rallies in London that have gone unclaimed, mostly opposing the war. I can't help but wonder how many of those were planned and executed by Lord Hungerton and Juliette."

"Juliette has claimed that she has been in England for years. What if she was telling the truth?" Simone asked.

"It would be a first for her," Caleb muttered. "I think she is a wolf in sheep's clothing."

"I must agree with Mr. Bolingbroke," Lady Hungerton stated.

"Caleb, if you don't mind, considering we will be family soon enough," he said.

Lady Hungerton's eyes held warmth as she responded, "I would like that very much, but only if you call me Rebecca."

"I would be honored to," Caleb said.

Simone glanced at the tall buildings that stood shoulder to shoulder in an impenetrable line. "We are far from home, Mother," she said. "It might be far more comfortable on the bench than on the floor."

"I do not wish to risk it," Lady Hungerton remarked. "I would rather stay hidden since my horrifying appearance would cause unnecessary attention in this elegant carriage."

Simone winced. "It is not 'horrifying,'" she attempted.

"You are a terrible liar," Lady Hungerton said.

Caleb grinned. "That is what I have told her as well."

"I am an excellent liar, when the situation warrants it," Simone defended.

Her mother tucked her tangled dark hair behind her ear. "I can't believe that I am out of that horrible place. In every direction were shadows and darkness. Even the rats reeked of despair." A small sigh came to her lips. "I named each and every one of the rats that came into my cell."

Simone looked at Caleb with sorrow in her eyes and he knew what she was thinking. She was blaming herself for not finding her mother sooner.

"You are wrong," Caleb said.

She didn't even attempt to deny what she was thinking. "How could I have not known that my own mother was still alive? I gave up on her when I should have been fighting for her all along."

Caleb wished that they were alone so he could reach for her and hold her in his arms. He needed her touch just as much as he suspected she needed his. "It is no one's fault but your father's. He did this to your mother."

"And Juliette," Simone said. "Do not forget her involvement in all of this."

Lady Hungerton stared up at her daughter, her gaze not straying. "This was not your fault, and I will not have you think like that."

Tears came into Simone's eyes. "What you have experienced these past two years…" Her words trailed off.

"I would not trade it for the world, knowing it kept you safe from your father," she said.

Simone swiped at the tears that were streaming down her face. "Father tried to sell off Grandmother's estate and deprive me of my inheritance."

Lady Hungerton's eyes grew wide. "What a ninnyhammer! How could he do such a thing- and to his own daughter?" she asked.

"Why did Grandmother leave me the estate and not you?" Simone inquired.

"Because my mother never did like Theodore, and she refused to leave one farthing of her money to him," Lady Hungerton admitted. "Theodore convinced me not to tell you about the inheritance until you reached your majority. Was he furious when you confronted him on it?"

Caleb reached into his jacket pocket and removed a handkerchief. As he extended it towards Simone, he revealed, "We have kept it from him until we deem the time is right."

Simone offered him a weak smile in response as she accepted the handkerchief. "I suspect that Father will disown me when he learns of the truth."

"Most likely, or worse, I'm afraid," Lady Hungerton said. "I never thought he would harm me but he had no qualms about locking me in Bedlam."

Caleb's eyes roamed over the pavement as the vendors attempted to hawk their goods. "This cottage will keep you safe for the time being," he said. "At least until we decide what we are going to do about this situation."

"There is nothing to decide," Lady Hungerton said. "I will remain in seclusion for the remainder of my days."

"No, that is a terrible idea," Simone admonished.

Lady Hungerton gave her an understanding look. "I am married to your father and he has control over where I go and what I do. I won't give him that power back," she stated. "I would rather live a quiet life in the countryside than return from the dead, so to speak."

"You can live with us once we are wed," Simone attempted.

"No, Child, I can't, and you know why," Lady Hungerton said. "The servants will talk and word will get out. I can't risk it."

Simone pursed her lips before saying, "So Father wins?" she asked.

"No, I never said that, but I must think of you as well," Lady Hungerton said. "You will be married soon and cannot have scandal surrounding you. That wouldn't be fair of me, especially since I have lived my life. It is time for you to live yours."

Caleb had tremendous respect for Lady Hungerton and how freely she was putting her daughter's needs before her own. But he refused to let her throw away her life. She deserved far better than hiding out in the countryside. After all, she had done nothing wrong to deserve such ill-treatment.

"I think for the time being it would be wise for you to remain out of sight, but you will always have a place in our home," Caleb said.

"Thank you," Lady Hungerton acknowledged. "That means a lot to me."

The coach came to a stop in front of Simone's townhouse and Caleb stepped out in such a fashion that kept Lady Hungerton hidden from view. He assisted Simone onto the pavement and closed the door behind him.

Simone sighed. "Is it sad that I do not want to go home?"

"Soon you won't have to," Caleb replied. "You will come home with me."

In a hushed voice, she said, "We need to tell Kendrick what we know about my father and Juliette. He will want to arrest them as soon as possible."

"I will send word right away," Caleb assured her. "Until then, do not confront your father with what you know. It might end very badly for you since he is surrounded by Juliette and Victor."

With a glance at the townhouse, Simone said, "It will be hard, considering my father is not the man I thought he was. He is a traitor, a cheat, and a liar."

"And that is on a good day," Caleb joked.

She laughed, just as he intended. "You are awful."

Caleb took a step closer to her. "This will all be over soon," he said. "We just have to stay the course for a little while longer."

"And if Juliette makes good on her promise to reveal that we are spies to the newssheets?" Simone asked.

Caleb curled the corners of his lips upward, knowing he was about to make Simone very happy. "With everything that went on, I forgot to mention that I received word from Kendrick this morning. Apparently, he contacted all the newssheets and asked the editors nicely to not take any spying allegations seriously."

"He asked nicely?" Simone asked.

"'Threatened' might be a better word, but not even Juliette can control what the newssheets write," Caleb said.

Simone smiled, but this time it was different. It was as if her soul were smiling. "I am just happy to hear that Juliette will not win."

"As am I." Caleb turned his attention towards the carriage. "I should go and get your mother situated at the cottage before dark."

"Thank you," Simone said as she stood on her tiptoes and kissed his cheek.

He watched as Simone turned on her heel and hurried into the townhouse, not quite believing what had just happened. Perhaps he was making more progress than he realized with her.

Stepping back into the carriage, a genuine smile adorned Caleb's face. He was happy, and it was all because of Simone.

Lady Hungerton's voice interrupted his musings. "You love my daughter, don't you?" she inquired, her tone carrying a shrewd understanding.

"I do," he replied, seeing no reason to deny it. Frankly, he didn't want to anymore.

"I can tell," she said.

Caleb kept his gaze straight ahead as he assured her, "You need not fear. We will keep you safe."

"Do you think you could get me a few daggers?" she asked. "If so, I can protect myself."

A slight chuckle escaped his lips. "You sound so much like your daughter."

Lady Hungerton gave him a knowing look. "Who do you think taught her to think that way?" she asked.

"You raised an amazing daughter," Caleb said. "My entire world is so beautiful because Simone is in it."

Lady Hungerton's face softened. "Have you told her this?"

"Not yet," he admitted.

"What is holding you back?"

Caleb leaned back in his seat as he pondered Lady Hungerton's words. What was holding him back? He had never needed anyone before, but he realized that he needed Simone in his life. But before he could confess how he felt, they needed to finish this assignment. That was their priority.

But that didn't mean he couldn't dwell on Simone for a little while longer. He felt such contentment when he was with her. How he longed to feel like that all his life.

Chapter Nineteen

Simone stepped into her townhouse and let out a sigh. She couldn't quite believe how brazen she had been by kissing Caleb on the cheek, but she had to express her gratitude for what he had done for her mother.

Her mother.

She was alive, and safe. Simone had no doubt that Caleb would ensure she arrived safely at Kendrick's cottage, where she would be protected from her father.

Her father.

How could her father have done such a thing to his own wife? What kind of man was he who would force his wife to live in such horrific conditions, all while carrying on as a grieving widower? He would get his comeuppance. She was sure of that. Once Kendrick arrested him for being a spy, he would disappear. She was aware of what his fate would be, but she didn't seem to care at the moment. Perhaps she would feel some sorrow for him, but it wouldn't be anytime soon.

As she walked up the stairs, she heard her father's booming voice echoing throughout the main level. "How could the contract have just disappeared?"

Simone suspected that her father was referring to the

contract for her grandmother's estate. She spun on her heel and headed towards his study.

When she arrived at the open door, she peered inside and saw Mr. Frickle standing in front of the desk as her father leaned forward in his chair.

Mr. Frickle's face was red and splotchy. She watched as he wiped the sweat off his brow with a handkerchief. "I don't know how it happened—"

Her father jumped up from his seat and slammed his fist on the desk. "I can't believe you are this incompetent. Now we will have to start this process all over again."

"Yes, but the buyers are still interested," Mr. Frickle assured him. "It will just take some additional time."

"I won't pay you for your mistake," her father grumbled. "You will fix this and don't come back until the deal is done. I need those funds, and I need them now!"

Mr. Frickle bobbed his head. "I understand."

Her father swiped his hand in front of him. "Get out of my sight. I can hardly look at you right now."

A visible sign of relief came to Mr. Frickle's face as he ducked his head and hurried from the room. Not wanting to be caught eavesdropping, Simone hurried into the parlor, ducking out of view from the corridor. She waited for the solicitor to pass by the door before she came out of her hiding spot. She should go up to her bedchamber and prepare for the upcoming ball. But she couldn't seem to leave well enough alone and decided to go speak to her father.

She approached the open door of the study and knocked. "Father?"

Her father had returned to his seat and was reviewing the ledger. Not bothering to look up, he asked, "What is it?" His voice was curt, and not at all engaging. He clearly was not pleased by the interruption.

"Is everything all right?" Simone asked, innocently. "I heard shouting."

"You do not need to concern yourself with that," he said.

Simone walked further into the room, unwilling to be dismissed so easily. "May I ask what contract went missing?"

"It doesn't matter, at least not to you," her father said, his eyes still reviewing the ledger. He couldn't even give her the courtesy of looking up at her.

She wanted to confront him with what she knew, but she was well aware this was not the time or the place to do so. But as she gazed upon her father, she didn't feel hatred for him, like she thought she would. No. It was most definitely not hatred. She felt a profound sadness, knowing the choices he had made had brought him to this point. Now that they knew that he was a French spy, there was no saving him. And she doubted she would have done so, regardless.

Her father glanced up at her with annoyance on his features. "What is it?" he demanded.

Simone forced a weak smile to her lips. "I was just thinking about how different our lives used to be before Mother died."

"Times were different, yes," he agreed, showing no slip in his mask. "I have work that I need to see to. You may go."

As she turned to leave, she was grateful that her father dismissed her so readily since she didn't think she could have played the innocent act for much longer. How could her father just lie to her face, and not feel the slightest bit guilty?

It wasn't long before she arrived at her bedchamber and she was pleased to see Felicity organizing her dressing table.

"You will never believe what happened," Simone said after she closed the door.

Felicity gave her an expectant look. "You found your mother?" she asked.

Simone smiled. "We did, and she is safe."

"That is wonderful news," Felicity acknowledged. "I have been staying in your bedchamber for hours now, just waiting for you to return." She took a step back. "I think I have moved around your bottles at least ten times now."

Coming to sit on the settee, Simone said, "My poor mother looks terrible and is in desperate need of a few good meals."

"I would imagine so after residing in Bedlam for two years," Felicity remarked as she sat down next to Simone.

"And it gets worse," Simone said.

Felicity looked doubtful. "How could it get worse?"

"My father is a French spy, right alongside Juliette and Victor," Simone revealed. "He confessed as much to my mother when he was transporting her to Bedlam nearly two years ago."

With wide eyes, Felicity asked, "How could Lord Hungerton betray his country, or his wife for that matter?"

"He will be arrested soon, along with Juliette and Victor," Simone said. "But due to his position in the House of Lords, he will just disappear until the newssheets no doubt report his untimely death. Most likely, he will die from an infectious fever."

Felicity reached for her hand. "How are you being so brave about this?"

"How could I not be?" she asked. "Look at what he did to my mother, what he tried to do to me. I just feel sadness for what could have been. We could have been a happy family, but his choices forever altered that."

"With his death, at least your mother will be free," Felicity remarked.

"True, but she wants to live out her days quietly in the countryside," Simone shared. "She doesn't want to return to Society so there won't be any scandal associated with my name."

Felicity offered her a sad smile. "That sounds like Lady Hungerton." She withdrew her hand. "I am so relieved that she is safe."

"Yes, Caleb is ensuring that," Simone said. "She will reside in a cottage on the outskirts of Town until we figure out what the next step will be."

"Will you reside with your mother or do you still intend to marry Mr. Bolingbroke?"

Simone pretended to consider Felicity's words, but she already knew the answer in her heart. She didn't want to question that still small voice that was telling her what path she should take. She couldn't believe she had been so afraid of what a marriage to Caleb would bring but she was different now. She was braver than she was just a few days ago.

Knowing her lady's maid was still waiting for a response, Simone replied, "I will marry Caleb, as planned."

A bright smile came to Felicity's lips. "I am pleased to hear that."

Simone bit her lower lip before admitting, "I kissed him on the cheek today, right on the pavement, in front of our townhouse."

Felicity's mouth dropped open. "You kissed him?" she asked. "That doesn't sound at all like you."

"I wanted to find a way to express my gratitude for what he did for my mother, and me," Simone said. "I did it before I thought it through."

"And now?"

Simone grinned. "I do not regret my actions."

"Good, because I wouldn't have let you feel guilty," Felicity declared. "It is about time that you acknowledge your feelings for Mr. Bolingbroke."

"I never said—" Simone started.

Felicity put her hand up, stilling her words. "I have known you for many years, and I can tell when you are keeping something from me. It was rather obvious to know what it was."

Simone started fidgeting with her hands. "It is rather foolish that I have fallen for him, is it not?"

"I think it is a good thing that you have genuine affection

for your fiancé," Felicity replied. "You can work as a spy and be happily married."

"But what if Caleb doesn't return the depths of my affection?" Simone asked.

Felicity looked amused. "Then threaten him with a dagger until he does so."

Simone made a face. "Do be serious."

Her lady's maid laughed. "It is much more fun to tease you, considering everyone with eyes can tell that he is enamored with you." She paused. "Well, except for you."

"I do not wish to presume," Simone said.

The wall clock chimed, alerting them of the time. Felicity jumped up from her seat and announced, "I have something for you." She walked over to the bed and reached under the mattress. "It is the key to Victor's room."

"How did you get this?" Simone asked.

"Would you believe me if I told you that I asked Mrs. Stanley nicely?" Felicity asked.

Simone shook her head. "No, I wouldn't, because the housekeeper is not one to hand out her keys freely."

"Regardless, Victor left this morning and he has yet to return," Felicity said. "It would be a good time for you to search his room."

Simone accepted the key and acknowledged, "Thank you."

Felicity waved off her praise. "Just go before you get caught."

With quick steps, Simone exited her bedchamber and walked down the corridor to Victor's room. She glanced over her shoulder, ensuring no one was privy to what she was about to do.

Finding herself alone, she slipped the key into the lock and opened the door. She stepped inside, closing the door behind her. Her eyes roamed over the room and they stopped at the blackish powder on the desk.

Gunpowder.

Simone approached the desk and ran her finger along the powder. What was he using gunpowder for, she wondered.

Other than the powder on the desk, nothing seemed out of place or suspicious. She started opening drawers but found them all empty; not even his clothes hung in the wardrobe. Approaching the bed, she slipped her hand under the mattress but found nothing.

There was still one place she hadn't looked. She crouched down and looked under the bed, finding a cast iron sphere with a fuse intact.

Her heart dropped.

It was a grenade. What was Victor doing with a grenade in his bedchamber? More importantly, were there more that were unaccounted for?

Simone rose and hurried out of Victor's bedchamber. She needed to send word to Caleb. He must know about what she discovered.

As she entered her bedchamber, Felicity glanced down at her hand and asked, "What is that?"

"It is a grenade," she revealed.

With confusion written on her face, Felicity asked, "Why would Victor be making grenades in his bedchamber?"

"I have a fairly good idea since the ball is tonight and General Merrell will be present," Simone said. "Each grenade is equivalent to a four-pound cannonball. If Victor releases more than one of these grenades into the ballroom, it could cause a tremendous amount of damage and could kill hundreds of people, including a vast majority of the members of the House of Lords. It would be a devastating blow to England if Victor succeeded."

Felicity took a step back as she looked warily at the grenade. "I hadn't realized that it was so dangerous."

"That is why only a specific type of soldier is tasked with throwing grenades during combat. They were known as grenadiers," Simone explained. "They stand in the forefront of the fight to light the fuse and know when the precise moment is to throw them. Furthermore, they have to be skilled enough to throw the grenades far enough away so as not to harm themselves or their comrades."

"How do you know so much about grenadiers?" Felicity asked.

"I have always found weapons of war to be interesting and hand grenades were only introduced a decade ago," Simone said.

Felicity furrowed her brow. "I think we should get rid of the grenade. We don't want to accidentally blow a hole in the townhouse."

Simone nodded. "I agree, although this one appears damaged. Do you see the small hole on the side?"

Felicity put her hand up. "I would prefer to remain where I am."

"I think that is why it was discarded and forgotten," Simone asserted. "I need to send word to Caleb. Can you ensure it is delivered at once?"

"I will deliver it personally."

Walking over to the vanity desk, Simone pulled out a drawer and removed a piece of paper. She gently placed the grenade down onto the table next to her. Now that they had an idea of what Victor was planning, they had to stop him before he released the grenades on a room full of innocent people.

The time had come to end this game.

Caleb had just returned to his townhouse after ensuring Lady Hungerton was safe at Kendrick's cottage. No one would be able to find her there. But as a precaution, Kendrick had placed two agents to guard the place.

As he stepped inside, his butler approached with a tray in his hand. "An urgent message was delivered for you, sir."

Caleb reached for the paper and unfolded it. He read the contents and crumpled the piece of paper in his hand. The letter had been from Simone, warning him of a pending attack at the ball this evening. An attack that would wreak havoc in England.

His mother stepped into the entry hall. "There you are," she greeted. "Why is it that I haven't seen you very much these past few days?"

"I have been busy, Mother," he responded.

"Doing what, may I ask?"

Caleb didn't have time for this, but he didn't dare be rude to his mother. "I have been spending my time with Simone." At least that much was true. The partial truth, but the truth none the less.

His mother nodded approvingly. "That is good. Did you have a chance to ask her what her favorite flower is?"

Drats. How had he forgotten to ask such a simple question? "I haven't gotten around to asking that," he admitted.

"Dare I ask what you two speak about?" his mother inquired.

Caleb worked hard to keep his face expressionless. His mother had no idea what kind of things he was involved in with Simone. "The weather, and whatnot," he replied vaguely.

His mother looked displeased by his response. "Fine. Do not tell me, but we do need to plan this luncheon."

"The luncheon can wait," Caleb said. "There are a few things I need to tend to first that are far more important."

"You and Simone are to be married in less than three weeks' time. It sounds like it is far off, but it will be here before you know it."

Caleb forced a smile to his lips. "As much as I enjoy this conversation, I need to go speak to Roswell at once."

"Why didn't you just say so?" his mother asked. "He is in the parlor with Anette and your father."

"Roswell is here?" Caleb asked.

His mother gave him a concerned look. "Isn't that what I just said?" she asked. "Are you even listening to me, dear?"

Caleb approached his mother and kissed her cheek. "We can start planning the luncheon tomorrow. I promise. I just have to get through tonight."

"I shall hold you to that promise," his mother responded.

"Now I must go speak to Roswell," Caleb said before he started walking towards the parlor. Once he arrived, he saw Roswell, Anette and his father sitting around a table, playing a card game. "Roswell."

His friend brought his gaze up. "Caleb," he greeted. "Come join us."

Caleb shook his head. "I need to speak to you. Privately, if you don't mind."

Roswell must have heard the seriousness in his tone because he promptly put his cards down. "I shall be right back."

Anette followed suit and rose. "I shall join you."

"That won't be necessary," Caleb said. "I just need to speak to Roswell."

With a mischievous smile, Anette responded, "You don't need to beg, Caleb. I would be happy to hear what you wish to say."

Knowing the urgency of the situation and aware he was in a losing battle with his sister, Caleb relented, "All right. You may join us."

"How gracious of you, Brother," Anette said.

Caleb stepped back into the hall and waited for Roswell and Anette to do the same. Once they were alone, he spoke in a hushed tone, "Simone believes that Victor is going to use grenades at the ball this evening to assassinate General Merrell and the attending members of the House of Lords."

Anette gasped. "Why would he do such a thing? That could kill hundreds of people, along with the general and members of the peerage."

"I know, which is why we have to stop him," Caleb said before addressing his next comment to Roswell. "I need you to go find Fredrick and inform him that we need his help to convince General Merrell to abandon the ball, along with the members of the House of Lords."

Roswell nodded. "Fredrick is familiar with General Merrell. He mentioned working with him on multiple occasions while serving under Wellington."

"Good, that association will come in handy," Caleb said.

"Why do you suspect they are targeting General Merrell, as well?" Roswell asked. "Not that I am questioning it, but I am merely curious."

With a slight shrug, Caleb replied, "The general is Wellington's right-hand man and has won many key battles against the French. If he died, it would leave a leadership void in the war efforts."

Anette spoke up. "What will you have me do?"

Caleb turned to his sister. "You have a very important task of ensuring Mother goes nowhere near that ball this evening."

"Why not tell her the truth?" Anette asked.

With a lifted brow, Caleb questioned, "Do you want to explain to Mother how we know that there is a pending attack?"

Anette looked thoughtful. "Good point," she replied. "I will think of something."

"I need to go speak to Kendrick about this. He must know what is going on," Caleb stated. "Oh, and Lord Hungerton is a French spy. Do not trust a word out of his mouth."

Roswell didn't seem fazed by his words. "I understand.

Also, I will go round up Greydon so he can help look for Victor."

"Good idea. We need all the help we can get," Caleb said.

With a solemn look, Roswell encouraged, "Be careful. I have seen the destruction that can be caused by a single grenade. If what you are saying is true, I can't imagine the devastation that could be caused by multiple grenades in a ballroom."

Caleb tipped his head. "If you will excuse me, I will see you at the ball this evening. Ensure that you bring your pistol with you."

"I always do," Roswell said.

Knowing time was of the essence, Caleb hurried out of the townhouse and was about to step into the waiting carriage when he noticed a shadowed figure already inside.

"Do come in," a familiar voice said.

Caleb recognized Kendrick's voice and went to sit across from him. "I see that you got my message."

"I did, but it was rather vague," Kendrick said. "Although, I am glad that you were able to rescue Lady Hungerton and she is safe from her husband's clutches. For now."

"We have a problem," Caleb announced.

Kendrick lifted his brow. "What is it?"

Caleb took a deep breath before sharing, "Lord Hungerton is a French spy and I do believe that they intend to blow up Lord Pendley's ballroom with makeshift grenades."

"Do you have any proof of this?"

"Simone informed me that Victor left behind a grenade in his bedchamber, but he hasn't returned since this morning," Caleb said.

Kendrick held his gaze. "And how is it that you confirmed Lord Hungerton is a French spy?"

"Lady Hungerton informed us of this," Caleb replied. "She told us that he admitted to it when he was transporting her to Bedlam."

"It is a good thing that I have sent agents to arrest them. Your time was up, anyways," Kendrick said.

Caleb bobbed his head in approval. "With any luck, they haven't left for the ball yet. That could complicate matters."

"That it could. However, more importantly, we need to find Victor, and quickly," Kendrick said. "I will send agents to scour the grounds of Lord Pendley's townhouse and see if they can locate him."

"Simone and I will go to the ball, as planned, and we will look for him as well," Caleb stated. "Furthermore, I intend to tell General Merrell and members of the House of Lords of the impending threat on their lives and encourage them to leave at once."

"If all those people did leave the ball, it would be a great insult to Lord Pendley," Kendrick remarked.

"But by removing them, it could save hundreds of lives."

Kendrick nodded in agreement. "I never said it was the wrong move, but it will be more difficult than you perceive."

"That is why I am recruiting Fredrick and Roswell to help me round them all up," Caleb said.

Kendrick grew silent. "I want you to be extra vigilant tonight," he encouraged. "I keep asking myself why Juliette hasn't told Lord Hungerton that his own daughter is a spy. It just seems unlikely, considering she is his mistress."

"I have thought something similar."

The spymaster reached up and hit the top of the coach. In response, it started to slow down. "I will be much happier when those three are locked away and we can interrogate them more fully."

"I will be, too," Caleb said.

After Kendrick departed from the coach, Caleb leaned back, lost in his thoughts. Doubts crept in- what if they were wrong? And even if they weren't, one misstep could result in numerous casualties.

They had to stop Victor before he released the grenades. But where was he?

Caleb looked out the window and noticed that the coach was just about to pass Simone's townhouse. He pounded on the roof and the coach gradually halted by the pavement.

Stepping out, Caleb walked to the main door and rapped on it. The butler opened the door, awaiting his arrival.

"Good evening, Mr. Bolingbroke," the butler said, opening the door wide. "Do come in."

"Would you inform Miss Delacourt that I need to speak to her?" he asked. "The matter is most urgent."

Simone's voice came from the top of the stairs. "Now you have me intrigued," she said in a teasing voice.

Caleb watched as she descended the stairs and he knew, without a doubt, that Simone was his future. He would fight for her love, to the ends of the earth, if necessary. He had no choice. If he ignored his heart, it would be a betrayal that he could never live with.

Simone came to a stop in front of him and said, "Let us speak in the drawing room." She lowered her voice. "We will only have a short time until my companion is sent in."

"Then we best not waste a moment of our time together."

"That is what I was thinking, as well," Simone said before she waved him towards the drawing room.

Once they were in the center of the room, Simone turned back around to face him. "My father and Juliette are gone, but that isn't the worst part." She paused. "The guards that were assigned to guard the townhouse are dead. Someone slashed their throats. I found their bodies in the alleyway, hidden behind some debris."

"They must know that we are on to them," Caleb stated.

Simone's face was expressionless, but her eyes gave away her inner turmoil. She was hurting; he was sure of that. "What is my father thinking?" she asked. "Surely he must know that this will not end well for him."

"He must have some sort of plan," Caleb said.

"No matter what he does, he can't come back from this," Simone remarked. "Once he is caught, Kendrick will show him no leniency."

Caleb reached out and touched her arm. "I'm sorry that it had to end this way."

Simone's voice betrayed her emotion. "When we started this assignment, I never thought this is where we would end up. I never thought my own father was a traitor to the Crown."

"You have handled this rather bravely."

She let out a disbelieving huff. "I don't feel brave," she admitted. "I am just mad at myself that I didn't see it sooner."

Caleb took a step closer to her. "Don't look in the past for the answers. You won't find them there. Not anymore. You must look towards the future."

Simone held his gaze, her eyes seeming to implore his. "How do you always know the right thing to say?"

"Years of practice," Caleb said with a smile. "Once this is all over with, I want to sit down and have a frank conversation about us and our future."

"I would like that, very much."

"Good. We are in agreement, then, because you deserve to be happy. Not tired, not hurt, not deceived, just happy," he responded.

Caleb had just uttered his words when Mrs. Fernsby stepped into the room, causing him to drop his arm and take a step back.

Mrs. Fernsby walked closer to them and squinted her eyes. "Mr. Bolingbroke?" she asked. "What are you doing here?"

"I came to see Miss Delacourt," he replied.

Mrs. Fernsby adjusted the round spectacles on her nose. "Very well, I suppose that is best since Theodore asked for us not to attend the ball this evening," she said.

"I am going to the ball, whether my father wants me there or not," Simone asserted.

The aged companion looked displeased. "You will risk your father's wrath if you go," she said. "I think it would be prudent if we remained home and worked on our needlework."

Simone kept her voice calm as she replied, "You may stay, but I am going to go." She turned towards Caleb. "Will you escort me?"

With a scoff, Mrs. Fernsby declared, "That is highly inappropriate, even for you. If you are so insistent on going, I shall take you."

Caleb bowed. "I shall take my leave and see you both at the ball," he said.

Simone smiled, and Caleb realized that he couldn't stop loving her even if he tried.

Chapter Twenty

Simone sat across from her companion as she waited for the coach to come to a stop in front of Lord Pendley's townhouse. Mrs. Fernsby was proving to be a hindrance, which was something she didn't have time for.

She had to find Victor and stop him before he killed anyone. But that was only the beginning. The next step was ensuring that her father and Juliette were arrested. It sounded simple enough, but she knew she needed all her wits about her to complete this assignment.

The coach came to a stop and it dipped to the side as a footman exited his perch. Once the door was opened, Simone accepted the footman's hand and stepped onto the pavement. She took a moment to adjust her long white gloves and smooth down her gold ballgown.

Caleb approached her and bowed. "Miss Delacourt," he greeted. "You look like a vision of perfection this evening."

Knowing what was expected of her, she curtsied. "Thank you, Mr. Bolingbroke," she said. "That is most kind of you."

"May I escort you inside?" he asked, extending his arm.

"Yes, thank you," Simone replied.

As she accepted his arm, Caleb shifted his gaze towards

Mrs. Fernsby. "I shall see to Miss Delacourt this evening." His tone was firm, unwavering.

Looking unsure, Mrs. Fernsby replied, "Lord Hungerton has tasked me to watch over Miss Delacourt."

"Yes, but she is my fiancée now and I am responsible for her welfare," Caleb stated. "You may return home for the evening."

Mrs. Fernby pursed her lips before saying, "I believe I shall wait in the ballroom for my charge so I can at least escort her home."

"Very well." Caleb started to lead her away from her companion as he said in a hushed voice, "There is no sign of Victor."

"Where could he be?" Simone asked.

Caleb shrugged one shoulder. "I don't know, but we will find him," he said. "But your father and Juliette are here."

"I suspected as much, but why did they come, knowing that we were on to them?" Simone asked.

"I suppose to see Victor's handiwork," Caleb suggested.

Simone frowned. "Something isn't right, but I am not sure what it is," she admitted. "Regardless, we need to convince General Merrell and the other lords to leave the ball at once. It isn't safe for them here."

They arrived in the entry hall of the grand townhouse and bypassed the receiving line. Once they arrived in the ballroom, Simone went on her tiptoes and her eyes roamed over the hall, trying to decide their next course of action.

Caleb pointed towards the rear of the ballroom. "I see General Merrell. Let's start with him," he said before he started leading her through the crowds of people.

Simone's gaze fell upon the tall general, resplendent in his military uniform. Contrary to her expectations, he appeared younger, though his dark hair bore distinguished streaks of white. His very presence exuded authority, casting an imposing aura that commanded attention.

"How do you want to handle this?" Caleb asked.

"We tell him the truth, all of it," Simone replied.

Caleb lifted his brow. "Are you sure?"

Simone nodded. "It is the only way," she said, squaring her shoulders. She didn't want to admit that she was an agent of the Crown, but time was of the essence.

The general's eyes watched her as she approached him. They were kind, but they had an alertness about them.

Simone came to a stop in front of him and decided to dispense with the pleasantries. "You need to leave the ball at once. Your life is in danger," she said.

He smiled. "My dear, my life is always in danger," he remarked.

Caleb spoke up. "It would be best if we introduced ourselves," he said. "My name is Mr. Bolingbroke." He patted Simone's hand. "And this is Miss Delacourt, my fiancée."

The general bowed. "Miss Delacourt, a pleasure," he said. "Now, why do you think my life is in danger?"

This was it. It was time to reveal the truth and hope that he had enough sense to believe her. "We have reason to suspect that a French spy is going to release grenades in the ballroom to kill you and the members of the House of Lords," she revealed.

Growing serious, the general asked, "How did you come by this information?"

She held his gaze. "I am an agent of the Crown."

The general didn't look surprised by her admission. "I see," he said. "And I must assume that Mr. Bolingbroke is a spy, as well."

"I am," Caleb confirmed. "If you don't leave, hundreds of people could be killed, including you."

With a glance at his guards that were standing a few feet back, the general said, "I understand your concern, but if I retreated every time someone threatened my life, I would never have accomplished all that I have."

Simone furrowed her brow. "What of all the innocent people that are in harm's way?"

The general gave her an understanding look. "If I left now, it would be a great insult to Lord Pendley and we need his help in Parliament to help with funding of the war effort," he said. "Furthermore, a soldier does not retreat when things look bleak."

"And if you are killed?" Simone asked.

"I won't be, if you do your job," the general responded. "Now run along and ensure this spy does not wreak havoc on the ballroom."

Simone stared at the general, not quite believing how he could be so calm about what they had just revealed.

The general turned to address the guests that came to speak to him, dismissing them.

While Caleb started to lead Simone away, he whispered, "We need to find Fredrick. Perhaps he can talk some sense into the general."

Simone's eyes scanned the crowded ballroom and she felt panic well up inside of her. This was a *crush*, and if they didn't stop Victor, hundreds of people could be killed.

Caleb's calm voice broke through the silence. "We will stop Victor."

"How?" Simone asked. "We don't even know where he is."

She had just spoken her words when her father broke through the crowd and stopped in front of her.

"We need to talk," her father said in a curt tone. It wasn't a suggestion, but rather an order. But she expected no different from him.

Simone tilted her chin. "We are talking."

Her father's eyes shifted towards Caleb. "Alone." He held out his hand. "Take a walk with me around the ballroom."

She glanced down at her father's hand. He was the enemy.

A traitor. A cheat. A monster. But she knew she needed to hear what he had to say. If not, she would regret it.

Caleb stepped in front of her. "Simone isn't going anywhere with you," he asserted.

Her father looked bored by Caleb's declaration. "I daresay that my daughter can protect herself or so I have been told. Am I mistaken?"

Simone knew that they were going to start drawing unwanted attention if she didn't act fast. And the last thing they needed was to be gossiped about. She came out from behind Caleb and said, "One turn around the ballroom. That is all."

"Simone…" Caleb started, the concern evident in his voice.

"It will be all right," Simone assured him as she accepted her father's hand. "My father wouldn't be foolish enough to cause a scene in front of all these people."

Her father didn't wait for Caleb's reply before he led her towards the side of the ballroom. "I know what you did," he growled.

"You will have to be more specific," she said.

He spared a glance at her. "You broke your mother out of Bedlam."

She gasped. "Mother is alive?" she asked.

Her father narrowed his eyes. "I am not a simpleton," he replied. "Juliette told me what you are and what you do."

Simone kept her face expressionless. "I don't know what you are talking about." So much for Juliette's promise not to tell her father. But she wasn't surprised. In fact, she expected it.

He stopped and turned her to face him. "You know precisely what I am talking about, and we don't have time for these games," he said. "You weren't supposed to come this evening. You need to leave."

"If what you are saying is true, you know why I can't," Simone stated.

"You will die, then," her father said.

Simone had so many questions for her father, but she didn't know quite where to start. Or if he would even be honest with her. There were so many lies between them that trusting him would be nearly impossible. "Why?" she asked.

Her father's jaw clenched. "Why, what?"

"Where should I start?" she asked. "You betrayed your country, treated Mother terribly, and tried to cheat me out of my inheritance."

His eyes flashed with surprise. "You know about your inheritance?"

"I have for many days now," Simone replied.

"I must assume you are the reason why the contract went missing," her father said dryly.

Simone took a step closer to him, not cowed by the angry expression on his face. "The missing contract is the least of your concerns. It is only a matter of time until you are arrested and get the comeuppance that you deserve."

Her father smirked. "I will get what I deserve, but it will not be from a prison cell."

She held her hands up. "Look around you," she said. "I have no doubt that agents are just waiting for you to leave so they can arrest you."

"You make it seem like I don't already know that," he said. "I have been doing this for far longer than you."

"Where is Juliette?"

With an amused look, he replied, "She is around. Although, she has rather enjoyed this cat and mouse game with you."

"It isn't a game, Father," Simone declared. "People could get killed, innocent people."

The humor left his expression and his eyes grew hard. "Then they shouldn't be following a tyrant blindly."

"Are you speaking of King George or Napoleon?"

Her father scoffed. "King George is mad, and his son is no better," he said. "Napoleon is a visionary, a true ruler."

"Who is the mad one now?" Simone asked.

Her father reached out and grabbed her arm. "Regardless, you have no business being here. Go home, where it is safe."

"I will not," Simone said, yanking her arm back. "I am curious as to why the sudden concern for my well-being."

"No matter what happens, you are still my daughter."

Simone could hear the faint sincerity in his voice, but she was not about to back down. She had a job to do and she refused to leave these people to their fate. "I'm sorry, but I can't in good conscience let you hurt these people."

Her father looked displeased by her remark. "Forget these people. Think of yourself. Don't you want to live another day?"

She stared up at him, disbelief on her features. "Do you not care about anyone but yourself?"

"I care about you," her father replied.

"You have a funny way of showing it, considering you tried to steal my inheritance from me," she challenged.

"Yes, but only because I needed that money," he stated. "Besides, you are a woman. You didn't need that money since you are marrying Mr. Bolingbroke."

Simone blinked. "That is your excuse."

"You seem to forget that I don't answer to you."

"It was my money to do what I wanted with, and that includes keeping the Earlshall estate," Simone responded.

Her father scoffed. "What are you going to do with a castle? Think, Simone. You don't have the mind for estate management."

With a shake of her head, Simone muttered, "You are a terrible father."

"Just go, Simone," her father said, a hint of pleading in his voice. "I can't do what I need to do and worry about you."

She took a step back. "I'm sorry, Father. I will stop you, and then I will ensure you are arrested and pay for your crimes."

"You can't stop this."

"I daresay that you are underestimating me. You always have," Simone said.

Her father put his hand out but dropped it to his side with a sigh. "Then this is a goodbye," he responded before he spun on his heel, disappearing into the crowd of people.

Simone remained rooted in her spot until she heard Caleb's voice coming from behind her. "What did your father want?"

"To say goodbye," Simone shared, turning to face him. "We have to stop him. My father isn't going to stop until everyone is dead."

Caleb's eyes grew determined. "Leave your father to the other agents. They will no doubt arrest him the moment he leaves the ballroom. But we must find Victor, and quickly. I have searched the ballroom, but I have seen no sign of him. Let's go search the gardens."

"I thought Kendrick already sent agents to do so."

"He did, but they might have missed something," Caleb replied.

Simone bobbed her head. "I think that is a brilliant idea."

***

Caleb knew of the precariousness of the situation they were facing. If they didn't stop Victor in time, the consequences would be dire.

He glanced at Simone and saw that her jaw was set in determination. He had meant what he had said earlier about her being brave. She was the bravest person that he knew. What she had experienced these past few days would have brought most people to their knees, but not Simone. She stood taller, grew more steadfast.

He was grateful to have Simone as his partner.

Simone's eyes roamed over the gardens as they stood on the veranda. "I don't see Victor, or Juliette, for that matter."

"They have to be out here," Caleb said. "No doubt they are hiding until they release the grenades."

"Perhaps we should go down a path," Simone suggested.

Caleb looked at the many paths in the gardens and asked, "Which one?"

As Simone looked thoughtful, a rustling of bushes came from down the far path, the one that was shrouded in shadows. "I think it is fairly obvious."

"It is no doubt a trap," Caleb said.

"What choice do we have?" Simone asked. "If Juliette or Victor are trying to contact us, we have to go see what they want."

Caleb glanced over his shoulder at the ballroom, knowing his friends were somewhere inside. Surely they would notice his absence if he left the veranda. But Simone was right. They had to investigate the noise, knowing what they knew.

Simone headed down the path without a hint of hesitation. Caleb followed closely behind, his pistol in hand, and his eyes alert. He had an uneasy feeling about this. It was just too convenient that they heard that noise when they did.

As they approached the bush, Juliette stepped out onto the path, holding a pistol in her hand, a smug smile on her lips. "I see that you got my message."

"We did," Simone said, coming to a stop. "What is it that you want?"

"For starters, I want Mr. Bolingbroke to put his pistol on the ground and for you to remove your dagger from the folds of your gown," Juliette replied.

Caleb brought his pistol up, pointing it at Juliette. "I do not think so," he responded. "You drop your weapon."

Juliette turned the pistol towards Simone. "I know you would rather shoot me than talk but would you really risk Simone's life?"

Uncertainty pierced his very soul as he shifted his gaze towards Simone, who looked upon him with fierce determination. He had seen that look before. Simone had a plan and he needed to trust her. He crouched down and tossed his pistol onto the path as Simone did the same with her dagger.

Juliette gestured with her pistol towards a cluster of trees just off the path. "Now I would prefer to have this conversation in private," she said. "Go on."

Caleb placed his hand on the small of Simone's back and led her into the trees. "What is the plan?" he whispered.

"Trust me," she responded.

Juliette's voice came from behind them. "That is far enough," she said. "We can't go too far into the trees or we won't be able to hear the music."

Simone lifted her brow as she turned around to face the French spy. "You have lost, Juliette. Agents are looking for you at this very moment to arrest you and your brother."

With a chuckle, Juliette said, "I took care of those agents that were searching the gardens. I must admit that I was not impressed at how easily I snuck up on them."

"When is the killing going to stop?" Simone asked.

"I don't know, but I will admit it is not as thrilling as my first kill was." Juliette cocked her head at Simone. "You have killed before, haven't you?"

Simone shifted in her stance. "I have not. I have never seen the need."

Juliette looked amused. "A spy that does not kill," she mocked. "How intriguing. Although, I bet your father will be relieved to hear you say that."

"I thought you had no intention of telling my father that I was a spy," Simone said.

"About that, yes, I lied. I do that sort of thing, you

know?" Juliette mocked. "I will admit that your father took the news rather hard that you were spying for England. He had halfway hoped that we could turn you into a spy for France."

Lord Hungerton stepped out from the shadows and came to stand next to Juliette. "Leave Simone alone," he ordered.

"I'm afraid we can't do that, not anymore," Juliette said. "We need them out of the way when Victor releases the grenades or we can just kill them now and be done with it."

"If you discharge a pistol now, it will draw unwanted attention and people will come to investigate," Lord Hungerton mused.

"Good point. We will just kill them when the grenades go off," Juliette said. "Then we will make our escape."

Caleb offered them a curious look. "Where will you go?" he asked. "Every agent in England will be looking for you. You will never be free."

"It is a good thing we are returning to France," Juliette replied. "We have already chartered our ride home and the ship will depart once we arrive this evening."

Simone shifted her gaze towards her father. "You are leaving England?" she asked.

"There is nothing left for me here," Lord Hungerton responded. "Napoleon has offered me a French title in exchange for what we are doing here tonight. I will be a *vicomte*. That is where your inheritance would have come in handy, but Juliette and I will have to make do with what he has graciously promised to bestow upon us."

Juliette beamed. "Napoleon has offered us a fortune for what we have had to sacrifice."

Lord Hungerton held his hands up. "Anyone of importance is at the ball this evening, including most of the members of the House of Lords and the Prime Minister. By killing so many influential people, it would cause mass chaos amongst all levels of our government. England would become vulnerable to outside threats, something which Napoleon intends to take advantage of."

"You would betray your own country for a new title and some money?" Caleb asked in disbelief.

Lord Hungerton's eyes grew hard. "What has my country done for me? I will tell you. Nothing. England has done nothing for me but tax me relentlessly. And why? So our Prince Regent can carry on with his mistress and spend money he doesn't have?"

Simone's eyes seemed to plead with her father. "You don't have to do this. You can do the right thing and walk away."

"If I walk away, I have nothing to show for it," Lord Hungerton stated. "No, I am in too deep to even entertain such a ludicrous idea."

Victor stepped out of the trees and stood next to his sister, holding a grenade in his hand. He had a belt tube around his waist, no doubt holding the match for lighting the fuse. "I am ready to release the grenades."

Juliette looked at her brother with pride. "Victor is one of the most celebrated grenadiers in all of France," she revealed. "When I heard of our next assignment, I knew we had to bring Victor in to help us, despite the risks."

"You have this all planned out, don't you?" Caleb asked.

"We do, especially since we have been working up to this bombing for years," Juliette said. "We have participated in many bombings all over England."

Simone glanced between her father and Juliette. "Is that why you hid my mother in Bedlam because she overheard your plans for one of the bombings?"

Juliette scoffed. "I wanted to kill your mother, but your father refused to do that. So I came up with the idea of tucking her away in Bedlam. Even if she did tell people about our plan, no one would believe her."

Simone's eyes burned with fury. "Do you even have any remorse for what you have done?"

"Why would I?" Juliette asked. "We are at war with your country, or did you forget that? I do what I must to live another day."

"You will pay for what you did to my mother, what you both did!" Simone declared.

Juliette grinned. "What are you going to do?" she asked. "The only reason you are still alive is because we haven't released the grenades."

The music in the ballroom started up again, indicating a set was about to begin.

In a commanding voice, Lord Hungerton ordered, "Release the grenades."

"No! Stop! You can't do that!" Caleb exclaimed. "Just think of what you are doing. All the people that you are going to kill."

Victor held up the grenade. "It will be so easy to release this one in the ballroom. It will roll right by people's feet and they won't be the wiser. Then when it explodes, during the chaos of the aftermath, I will release another one. And another one."

Simone took a step forward. "I won't let you do that."

Juliette cocked her pistol, causing Simone to come to an abrupt stop. "I should have known you would be difficult about all of this."

"Once all the explosions have gone off, we will depart for the ship, and leave this despicable country behind," Victor shared.

Lord Hungerton met Victor's gaze. "Go. Now."

Victor tipped his head before he disappeared back into the trees.

Turning towards Simone, Lord Hungerton said, "It isn't too late for you. You can join us on our journey to France."

"She can?" Juliette asked, a stunned look on her features.

"Yes. She is, after all, my daughter," Lord Hungerton replied.

Juliette frowned. "I gave you my word that I wouldn't hurt her, assuming she didn't get in our way. But she is the enemy, or did you forget that?"

Lord Hungerton didn't acknowledge Juliette's remark as he asked Simone, "Will you come with me?"

Simone visibly stiffened. "How could you ask me such a thing?" she questioned. "Do you even know me at all?"

Disappointment showed on Lord Hungerton's features. "Very well, then. If you want to die, I won't stop you."

The sound of an explosion could be heard in the distance, and it was followed by an eerie silence.

Juliette's eyes lit up. "That was the first one. Now we wait for the second explosion."

Caleb had never felt such raw emotion as he was feeling right now. He couldn't even imagine the destruction that the grenade had caused and how many people had died. And he and Simone were helpless to stop it.

As they waited for the second explosion, Juliette asked, "Shall we kill them now?"

"There is no reason to stop the inevitable," Lord Hungerton replied.

Caleb stepped in front of Simone. "You are going to have to kill me first," he stated.

Juliette pointed her pistol at him. "My pleasure," she said.

While he braced for being shot, Simone stepped out from behind him and released a dagger, which embedded itself in Juliette's chest.

Juliette dropped her pistol and pulled out the dagger. "What have you done, you stupid chit?" she asked, her voice breathless. She took a few raspy breaths before she collapsed onto the ground.

Lord Hungerton retrieved a pistol and brought it up. "How could you?" he demanded.

Simone held her father's gaze. "I wasn't about to let Juliette kill Caleb," she replied. "Are you going to kill me- your own daughter?"

"Yes," Lord Hungerton said, tightening his hold on the pistol. "You left me with little choice."

In a swift motion, Caleb reached down and retrieved the muff pistol from his right boot. He brought it up, pointing it at Lord Hungerton. "Put your pistol down or I will have no choice but to shoot you."

"You are bluffing."

Caleb clenched his jaw. "I am many things, but bluffing is not one of them. If your finger so much as twitches on that trigger, I will kill you."

Doubt crept into Lord Hungerton's eyes. "This is not how it is supposed to end. I am supposed to be a *vicomte*."

"Your greed and ambition have ruined this family, Father," Simone declared. "You don't need to die today."

"But for how long?" Lord Hungerton asked. "We both know that I don't have long."

"That is your doing," Simone asserted. "You only have yourself to blame."

Lord Hungerton's eyes narrowed to slits. "You impertinent girl. You think you are better than me?"

"No, I have never thought that," Simone said with a shake of her head. "But I do think you need to pay for what you have done."

Caleb saw Lord Hungerton grow tense at Simone's words and he knew he needed to end this. He wouldn't risk Simone getting shot. Cocking his pistol, he fired, aiming at Lord Hungerton's hand that gripped the pistol.

Lord Hungerton dropped the pistol and cradled his right hand. "You shot me!" he exclaimed.

Approaching Lord Hungerton, Caleb crouched down to retrieve the pistol. "It is over," he declared, walking back over to Simone.

With a ruthless laugh, Lord Hungerton insisted, "This isn't over. The second grenade will go off any minute, killing more people. You have stopped nothing."

Fredrick's voice echoed from behind Lord Hungerton. "You are wrong," he stated, emerging from the trees.

A moment later, Roswell and Greydon came to stand next to Fredrick, all pointing pistols at Lord Hungerton.

Lord Hungerton's eyes grew frantic. "What are you doing here?" he asked. "You should all be dead."

Roswell grinned at his brother. "Do you want to tell him or should I?"

"You do the honors," Fredrick replied.

Roswell stepped forward. "We located Victor before he released the grenade and we set it off in a secluded part of the gardens. So you see, no one died."

"Except for Victor," Greydon interjected. "And, apparently, Juliette."

Simone took a step towards her father and Caleb placed his hand on her sleeve to stop her. "I wouldn't do that if I were you."

"It is all right," Simone assured him.

Lord Hungerton watched her as she came closer. "Do you want to gloat?" he half-asked, half-demanded.

"No, I want you to know that I will not think of you after today, but I am sure you will think of me every moment until you die," Simone said, coming to a stop in front of him. "You have no power over me or Mother anymore. We have won. You have lost. And now you will finally receive the comeuppance you so desperately deserve."

With defiance in his eyes, Lord Hungerton held Simone's gaze, remaining silent.

Fredrick grabbed Lord Hungerton's arm. "Do you even want to say goodbye?" he asked.

"I already said my goodbyes earlier," Lord Hungerton responded, showing no hint of remorse for what he had done.

While Fredrick and Roswell led Lord Hungerton away, Caleb watched Simone as her eyes remained on her father's retreating figure, her expression giving nothing away.

Chapter Twenty-One

Simone watched as her father was being led away, knowing this would be the last time she would ever see him. She needed to stop holding on to him since he had already let go of her long ago. She was free of him, and more importantly, so was her mother.

Caleb's voice came from behind her. "Are you all right?"

"I will be."

He gently touched her arm and turned her to face him. "He is gone," he said. "He will never be able to hurt you again."

"I know, and all I feel is relief. Is that wrong of me?" she asked.

Caleb shook his head. "I do not think so, especially after what he put you through."

With a glance at Juliette's lifeless body, she asked, "What will happen to her?"

"The agents will be by to collect her body so there is no trace of what happened here this evening," he replied. "Would you like me to collect your dagger?"

"No, I want nothing to remind me of this night," Simone

replied. She hadn't meant to kill Juliette, but she was left with little choice when Caleb's life had been threatened.

Caleb gave her an understanding look. "You saved my life... again. Although, I would have preferred if you hadn't put yourself in harm's way."

"A simple 'thank you' would suffice, considering I correctly assumed I would need more than one dagger this evening," Simone teased.

He smiled. "Thank you," he said. "Although, I would like to point out that I saved your life as well."

"That is true. Thank you."

Caleb's smile faded as his eyes dropped to Juliette's body. "We should return to the ball before anyone comes looking for us."

"I think that is a fine idea," she responded, accepting his arm.

As they stepped back onto the path, Caleb asked, "Where do we go from here?"

"I suppose anywhere we want to."

Caleb kept his gaze straight-ahead as he said, "I think it would be a shame if we didn't keep working as a team."

Simone pretended to consider his words, but she already knew the answer. "I would agree. Do you think Kendrick would have any objections?"

"No, he has said as much, especially since we are to be married soon," Caleb said.

They arrived at the empty veranda and Simone felt no urgency to return to the ball. She would prefer to remain with Caleb outside rather than return to a stuffy, crowded ballroom. Fortunately, he seemed to feel the same way because he came to a stop near the iron railing.

Caleb dropped his arm and leaned against the railing. "It is a beautiful night, is it not?"

"It is," she rushed to agree. Drats. Now they were talking about the weather. Could anything be more of a bore?

He grew solemn. "I was hoping you would be willing to have that discussion now about us," he said, appearing to hold his breath.

"I am not opposed to it."

"Good," he replied. "Because I have much to say on the subject."

Simone gave him an expectant look, choosing to remain silent. If she was brave, she would admit that she loved him. But she wasn't that brave. What if he didn't return her affection? She knew he cared for her, but that was not the same as being desperately in love with someone.

Caleb appeared nervous, which was in stark contrast to how he usually was. "I was hoping that we could change the terms of our agreement."

"You were?" she asked, unsure of his meaning.

He nodded. "Yes," he replied. "When we agreed to marry, I promised that it would be in name only."

"I remember."

"But things have changed between us," he hesitated, "at least I think they have changed. Am I wrong?"

Finding strength in herself that she didn't know she had, she said, "You are not wrong."

A soft sigh escaped his lips. "I am pleased to hear you say that because I may never find enough words that are beautiful enough to describe how much I love you, but I will spend the rest of my life searching for them, if you will allow me to."

Fearing that she had misheard him, she asked, "You love me?"

"How could I not? From the day I met you, all at once my whole world began to change," he said. "Put aside that you have saved me twice now, you have also saved me from myself. The way you have accepted me and all my flaws made me love you even more."

Simone's lips twitched. "You do have a lot of flaws," she joked.

He chuckled. "I am well aware," he said. "But these past few days, I have second-guessed every word, every action, every moment, as I hoped that you might care for me as I do you."

Feeling a need to tease him, she remarked, "I do find you tolerable."

"Only tolerable?" he asked with a hopeful expression.

She shrugged one shoulder. "Maybe just a smidgeon more than tolerable," she replied lightly.

"I will take that, for now." He took a step closer to her, causing her to tilt her head to look up at him. "But do you want to know what I think?"

Attempting to appear unaffected by his nearness, she kept her voice steady as she replied, "What is that?"

He leaned closer and whispered, "I think you love me, too."

Simone made the mistake of turning her head, making their faces only inches apart. Her eyes darted towards his lips for the briefest of moments. "I… uh…" It was true. He wasn't wrong. However, she couldn't think with him being so close.

Caleb seemed to take pity on her and leaned back. "It is all right if you don't wish to admit it but I love you. For I can't deny it any longer."

Knowing she would never be able to escape from her heart, Simone thought it was best if she just told him how she truly felt. It was scary for her to be so vulnerable with anyone. But Caleb was different. He made her feel as if she deserved to be loved.

Simone brought her hand up and gently placed it on his chest. "I love, love…" She paused, collecting her strength. "I love you, Caleb."

He reached up and encompassed her hand with his own. "I know, Simone. And I promise that your love is safe with me."

Caleb looked at her with so much love in his eyes that

Simone knew he spoke true. Now that their declarations of love were out of the way, Simone asked, "Are we not supposed to kiss on it?"

His eyes darted towards the ballroom. "Do you think that is a good idea?"

"No, it is a terrible idea," she replied. "Our kiss would no doubt cause a scandal."

"It would, most definitely," he said, bringing his gaze back to hers.

She leaned closer to him with a coy smile playing on her lips. "But I am willing to risk it, assuming you are."

His eyes dropped to her lips. "Well, we are engaged," he said. "In the eyes of the *ton*, we are practically married."

"That we are," she agreed.

"Then there is no reason for us not to kiss. Is there?" he asked as he brought his head closer to hers.

Simone could feel the warmth of his breath on her lips as she tried to ignore the racing of her heart. "I cannot think of one."

The moment her words left her mouth, Caleb pressed his lips against hers. It was a gentle kiss, a mingling of warmth and vulnerability, telling her everything she needed to know. He loved her. And she loved him. He completed her in a way that she couldn't explain; she didn't want to explain. Because it just made sense for them to love each other as much as they did.

In that stolen breath of time, the outside world seemed to fade away, leaving only the echo of their shared affection- a whisper of promises.

Caleb broke the kiss but remained close. "You must promise me that you will always kiss me like that, always."

"I promise."

"Good, because it was perfect," Caleb said. "You are perfect."

She let out a slight laugh. "Now I know you are exaggerating."

A clearing of a throat came from next to them, startling them both. Simone turned her head and saw General Merrell standing a short distance away.

Caleb dropped his arms and took a step back. "General," he said with a slight bow.

The general's eyes held amusement. "I see that spies handle the completion of their assignments very differently on English soil."

"My apologies, but Miss Delacourt is my fiancée—" Caleb started.

He put his hand up, stilling Caleb's words. "You do not need to explain yourself to me," he said. "I came to thank you. I assume the earlier explosion in the gardens was your doing."

Caleb exchanged a glance with Simone before admitting, "My friends had something to do with that. We were handling another threat that arose."

"Well, be sure to pass along my thanks to them," the general said. "Is it safe to assume that the threat on my life is over now?"

"It is," Simone confirmed.

The general nodded approvingly. "It is time that I return to the ballroom and I suggest that you do the same," he said. "I do trust that my guards gave you enough time to resolve everything."

Unsure of his meaning, Simone asked, "Sir?"

A knowing smile came to his lips. "Fredrick explained to me that you two hadn't come to terms with the depths of your feelings and suggested you could use some privacy on the veranda."

Simone felt a blush come to her cheeks. Had her affections been so obvious that others had seen right through her?

314

As the general stepped back into the ballroom, Caleb asked, "You aren't having any regrets, are you?"

"None," Simone replied.

Caleb stepped forward and reached for her hand. "Good, because I intend to dance with you twice this evening."

"I do hope that one of those dances is the waltz," Simone said.

He brought her hand up to his lips. "It most assuredly will be."

Fredrick and Roswell stepped out onto the veranda, feigning disappointment. "It wasn't enough that we saved the day, but now we have to watch our friend turn sappy."

"I have not turned sappy, and you only *helped* save the day," Caleb remarked.

With a smirk on his lips, Fredrick said, "No, I'm pretty sure we saved the day while you were having a very long and tedious conversation with Lord Hungerton and Juliette."

"We do need to give credit where credit is due," Simone acknowledged. "Thank you."

"When we saw you two leave the ballroom, we followed you and we were able to intercept Victor as he left to dispatch the grenade," Roswell explained.

"I had been hoping that was the case," Caleb said.

"Regardless, Anette will be sad that she missed this," Roswell stated. "We were placing bets on when you two would declare your love."

Fredrick lifted his brow. "Who won?"

"Anette," Roswell admitted. "But in all fairness, she is like a love expert."

Simone laughed, feeling freer than she had been in a long time. She truly couldn't think of a time when she was this happy.

Caleb kept hold of her hand and moved it to the crook of his arm. "Shall we go dance, my love?"

My love.

She thought her heart would now burst from happiness. Who would have thought that those two simple words would have such a profound effect on her?

Caleb descended the stairs with a smile on his lips. He couldn't help it. He hadn't been able to stop smiling since last night when he had declared his love for Simone. After that kiss, they returned to the ballroom and danced two sets. Two magical sets. He wasn't one for dancing, but he loved nothing more than to hold Simone in his arms.

He was going to quite like being married to Simone. She challenged him to be better, in all aspects of his life.

As he stepped into the dining room, he saw his sister was sitting at the table with the newssheets in her hand.

"Good morning," he greeted.

Anette lowered the paper to the table. "Good morning, Brother."

"Not that I am complaining, but why are you here?" Caleb asked as he sat down across from her.

She smiled broadly. A little too broadly. His sister was up to something. "I came to see you," she said. "But while I was waiting, I read the most fascinating article."

"Did you, now?" he asked.

"Yes, apparently, Lady Hungerton had amnesia these past two years and was working at a boarding school in the countryside," Anette said.

Caleb leaned to the side as a footman placed a plate of food in front of him. "That is interesting."

"I thought so, as well, making me wonder if it is hogwash," Anette remarked.

"Language, Sister," Caleb teased.

Anette laughed. "You are far too sensitive if you find that

word offensive," she said. "I just wonder why you didn't tell me that Lady Hungerton had returned."

"It was not my place to do so."

Lowering her voice, Anette asked, "What really happened to Lady Hungerton?"

"You wouldn't believe me if I told you."

"Try me," she insisted.

Caleb reached for his fork and knife and said, "I'm afraid it is not my story to share."

Anette looked put out. "You are no fun."

With a curious look, Caleb asked, "What else was said in the article about Lady Hungerton?"

"Only that Lord Hungerton is thrilled for his wife's return and that they will retire to their country estate for the remainder of the Season," Anette shared.

Caleb bobbed his head, knowing it was only a matter of time before Lord Hungerton's untimely death was announced.

Anette looked dubious. "Is any of that true?"

"I'm afraid not."

"That is what I assumed, considering you told us that Lord Hungerton was a French spy," Anette said. "I must imagine no one will see Lord Hungerton again."

"You would be correct in your assumption."

Anette folded the paper and placed it next to her on the table. "Roswell mentioned that he saw you kissing Simone."

"It is true," Caleb said, seeing no reason to deny it.

"I am happy for you, and Simone," Anette stated. "You both deserve to be happy."

"Thank you."

Anette considered him for a moment before saying, "But I was right all along about Simone." She reached for her glass and took a sip. "Are you going to let Simone continue working as a spy?"

Caleb placed his fork and knife down onto the plate. "I am

not going to *let* Simone do anything. It is her choice, not mine."

"That is very progressive of you," Anette said in an approving tone.

"I love Simone, and I just want her to be happy," Caleb stated.

Anette arched an eyebrow. "Have you discovered what her favorite flower is?"

Caleb groaned. "No, I haven't. But in my defense, we were focused on our assignment, which was far more important."

"I know, but Mother won't understand," Anette said.

The long clock in the corner chimed and it was finally a respectable hour that he could call upon Simone. He shoved back his chair and rose. "If you will excuse me, I am going to call on Simone now," he informed his sister.

Anette's eyes held amusement. "Of course you are," she said. "But do try to remember to ask her what her favorite flower is."

"I will," Caleb responded before he departed from the dining room.

It wasn't long before he found himself sitting in the coach. He was rather eager to see Simone, almost too eager. How he loved her. His life had changed for the better when he had met her. He didn't know it at the time, considering they were at odds with one another.

The coach rolled forward to merge into traffic but came to an abrupt stop. The door opened and Kendrick stepped inside.

Once he sat across from Caleb, Kendrick closed the door and said, "I must assume you are on your way to see Miss Delacourt."

"I am," Caleb confirmed.

"Good," Kendrick said. "You can break the news to her that her father died from an infectious fever last night."

Caleb lifted his brow. "We both know that isn't true."

"True, but it sounds so much more pleasant than saying he was tortured and killed," Kendrick remarked. "Lord Hungerton admitted to many bombings over the course of the past three years. His treachery ran deep, I'm afraid."

"I will inform Simone of the news."

"See that you do," Kendrick said. "Did you read the newssheets this morning?"

Caleb bobbed his head. "I did. Amnesia was an interesting choice."

"In exchange for the newssheets to not print what Juliette had leaked to them about spies and whatnot, I agreed to share some unprecedented stories," Kendrick shared. "Although, it took much convincing on my part to persuade Lady Hungerton that she shouldn't remain in hiding. She did nothing wrong and she deserves to have a life."

"Do you think she will return to high Society?"

Kendrick shrugged. "I don't know, but as far as the *ton* is concerned, she is alive and well," he replied. "She only agreed to leave the cottage if she could see her husband one more time."

"You allowed such a thing?" Caleb asked.

"I did, knowing she needed to address what he did to her," Kendrick responded. "Lady Hungerton only spent five minutes with him, but it was enough time for her to say what needed to be said. Unfortunately for her, she will be going into mourning to at least pretend to grieve the loss of her husband."

"Not that there is much to mourn," Caleb muttered.

"We both know that, but the *ton* doesn't," Kendrick said. "Since your engagement has already been announced, it is still acceptable for you to wed Simone during the mourning period."

Caleb gave him a knowing look. "I would have married Simone whether it was acceptable or not."

With a chuckle, Kendrick said, "I will admit that you and Miss Delacourt weren't awful as partners."

Caleb grinned. "Was that a compliment?"

Kendrick hit the top of the coach and it started to slow down. "That is as close as you get to one," he said. "Good luck with Miss Delacourt."

"I don't need luck."

Placing his hand on the handle, Kendrick responded, "I knew you two needed one another, which is why I decided to partner you together in the first place."

"Sir?" he questioned. Had the spymaster truly played the role of matchmaker?

Kendrick opened the door. "Do not read too much into this, Agent," he said in his usual gruff voice. "You two were terribly distracted, but you eventually figured things out. Just as I knew you would."

Once the spymaster departed from the coach, it traveled the short distance to Simone's townhouse. He exited the conveyance and hurried up the steps.

The door was promptly opened and the butler greeted him with a kind smile. "Good morning, Mr. Bolingbroke."

"Is Miss Delacourt available for callers?" he asked.

The butler nodded. "For you, she is," he replied. "Please follow me. She is in the drawing room with Lady Hungerton."

Caleb followed the butler into the drawing room, not bothering to wait to be announced. He saw Simone was sitting next to her mother on the settee, a bright smile on her lips. He thought he would have grown accustomed to her beauty by now, but every time he looked at her, she became more beautiful.

"Simone," he greeted.

She rose from her seat. "Caleb," she said. "It is good to see you."

"I hope I did not come too early," he responded.

"You could do no such thing."

Caleb returned her smile as he stared at her a moment longer than what would be considered proper. He reluctantly shifted his gaze to Lady Hungerton to acknowledge her. "My lady," he greeted with a slight bow.

He was pleased to see that Lady Hungerton's coloring had returned to her face but she still looked entirely too thin for his liking. Her hair was neatly coiffed, and she was dressed in a fine gown, one worthy of her social standing.

Lady Hungerton tipped her head. "Caleb," she said. "You are always welcome in our home, at any hour of the day."

"Thank you," he responded.

With a knowing smile at her daughter, Lady Hungerton remarked, "I know that Caleb did not come to see me. Why don't you two take a turn around the gardens?"

"You don't mind?" Simone asked.

Lady Hungerton waved her hand in front of her. "It is nice to see two such deserving people in love. I want you to enjoy it. I will be fine. You need not worry about me."

Caleb stepped forward and lowered his voice. "Before I escort Simone to the gardens, I thought you both should know that Lord Hungerton has died."

Lady Hungerton's eyes held a profound sadness. "Kendrick told me as much, but I wish it hadn't come to this."

"I am just glad that my mother is safe now. My father won't be able to hurt her ever again," Simone remarked.

"Or you," Caleb pointed out as he offered his arm. "Shall we tour the gardens now?"

Simone accepted his arm and he led her from the room.

While they walked down the corridor, he inquired, "Before we go on, I need to know what your favorite flower is."

"I don't have one," Simone responded.

Caleb grinned. "My mother will be disappointed by that fact. She is attempting to plan our wedding and apparently flowers set the scene."

"I would prefer a small, intimate wedding," Simone admitted.

"I knew I loved you for a reason," Caleb said before growing solemn. "How is your mother truly faring?"

"She claims she is all right, but I have my reservations about that. How could she not struggle at least somewhat after what she had endured those two years?" Simone asked. "But I do find that I am most appreciative of Kendrick. He allowed her to say her final goodbyes to my father before she returned home to me, at least until we are wed."

"Your mother will always have a home with us," Caleb stated.

Simone's eyes seemed to light up. "Do you think your parents would mind?"

"They will be thrilled to have your mother living with us," Caleb replied as they stepped out onto the veranda. "If it makes you happy, it makes me happy."

"You are too kind," she said. "My mother asked if I would go retrieve Lucy. She is hopeful she will return as her lady's maid now that this is all over. Apparently, my mother had told Lucy of her suspicions about my father, but Lucy knew she couldn't prove he had anything to do with her disappearance."

"I would be happy to help you track Lucy down, assuming you have no objections."

"I have none."

Caleb stopped and turned to face her, his boots grinding on the gravel path. "I hope you know how much I love you. I would do anything to ensure your happiness."

"You say that now..."

"I will say that always," he declared, speaking over her. "From this day forward, you and I are a team. Partners in life, and in the next, if I have my way."

Simone's face softened. "I love you, too."

Caleb took a step closer. "This is only the beginning. Just think of the adventures we will have together."

A slight sigh escaped her lips. "I can't wait."

Caleb tucked an errant lock of hair behind Simone's ear, his fingers lingering on her delicate skin. "I certainly did not think this was where we would end up when we first met but I am so glad that we did. All I know is that I could never love anyone as much as I love you." He paused as his emotions got the best of him. "You are all that I ever wanted- just you."

Simone rose on her tiptoes and pressed her lips against his. She leaned back just slightly enough to whisper against his lips, "It was taking far too long for you to kiss me."

"My apologies. That will not happen again," he responded before returning the kiss.

Epilogue

Nine years later

Simone watched as her daughter released the dagger and it embedded in the center of the target, just a short distance away.

Caroline smiled broadly. "I did it!" she said, jumping up and down in enthusiasm.

"That you did," Simone acknowledged. "You are better than I was at your age, but you still have to practice. Then you must practice some more."

"When do you think I can throw a dagger as far as you?" Caroline asked.

Simone pretended to mull it over. "How old are you now?"

Caroline stood up straight and held up eight fingers. "I am eight years and three months."

"That is right," Simone said with a smile. "I think you should be able to handle the farther distance when you are nine."

As Caroline skipped to the target to retrieve her dagger, ·

Simone felt such gratitude for what she had in her life. She had everything that she could ever want. A loving husband, three beautiful children, and she still was able to work as a spy.

She never thought she could be this happy. Quite frankly, she never thought she deserved to be this happy. But Caleb had convinced her otherwise. With him by her side, she felt seen and heard and loved.

"Mother, watch me!" Caroline exclaimed before she brought the dagger up.

"Remember your footing," Simone advised.

Caroline adjusted her feet, making them shoulder-width apart. "Is that better?"

"It is," Simone replied.

In a smooth motion, Caroline reared her hand back and released the dagger. Only this time, it sailed past the target, missing it entirely.

A pout came to Caroline's face. "That was an awful throw."

"It is all right," Simone encouraged. "We learn from the failed attempts just as much as we learn from the good ones."

Simone's mother's voice came from behind them. "Now where have I heard that before?" she asked lightly.

Simone turned to face her mother. "Someone very wise told me that," she said.

"Yes, but if I recall correctly, you didn't believe me when you were younger," her mother responded. "You were disappointed every time you didn't hit the center."

Caroline spoke up. "Did you come to watch me, Grandmother?"

"I did," Simone's mother replied. "But I find that I need a hug before your next throw."

Simone watched as Caroline ran past her and into her mother's open arms, causing her to smile at the tender scene. Her mother was a doting grandmother, just as she thought she would be. There was so much love in their home and Simone would have it no other way.

Simone's mother released Caroline and said, "Go collect your dagger and show me what you learned."

Caroline bobbed her head before she ran to collect her dagger.

"Caroline reminds me so much of you at this age," her mother remarked, her eyes remaining fixed on her granddaughter.

"She is rather opinionated and stubborn," Simone remarked.

"As were you," her mother said. "Would you have it any other way?"

Simone shook her head. "No, she is perfect."

She had just uttered her words when she saw Caleb approaching and she felt the familiar thudding of her heart. She wondered when she would stop having such a reaction to seeing her husband. But with every moment she spent with him, she loved him more.

As Caleb drew near, he kissed her on the cheek and whispered next to her ear, "Kendrick needs to see us."

"Very well." Simone turned towards her mother. "We have an errand that we need to see to. Will you ensure the children are tended to?"

Her mother tipped her head. "Go. We will be just fine until you get back."

"You are leaving?" Caroline asked, looking up at Caleb.

Caleb crouched down in front of his daughter. "We have to go, but we will be back before supper. I promise."

Caroline pressed her lips together. "Will you bring me back some dry sweetmeat?"

"Deal," Caleb replied.

She wrapped her arms around her father's neck. "I love you, Father."

Caleb returned her embrace and said, "I love you, too, little one."

After a long moment, Caroline dropped her arms and took a step back. "You and Mother can go now. Grandmother is going to watch me throw the dagger."

Simone slipped her hand into the crook of Caleb's arm. "We will be back shortly," she promised before Caleb started to lead her down the path.

"Do you need to change before we depart for headquarters?" Caleb asked.

She glanced down at her jonquil gown. "It depends," she replied. "Do you know what the assignment is?"

Caleb shrugged. "I don't, but it could be anything."

"I will take my chances."

It was only a few moments before they stepped into the waiting coach, and it merged into traffic. Caleb reached for her hand and said, "You are looking especially lovely today."

"Flattery?" Simone teased. "It is much too early for that."

He leaned closer to her. "You do realize that we are alone right now, which hardly happens now that we have three children."

"That was just as much your fault as my own," Simone joked.

Caleb chuckled. "It is, and I have no complaints." He brought her hand up to his lips. "Whether I am awake or asleep, I dream of you all the same."

Simone nudged her shoulder against his. "What do you want?" she asked. "You are being far too complimentary."

Caleb smiled. "Can I not just compliment my wife without being accused of an ulterior motive?"

"Now I know you are keeping something from me."

His smile grew. "You are far too suspicious, Wife," he said.

"It is the nature of the job."

Leaning closer, Caleb brought their faces just inches apart, his warm breath on her lips. "You are right. I do want something."

"I knew it."

His eyes darted towards her lips. "I want a kiss."

"You don't need to ask," Simone said. "That is the advantage of being married. We can kiss each other any time we want."

Caleb pressed his lips against hers and Simone relaxed into his arms. This was her life. Not the life she had once envisioned, but one that had been built with care and attention. And it was far better than she could have ever imagined.

The End

New Series Announcement

THE LOCKWOOD FAMILY

Lady Edwina Lockwood grapples with the loss of her father when her cousin extends an invitation to Lord Hilgrove to visit Brockhall Manor. She intends to avoid this houseguest, but he quickly becomes a constant presence, much to her annoyance.

Despite her initial reluctance, Edwina discovers she can offer support to Lord Hilgrove as he copes with his own grief.

Miles Burke, the Earl of Hilgrove, remains consumed by sorrow after losing his wife and brother nearly a year ago. Accepting the invitation to visit a friend seemed like a good idea at the time, but upon arrival, he immediately regrets it. The only bright spot is Lady Edwina, who offers him unexpected solace.

As Edwina and Miles spend more time together, they find comfort in each other's company and begin to heal. Together, they unearth secrets that were meant to remain buried. Delving deeper into the mysteries surrounding them, Miles finds himself risking everything to protect her. But can he give her the one thing that she desires the most- his heart?

Other series by Laura Beers include **The Beckett Files**, **Regency Brides: A Promise of Love**, **Proper Regency Matchmakers**, **Regency Spies & Secrets**, **Gentlemen of London** and **Lords & Ladies of Mayfair**.

About the Author

Laura Beers is an award-winning author. She attended Brigham Young University, earning a Bachelor of Science degree in Construction Management. She can't sing, doesn't dance and loves naps.

Laura lives in Utah with her husband, three kids, and her dysfunctional dog. When not writing regency romance, she loves skiing, hiking, and drinking Dr Pepper.

You can connect with Laura on Facebook, Instagram, or on her site at www.authorlaurabeers.com.